NATIVE SEERESS:
Woman of Magic

by

Ron Maier

To Joyce
Best wishes & God bless
Ron Maier

PublishAmerica
Baltimore

First printing

ISBN: 1-4137-1688-1
PUBLISHED BY PUBLISHAMERICA, LLLP
www.publishamerica.com
Baltimore

Printed in the United States of America

DEDICATION

To Ms. Scout Cloud Lee
whose talk on women's spirituality
led me to–What If...
Also to Prairie Wind Writers
my critique group.
And, as always, to Pat
a reader who puts up with a writer.

CHAPTER ONE

Sacred Grove loomed ahead, lush, and filled with sycamore trees. Ancient urges called him. Should he test his courage before returning to the Horse People? If the tribe knew he'd challenged the spirits they'd...

An ear-splitting whistle startled him.

Clayfoot slipped from his horse. Beyond the peeling bark of an old sycamore tree he saw a woman rip a slender furrow in the black soil. A few steps later she ripped another rut with her strange moccasins.

His gaze lingered over the white deerskin skirt clinging to her slender thighs. Colorful flowers circled her head in a snug band that held shining black braids close to a high-boned face. An iridescent, wide collar draped her shoulders highlighting a face more beautiful than any he'd ever seen. She looked fair, only slightly darker than the sand by the pool. A lone eagle feather jutted from the back of her headband.

This woman was not of the Horse People.

Awestruck, he watched birds of every color and kind flutter to the fresh-turned earth. At a chirping sound from her, noisy, colorful males moved grudgingly to allow their mates to join them.

"Wheeeet-Eeeet." Again, her whistle split the air.

A glistening raven swooped to her shoulder, bringing with it a large cluster of wild grapes. The black bird pranced across her shoulder while she ate, refusing when she offered it a grape.

For a carrion eater to bring fruit seemed peculiar. Its black feathers would fetch the heart of many maidens in the village as would the colorful feathers of the birds feeding at the trenches. No longer would they call him Clayfoot, the coward. He led Mah-ki, his red-speckled white horse, among the trees to a better vantage point.

The young braves would stop tormenting him if he captured this spirit-maiden with power over birds. They would be jealous if he returned with her slung over his horse.

He hid behind a large cedar trying to infringe on the sycamore grove. For an instant, she stopped eating and scanned the edge of the clearing. She looked directly at him while the raven pranced across her shoulder.

Experience taught him when his prey sensed danger.

Why did he feel the need to work up his courage to swoop down on this strange woman? It goaded him. No woman could be greater than a man. Easing to Mah-ki's back, he wondered why the horse trembled, refusing to advance.

He jabbed his heels into its sides.

"Hee–hee–hiha," he screamed, working up his courage. Her blood should thicken and freeze and he could lean wide to scoop her in front of him. Easy prey.

A shriek burst from the large bird. It leaped from her shoulder, claws spread to attack. Clayfoot kneed the horse to weave from the bird's onslaught, but the bird swerved to meet him head on.

Over pounding hoofbeats and his war cry, a sharp whistle split the air. The black bird veered, wings spread wide. A claw raked his left shoulder. Pain seared down his back, different from any wound he'd ever had. It spread across his shoulders and down his arm like fire. Half-paralyzed, he leaned wide to grasp her waist.

Her palm shot out as if to ward him off. Instead, Mah-ki stopped in mid-charge, planted its hooves, and sent him flying over its head to land on his belly.

Humiliated, he spewed dirt and grass from his mouth. No one had ever stopped Mah-ki in mid-charge...especially not a woman. His vision cleared, focusing on her strange moccasins; hard-soled with narrow straps criss-crossing up her legs to disappear under the fringe of her skirt. It was not deerskin! Gone was the lust he'd felt earlier, replaced by fury. Fury at what she'd done, but mostly at himself. He should have stalked her for the spirit she seemed, then sent an arrow...

Clayfoot flung off her cool hand when she grasped him just above the medicine band on his arm. Stumbling back from his angry thrust, she teetered on the edge of falling. Instantly, the raven swooped to her shoulder, one claw

6

raised to protect its mistress.

Do not be angry with me.

Her words echoed in his mind. She spoke without speaking. How did she get here? Horse People avoided Sacred Grove as a place of death, but he needed to test his courage. As a youth he'd known terror when a young bull buffalo charged and he failed the becoming-a-man ceremony.

She didn't seem like a spirit woman...unless she could change into one. Her touch felt soft...and she smelled like...like fresh water?

The only mystery he'd seen in this place of death were unfamiliar tracks in the sand by the pool. Struggling to his feet, he towered over her and arranged the feather in his right braid. He tightened the muscles across his belly.

Jutting his jaw, he said, "I do not fear you."

Then why does your belly tremble like a Cottonwood leaf in the wind?

Clayfoot clasped his hands over his ears to shut out words that came into his mind, not from her mouth. Was this a woman shaman of great power? Or a new, strange spirit who haunted the grove?

He sucked a deep breath to quiet his dread. "Who are you, woman-who-controls-birds?"

Her gaze flicked to the distant snow-capped mountains. *I am Kah-tay from beyond the White Hills of Death.*

"Must you always speak in my mind? Don't you have a tongue?" Backing away as he talked, he felt the heaving horse against his spine. Furious, he turned on the animal.

"And you, Mah-ki," he shouted at his sweating horse, "why did you stop like never before and toss Clayfoot in the dirt at the feet of this–this–woman?"

Out of the corner of his eye he saw her clenched fist. Mah-ki nudged him toward her. His thoughts lingered on his horse stopping at her outstretched palm.

She controls more than birds.

Don't blame your horse, Clayfoot. Mah-ki only followed my command.

"Why have you come to this place of death?"

It's not a place of death. It's a place where animals refuse to dwell. Come. I'll show you why.

She slipped her hand in his but he jerked away, suspicious, and followed her from the clearing.

A faint roar caught his attention. Toward distant white-capped peaks, half-way up a high cliff, a waterfall spewed from a cavern. It cascaded to a granite-lined pocket. He'd found solace there after his first outcast.

The stream slowed to a silent, pale blue pond where it spent its way toward an ancient beaver dam. Beaver no longer lived in these waters.

Across the pond, boulders lined the edge sending small eddies of water swirling to the center. Occasional bubbles rose to the surface, followed by others on the far side.

Beyond lay Dark Forest where only fools ventured.

Kah-tay knelt on a place where water lapped at sand only a shade lighter than her skin. Very beautiful, this spirit woman. Temptation filled his heart. Who would know? Clayfoot swelled his chest to invoke courage. She possessed spirit power...power he must overcome before carrying her back to the village. He reached for her shoulder.

I'm pleased you did not try to force me, Clayfoot. You may not think me so beautiful after we talk. Will you grant me a wish?

Startled, he drew away from this woman who knew his thoughts. "What wish? I never walk into a cave without a torch, spirit woman."

Say you will grant me a wish.

Her smile seemed sparse, almost pleading, but the shine in her black eyes held promise. Would she turn him into a raven, forever to do her bidding? What difference would it make? The tribe had mocked him since he was a boy for failing the becoming-a-man ceremony. No woman would speak to him except to sneer. If she turned him into a raven, or some beast roaming the forest, at least he'd be with her.

After a long pause he nodded.

"Maybe."

You have been chosen to accept me as your mate.

His lip curled and lust filled his mind. What good fortune! Perhaps she will be as good as her beauty when she wraps her legs around my hips. She would make me the envy of the tribe.

You may not enjoy the bargain after you hear me.

What could she tell that would turn him away?

She pointed to the distant mountains, hazy from blowing snow. Clayfoot knew the dangerous, craggy range. Once, wrapped in a buffalo robe, he'd gone far up their slopes when the tribe's rejection brought him to the brink of deep pain. Near death from the wind-whipped snow, he decided their taunts were more comfortable and returned to the warm plain.

Again her words filled his mind.

I came from a tribe far beyond the other side of the tall death. My people became angry when they didn't understand the power granted me by The

8

Great One. Birds and grass-eating animals tended me wherever I went. And I can do this...

She ran her finger over the raw place on his shoulder where the raven's claw raked a deep gash. Instantly, the stinging wound healed...warmth tingled up his back. His mouth gaped as realization sunk in. What a great friend she would be in battle. Our warriors would never die...they could live forever.

Fool. I cannot extend life. I heal sick and injured, not warriors. That's why my people grew angry. Plus the Elders were jealous and lied to have me cast out. He didn't need to know the full story...at least not at this time.

"It is their loss." He felt she was not telling all, but she still offered to mate with him. Why? And how had she crossed the White Death of the Mountains? Even in summer their peaks and valleys were deep with snow.

A sly smile crossed her lips.

I had help.

Clayfoot studied her with disbelief. What friends? Birds could not guide her over snow-filled crevasses and winds no man could walk against.

Unless she could change into....

Do not trouble yourself with my powers.

"Then why do you need a mate? If you have the power to cross them," he stabbed a finger at the mountain range, "and know a man's thoughts–"

I'll tell you why. But remember your promise to be my mate. Since the last full moon I've known I carry The Great One's child. It's a girl and I do not want her to come into the world without an earthly father. She would not survive. There is much danger in this land.

"With your power how could she not survive?"

She must have an earthly father. I'm to take the first man to enter this grove. I'm pleased you are handsome.

Clayfoot's thoughts raced to his good fortune and she would keep him from injury and...

What is your answer? Will you keep your promise to grant me a wish?

"Will you be a true mate? I don't intend to sleep alone on my bearskin." His gaze lingered on her body.

Kah-tay placed her head against his chest, then looked up at him, her eyes darker than a moonless night.

You mean like this?

Blood coursed though his body, every nerve on fire as passion ran its course.

"Yes–yes," he gasped.

It will be better than that.

"Come." He grasped her hand. "Let's seal this bargain now–in the meadow."

No!

"But you said–"

There are other tasks before us. You should return to the village in triumph, a mate across your horse and dragging the monsters from this grove.

Clayfoot scanned the clearing for strange beasts. What monsters? Nonplused, he went to Mah-ki and retrieved his lance and bow and a quiver of arrows.

Have you noticed the strange tracks in the sand?

"Many times. They are unknown to me, but I do not fear them." He straddled the three-toed tracks coming from the pond and the wavering groove between them. She led him further upstream, pointing to similar tracks leading from the grove back to the pond.

They leave the water at night and return after their kill. The beasts roam farther each night to satisfy their hunger. Someday they will reach your village and...

"No! I must kill this thing."

It will be more difficult than you think. The beast is mated and quite large. They are very dangerous. I don't know how they arrived this far inland.

"How could such a beast get here?" Wary, he scanned the surface of the pool but saw nothing. "Are they Noc-Muks, the spirit beasts?"

No. They were probably carried through the air by The Great Twisting Wind. Such things happen when nothing can withstand its force. She pointed to a stream of bubbles bursting as they rose to the surface.

Clayfoot watched for what seemed a short shadow stick then shrugged when nothing happened. He joined her on the beach.

Be ready with your lance. It will soon come to my call. I do not wish to kill it. In fact, I cannot kill. It is something you must do. Do not let it frighten you, Clayfoot. Every beast has its weak place. This one's is straight down between its eyes. You must pin it to the ground until it is dead. Avoid its lashing tail.

She knows more than she's telling, he thought, watching the bubbles draw near. Stealing a nervous glance, he saw Kah-tay clasp her hands in a tight grip and close her eyes.

A long snout broke the quiet pond. The Noc-Muk slithered forward until its short, three-toed legs reached dry sand. Glistening wet bumps covered its body. The spirit beast lunged, jaws wide, a throaty hiss roaring over its jagged teeth. More angry than a mother bear protecting her cubs, it charged again lashing its scaly tail. Longer than twenty arm lengths, it gave a loud hiss. Terrified, he stumbled back, fell once, then on his back pushed himself with quick thrusts of his legs up the sandy bank to safety.

Overcome your fear, Clayfoot, lest the beast turns on me.

His lance and bow were scattered in the sand amid his treasured arrows. Shame coated with fear raged through his mind as the Noc-Muk turned on Kah-tay. Its jaws snapped. When she clenched both fists the ugly monster stopped its forward momentum. It hugged the sand, hissing its anger.

Would she turn it into a bird?

The standoff continued long moments until the Noc-Muk inched itself against her power. She did not speak in his mind. Without her telling him, he realized she had to be using all her power to repel this evil spirit. If he didn't act he'd lose this beautiful medicine woman who asked him to be her mate.

Gulping his fear, Clayfoot leaped to his lance and straddled the scaly body. A powerful thrust between its eyes pinned it to the sand. Half his lance lay buried in the sand below the beast. A stench of stagnant water gushed from its jaws.

Kah-tay slumped after a deep breath. Her glance radiated shame at his disgraceful loss of courage. His arms trembled and his chest heaved from exertion. Fear snaked up his back. Where could such a large Noc-Muk come from?

It's no time to lose courage, Clayfoot. Its mate approaches, angry that she may lose her hatchlings. We must find her nest.

Thoughts of an angry bear defending her cubs goaded him. Only a fool would fight a mother defending her cubs. This woman called Kah-tay might lose her power when defied by a female. Should he risk his life to save her?

After a glance at the water's surface, he grasped Kah-tay around her slender waist and rushed her up the bank. He dumped her unceremoniously in the clearing.

The Noc-Muk quivered death throes when he returned to retrieve his lance. Again, he searched the pond. Its smooth surface calmed his tense muscles. Had its mate fled to avoid the fate he'd given the first spirit beast?

Scrutinizing the area, he saw nothing but a small movement in the tall reeds. Could it be it hiding there?

Cautious, his lance gripped for an instant thrust, he approached the tangled growth. Nothing moved, yet Kah-tay seemed certain a mate guarded her den.

Clayfoot shrugged and went up the sandy slope, hoping to seal their bargain in the clearing.

All at once the pool roiled and foamed next to the reeds. A quick lunge of a long snout accompanied by a throaty roar and snapping teeth drove him high-stepping across the sand. A second snap scraped his heal. Pain shot up his leg. Near the top ridge of sand he stole a glance to see if it followed.

The Noc-Muk had stopped, half curled, lashing its tail. Rotten grumbles spewed from its open jaws. For some reason it refused to charge him.

It acted like an angry she-bear and he recognized the behavior. "Guarding your cubs, mother spirit," he sneered, working up his courage. Clayfoot knew the beast would be too dangerous to frighten away...it could lunge and snap his legs like twigs. He longed for his bow and quiver of arrows scattered in the sand. From his vantage point he could send arrow after arrow into its bumpy hide.

A quick glance told him Kah-tay would be no help. She curled on the grass as if half dead from her struggle to ward off the first spirit beast. He would have to kill its mate by himself...and it would be angrier than the mean-spirited male. Tightening his grip on the lance, he shouted a war cry to build his courage.

"Hee-hee, hyah," he screamed and charged the snouted spirit.

Hissing, jaws wide, it turned to face him. When he drew too close to miss, Clayfoot hurled the lance into its open maw. The weapon sailed over jagged teeth to emerge behind its snake-like eyes. In one quick bite the hard shaft snapped as if it had been cut with a flint hand ax. The Noc-Muk lashed its tail, twisting and rolling, as it tried to expel the lance.

Snatching his bow and several arrows, he sent three quick shafts into its yellow under belly. Minutes later it quivered and lay still. He started to dance and sing around the lifeless Noc-Muk's when Kah-tay's voice entered his mind. She stood behind him.

Remember its eggs and soon-to-be hatchlings. If you fail to retrieve every one your battle with the evil beasts will be in vain.

At her calming touch, he followed Kah-tay near the clump of reeds. She pointed to a small mound. Probing with his knife, he uncovered several large eggs, alarmed that four were cracked and wiggling. One lay completely open. A baby Noc-Muk scampered toward the nearby water. Just as it reached safety a quick thrust severed its head. Clayfoot trampled the remaining eggs under his heel, then slashed them into small pieces.

No longer would these waters and the flowered clearing be feared.

Exhausted, more from fear than exertion, he collapsed in the sand. Pain burned his heel where the mother spirit had ripped a deep gash.

Kah-tay fell to her knees and touched the wound. Immediately the pain stopped. Clayfoot's eyes grew round when the wound sealed its torn edges.

"Truly you are a spirit woman," he whispered. "You stopped the first beast so I could kill–"

I did not hold it for you. The lizard from distant waters had power from the Evil One. It took all my power to protect myself. What made you gain courage?

"It moved toward you, very slow. I feared it would–I feared I would lose..."

Yes, Clayfoot. You finally gained courage to do something I cannot do, but mostly, so you could be called a man by your people–and, I think, to keep your promise to grant my wish. You were chosen to become my mate. Remember, the child I carry is not yours.

"You told me of the child's father. Only a fool would argue with The Great Spirit?" He motioned to the clearing. "Come, let us seal our bargain."

No! It will be sealed later.

Irritated by her maidenly toying he grasped her around the waist and carried her to the clearing. She seemed light, almost fragile, when he tossed her to the soft grass. Her legs went wide when she rolled on her back.

A glimpse of what lay higher up inflamed him. He would have her now. He'd forgotten the Raven until agonizing pain tore across his back. His lust diminished as he waved a protective arm at the bird. It struck again, tearing away the medicine band above the muscle on his right arm. Refusing to leave, the bird pecked at his face, missing his right eye by the width of a finger.

"Call it away–call it away!"

At her low whistle the bird settled on her shoulder.

You call yourself a man. Didn't you feel my power and the bird's anger the first time–when you lay in the dirt at my feet? Do you always freeze like ice when a strange beast presents its backside to you? And now you would force a woman to satisfy yourself. Shame.

Clayfoot slipped to the ground, head between his knees. This woman is right. He is a coward...and a forcer of women; something he had never done.

"I beg–"

Say no more. Cut two vines three times a man's length and bring them while I wash this evil stench from me.

From his perch in a tall tree, Clayfoot watched her rise in the clear pool, naked, then dive to its depth. She surfaced, a large fish wiggling in her grasp, then she lowered it to the water.

An aura of light surrounded her when the sun broke through the clouds...except the sky had been cloudless. She lifted her face to the heavens, arms spread wide. For a moment she glowed more beautiful than ever.

Teeth clenched to suppress his desire, he cut the vines and stepped to the lower branches. Why did she need long vines? At the edge of the clearing Clayfoot bit his lip when she left the water. Kah-tay extended her hand for a lift up the low ridge at the top of the beach. As she slipped by, smelling like fresh water, her soft, cool breast brushed his arm. Anger surfaced. She did that deliberately. His wrath faded as fear of this strange woman grew. For now, he would do as she wished. Stretching on the soft grass, she reclined, tantalizing, as if testing his endurance.

Her voice came into his mind.

You're learning, Clayfoot. While the wind dries me, wrap a vine behind the legs and head of your Noc-Muks. Then stretch the vines up the slope to the clearing.

Grudgingly, he did as asked, wondering what foolish thing she'd want next.

Because you need to drag them to your village to show what a great warrior you are. You can demand our mating ceremony as soon as you stop bragging. Then we will...

Clayfoot averted his eyes while she dressed, then brought his horse at her demand. Mah-ki seemed strangely calm. It had to be her power. He made a stout drag as she directed, then loaded the dead Noc-Mucs with Mah-ki's help. Finished, he lifted her to the horse's back then leaped up behind her.

Pain shot across his back, reminding him of the ever present raven circling overhead.

"Heal the pain in my back and face, Kah-tay. I beg you."

No. Let it be a lesson to you until we mate.

He'd learned the lesson, but his thoughts went to the Noc-Muks and this woman's power. Would the Horse People accept a spirit woman when they saw the fearsome beasts? He might have to fight to keep her. Her own people cast her out, she said...but if they could not stay in his village they would find another...or build their own.

Yes, Clayfoot. Even though my power is now greater, your battles are just beginning. The fight to keep me will bring you much pain.

CHAPTER TWO

Clayfoot stopped to rest. He had been leading Mah-ki to ease the burden of Kah-tay on its back and pulling the drag containing the two lizards. Pointing to a distant circle of hide-covered poles, he said, "There. My people. The tribe of the Horse."

Your village is on the ground? My people dwell in rooms of stone high above a canyon floor.

She didn't project her thoughts as she wondered what must have been a short ride to the grove for him that morning had become a slow trip back to his camp. They stopped once to repair his lance, then moved on. The sweet odor of smokey cook-fires drifting in the air made her stomach rumble. What did his people eat? Studying the irregular cook fires scattered among the hide covered circle of poles, Kah-tay sensed this was a permanent camp, not because Clayfoot's people were lazy; they had everything they needed; water, game, and maize. Over one hundred odd-shaped tents circled a large fire on an expanse of packed earth. Several men were talking, gesturing wildly, while their women stood in the background. Her thoughts were interrupted.

"Mah-ki has rested enough." He leaped on the horse's back behind her.

A sudden gust of wind felt cool on her cheek when the sweat-stained horse reared almost unseating him. She pressed her hand behind its ears, immediately calming the horse.

He smells the dead beasts. Go quickly to your village. There will be battles enough after we get there.

"Will you always speak in my mind? The Shaman will think you have no tongue. He may–"

I am learning your speech. Whenever you speak I learn a new word and how it twists my mouth and tongue. Before this night is over I may teach your Shaman what power means. Is he your only leader?

"Chief Ra-ton is old."

When Clayfoot thought of the struggle for power waged long ago between the old Chief and Nah-mo the Shaman, she knew his thoughts. Not everything was known, except Ra-ton let Nah-mo speak for him. Peyote may be the reason. Ra-ton often staggered, his speech slurred when he told of strange dreams.

I will restore him when he is ready.

"Look." He pointed at a group of children. "They see Mah-ki pulling a drag. I hate their taunts and constant ridicule saying I'm a coward. I wish one of the beasts could come to life and eat them." His expression went dour. "Then they'll fear me."

Everyone knows fear, Clayfoot. It's overcoming fear that makes a man what he is.

"Does Kah-tay know fear?"

Many times. My power brings fear that I may use it wrongly—and I fear for the child in my belly. She nodded at the distant, chanting children. *Why do they taunt you?*

"Before the becoming-a-man-ceremony my father took me hunting with the other boys and their fathers. A very large buffalo charged. Its horns were bloody—and it came at me. I was so frightened I threw down my small bow and ran. The men and other boys jeered me. I was truly a child with feet of clay, but someday they will call me a man. Today they ordered me to leave."

She read his thoughts of that day and the torments he'd suffered; disowned and never allowed to take the becoming-a-man-ceremony. Later, he'd grown indifferent; a head taller and more muscular than other men. But he was quiet, soft hearted, enduring the ridicule until their sneers and scorn became too great. Then he'd leave for days, wandering the forests and plains, seeking courage.

You must have been lonely. How did you get your iron-tipped lance and the blade of iron at your side? And this great horse? She leaned back against his powerful chest. *The choice is right...and his heart is tender.*

"You know my thoughts, Kah-tay. Far to the South I found a strange man with white skin and hair growing on his face. He was dying from a wound in his belly. His horse was dead and little Mah-ki nuzzled and cried for his mother. I offered the baby horse dried meat, but he would not eat it. A handful of grain from a leather bag on the stranger's dead horse made Mah-ki happy. Like a sticky fly, he followed me, wanting more grain.

"The man motioned me closer, but I could not understand his strange tongue. When he took this knife from his belt and motioned me to cut his throat–I understood. An old belly wound is a painful way to die. He motioned me to take what I wanted. 'Mah-ki'? I pointed to the little horse. He nodded. I gave him a drink of water and he smiled. Then he made a strange hand movement to his head and heart, ending at his shoulders. I cut his throat."

You were very kind, Clayfoot. An old wound in the belly never heals. He asked you to end his suffering.

"I took his strange lance and the knife. His iron shirt smelled like rotten meat so I buried it with him. Everyone mocked me when I returned with my little horse.

"They had just come from a war party against the strange white men who wore shirts of iron. Many had horses and knives. Only one of my people took the iron shirt. He stunk many days from it. I was told it is very hot to wear in the summer and cold in the winter. My brother is a dangerous fool, but he will not part with the iron shirt."

You're thinking of Ironskin, your tormenter. Will you fight him again?

Clayfoot smiled. "Are there no secrets from you, Woman of Magic? You know my every thought. I always have to fight him. He never learns. But he knows I will not kill any of my people."

Will you fight him for me?

He looked into her eyes when she turned to him. "You asked me to grant you a wish. Do you now want the one who is the best warrior? I have to fight him for anything of value I bring to the village. If he wins, the fool will treat you the same as all women he knows.

For the price of a fur or pretty stones, his squaws straddle the road as far as the eye can see. No decent woman will have him. It is said he is a forcer of woman."

Nevertheless, you will fight him.

Kah-tay smiled at his attempt to hide his thoughts. She read every emotion. Ironskin bore many scars from their previous battles; over Mah-ki, then over the lance with which Clayfoot cut two toes from Ironskin's left foot. Kah-tay leaned her head against his chest as they approached the taunting row of children. After seeing what lay on the drag they ran screaming to their mothers.

Kah-tay will use her power to...

No. I will not kill.

"You mean with your new power you would accept...?"

Kah-tay refused to answer and noticed he tightened his lips. He would fight–perhaps this time kill. Her braids rubbed against his chest when he took a deep breath. This man would do. An almost forgotten urge settled on her. Remembering, she relished the smell of clean sweat, the scent of flowers and the taste of tender lips. She felt a shiver rippling up his spine, sensing his resignation to whatever fate this battle would bring. Ironskin would challenge him for his woman.

Am I your woman?

He grunted, "You know the answer."

Murmurs rumbled through the crowd as they made room for Clayfoot and the strange woman and fearsome beasts. When they reached the center of packed earth, near the flickering light from the council fire, he helped her from the horse.

"See? I bring my woman and these Noc-Muks, the spirit-beasts from the grove. They fought with evil spells and teeth that burn when they bite. My lance pinned the evil beasts to the ground. It takes great courage to fight spirits like these."

Clayfoot cut the bindings holding the lizards to the drag. After rolling them off, he placed a foot on the biggest of the Noc-Muks and crossed his arms. Again Mah-ki smelled the dead carcasses and reared. Kah-tay touched its neck, murmured, and the horse became calm.

"My woman is Kah-tay from beyond the White Hills of Death."

She noticed him glance across the circle to a man in an iron shirt, knowing he saw her soothe the horse's fear. *Ironskin is no fool. He knows which is more valuable...and there is evil in his eyes.*

Ra-ton, head dress askew, and Nah-mo shaking his gourd to ward off spirits, inspected the foul smelling lizards.

The old Chief smiled over his toothless gums. "You have done well for a man with no courage. I think you have been fooling us all these years playing the coward."

Kah-tay suppressed a smile when Clayfoot tried not to let his pride show while telling the story of how he slew the spirit-beasts. He left out the part she played in his success.

Enjoy your fame, famous warrior. I sense jealousy and hatred among the council. Not all consider you a man.

His look became angry, but she shrugged and moved toward the women. Among them she noticed a young girl with a club foot hiding behind her mother's skirt. Ba-chey? Is that what Clayfoot's thoughts named her? Her fingers passed over the child's face, then dropped to caress the deformed limb. In moments the foot became perfect.

Amazed gasps came from the women. Immediately, Shaman Nah-mo ignored the rest of Clayfoot's tale and strode to her. A slight smile played across her lips as she projected her thoughts to Clayfoot.

He must perform another spirit cleansing ceremony. Nah-mo enjoys his power over your people.

She let the Shaman dance around her, shaking his gourd rattle. Kah-tay saw fear in his eyes when he peered at her body and watched his fear change to desire. When Nah-mo reached to touch her, Clayfoot hurled his lance, planting it in the ground between the Shaman's feet.

"No man may touch another's woman, Nah-mo. You know our law." Retrieving his lance, he stepped in front of her, arms crossed, watching as the humiliated Shaman went back to his seat beside Ra-ton.

The old Chief's cunning grin told her Clayfoot's troubles were not over. Ra-ton reached in a beaded bag and retrieved a peyote button.

His healing begins. Clenching her fist, she stepped beside Clayfoot. *Watch.*

Ra-ton cut a small bit of the button and rubbed it over his gums before placing it in his mouth. Immediately, he spit the peyote to the ground.

"Buffalo droppings," he muttered and reached for another button.

Again her fist clenched. Old Ra-ton flung the bag aside. Several scorpions crawled up his arm, lashing their barbed tails. He screamed when they stung, repeatedly, then dropped from his arm. In moments, his arm swelled to twice its size.

His days with peyote are over. Whenever he has the urge to eat them he'll remember the scorpions.

The scene was broken by a shrill voice behind the Chief. Ironskin stepped into the flickering circle of night fire, an arrow knocked in his bow.

"I fight you for this woman, coward. She will use what little beauty she has to pleasure me."

Kah-tay felt Clayfoot's rage. Ironskin wanted to fight from a distance with arrows. Hefting his lance, Clayfoot stepped to the face the challenge.

No. Once you throw the lance you cannot win. Use your knife and circle to the left. Never stop moving left until you see an opening. You'll know it when you see it. Be careful. I sense treachery from this one. Remember, you are a man among men, but I cannot help you.

***

For once Clayfoot never questioned her thoughts. A surge of pride went across his chest. A man among men she said. He knew Ironskin's trickery. By circling left he'd put pressure on Ironskin's old foot wound. Handing his lance to her, he pulled the knife from his belt.

"You are the coward, Ironskin. You would stand far off and send arrows at my naked chest?"

"I will fight with the knife," Ironskin sneered. "You have seen my skill with the iron blade before. I'll give you another lesson. Admit defeat now, coward, or I'll make woman's hair ribbons from your chest." He tossed his bow aside and pulled a long blade from its sheath. "I'll be good to your woman–as long as she pleases me."

Ironskin's chest was protected front and back by the rusting iron shirt. Crouched low, his enemy started to circle right, waving the long blade. Clayfoot refused to follow his lead. He feinted once to put Ironskin on guard, then circled left. It would be difficult to find a place to slip his blade. Several times Ironskin tried to change and move to the right, but a quick lunge put the boring infighting on track. They continued feints and lunges to the taunts of jeering warriors.

Not a thought came from Kah-tay. She said she would not help him. The only sound came from their feet padding and scraping the packed earth as they circled for advantage. Orange light flickered across Ironskin's shirt and the sinister grin on his face. If Kah-tay fell under Ironskin's control...

Ironskin shifted his knife to his left hand and made a quick upward thrust. A red streak went up Clayfoot's chest, bringing with it a sense of terror.

The crowd cheered when they saw the bloody streak.

"Admit defeat, coward. My next cut will be in your heart. The woman is as good as mine."

Clayfoot said nothing. He locked eyes with his enemy, knowing the opening would appear first in the man's eyes. His stomach muscles tensed when he momentarily dropped his guard. If he failed...

It came when the over-confident man in the iron shirt rushed forward, slashing at his chest. Stepping left, he spun away from Ironskin. The man's back was exposed beneath the iron shirt. His blade flashed in the light from the blazing fire. Leaping forward, his foot struck a log protruding from the fire, throwing him off balance. What was supposed to be the killing thrust merely scraped rust-colored sweaty skin from the warrior's back.

"I could have cut your bones, Ironskin. You would beg for death to keep from crawling to the woods and squat like a woman." Clayfoot made a hacking gesture with his knife.

Smirking, Ironskin said, "Fight, coward. You can scrape skin, but never kill."

The warrior tried to circle right apparently to relieve the pressure on his left foot, but Clayfoot insisted they continue to the left. His arm grew tired and he shifted the weapon to his left hand. Immediately, Ironskin took advantage and slashed Clayfoot's chest, again drawing blood.

The crowd roared their approval. Ironskin lunged again, missed, and rolled to the ground. Clayfoot saw him grasp a handful of dirt. Loathing seized him. The braggart would use anything to win. He suppressed his disgust and teased his brother.

"Would you use dirt to cloud my eyes, man-who-stinks? Am I too strong for you?"

He raised a sweat-streaked arm to ward off the shower of dirt and swung left, always following Kah-tay's advice. Grit showered his face. Ironskin shifted his blade to his right hand and lunged, aiming for the heart. Through dirt-filled eyes he saw what Kah-tay meant. Knives screeched as blade struck blade. Ironskin missed by the width of a leaf of grass. Cautious, Clayfoot crouched as Ironskin lunged again. Quickly, he grasped Ironskin's hand and with one chopping motion he severed it at the wrist. His rival fell away, howling as blood spurted into the council fire. Horror-stricken, Clayfoot watched the grasping hand crawl across the ground. Eerie light from the fire played across its moving fingers. Had Kah-tay made the hand move? His spine tingled from the thought.

"Now you can relieve yourself with your left hand. Or maybe you'll squat like a woman. I warned you once." Clayfoot turned his back and walked away.

Raise your left fist.

Why, he wondered, but he did as she ordered.

Angry in defeat, Ironskin hurled his knife left-handed. Unerringly, it came toward its mark then shifted upwards to lodge in Clayfoot's clenched fist. It appeared as if he'd caught the knife in midair.

The crowed gasped at his display of magic.

"He can catch a weapon in flight," muttered one.

Clayfoot nodded. "You said you wouldn't help me," he muttered.

Not during the fight. Nor would I have you slain after a fair fight, my warrior. But did you have to taunt him? Why didn't you cut his throat when you had the chance?

"It was too easy–and I didn't think it was what you wanted."

You may regret your decision. That man is evil and can do further harm. Now I must heal part of him.

Kah-tay clenched her fist. Blood stopped flowing from Ironskin's arm. Warriors and women who'd cheered him to victory now taunted the defeated warrior. Ironskin rushed though their ranks to his tipi. Clayfoot turned his attention to the Chief.

"Ra-ton. I give you the beasts. They–"

Not the belly of the large one. I need it to make something for my child.

"...are fearsome," said Clayfoot. "But I must keep the belly of the large one for a totem."

"Are they good to eat?" Ra-ton shuffled to the big Noc-Muk. After prodding it with his foot he said, "Let us feast on these spirits. By eating them we will gain their strength."

***

Kah-tay put a hand over her mouth to hide a smile trying to surface. She should warn them about eating crocodile flesh.

Their meat is stringy and tough. Some think it is bitter. Warn them it is a flesh eater.

Clayfoot told them then turned to her. "Why must I always speak for you? Haven't you learned our tongue yet?"

Yes, but the time is not right. I would have you play the champion a while longer to prove what I already know. You are a man. I'll speak in their minds soon, but you will hear the words, too.

Women clustered around the Noc-Muks at Nah-mo's orders. "Remember, the large one's belly skin belongs to Clayfoot," he said.

The skinners grumbled about the tough hide wondering what it could be used for. It was not soft like deerskin. For some reason Nah-mo wanted the beast's heads. The Shaman ordered them to put the heads on an anthill. Much power would come from wearing the head of these spirit beasts instead of the buffalo head he'd inherited from his father.

"I will have one head, Nah-mo," said Ra-ton shaking his eagle feather head dress.

The Shaman turned to the old Chief. "Go eat your peyote, old man."

"I no longer feel the need for it."

I sense another battle for control of your people.

"They fight forever, Kah-tay. After the meat is eaten I will ask Ra-ton to have the mating ceremony." He looked down at her with tender lust in his heart. Their glances were interrupted by the young girl whose foot Kah-tay healed. Ba-chey tugged at her skirt.

"Mother wishes to speak with you."

Clayfoot. Tell her I will speak tomorrow.

"Kah-tay will talk to your mother tomorrow, Ba-chey." The girl ran back to the carving women.

Clayfoot nudged Kah-tay and nodded across the circle. Nah-mo was staring at them with narrowed eyes.

"He knows about your power. What will you do?"

***

Kah-tay sent her thoughts to the Shaman and Clayfoot.

I will not interfere with your fight for control, Shaman. But you must remember who is Chief. My power comes from The Great One. It is not for you to use.

Clayfoot laughed as her words sent the Shaman into a frenzy. Words in his head must have driven him mad. Nah-mo jerked the aged buffalo-horn totem from his head and flung it to the ground. Still laughing, Clayfoot brushed the back of his hand across her cheek. She closed her eyes. He was right for her.

She sensed the meat tasted too strong for Clayfoot, but he swallowed it then passed his share to a warrior. After each had eaten the stingy flesh the drums beat faster, changing tone and rhythm. Kah-tay watched Clayfoot when the women formed a circle around the council fire and began a dance. She sensed Clayfoot never dreamed this dance would be performed for him. Nah-mo raised his gourd rattle and the drums stopped. Raising the rattle, he walked around the couple three times, shaking the gourd.

Four young women came to Kah-tay, motioning her to follow them. Giggling amongst themselves, the main thought pattern she heard was the size of Clayfoot's manhood. The rest seemed silly chatter. Since Clayfoot stood taller and more muscular, said one, surely he was well equipped to satisfy a woman.

"We will dress you for the mating ceremony."

One girl, who appeared to be older, brought a white deerskin garment covered with colorful beads and silver ornaments. Kah-tay sensed it was a long wedding shirt and stood patiently while the girls removed her clothes.

Their thoughts centered on her light skin, strange moccasins, and the golden cowl over her shoulders. Some day she would tell why her people wore hard soles and leg wraps.

"Come. You must bathe."

Through an opening in the back of the tipi they surrounded her in the dark and led her to a pond. While she washed, Kah-tay thought of other ceremonies; some more elaborate, one as simple as jumping over a log holding hands. This mating would be the most important of all. For the first time she bore a child of The Great One. Not only handsome and muscular, he'd promised to care for her child as if it were his own. A certain once-learned-always-remembered intelligence lingered about him. He was truly a man and now a champion among his people.

A few still had their old bigotry about boy-hood cowardice clouding their minds, but tonight's battle with Ironskin should put an end to his problems.

The oldest maiden approached. "Come."

After drying her with furs they dressed her in the beaded wedding garment. The maiden braided her hair, entwining it with bright feathers.

The crowd gasped when they led her to the circle...Clayfoot loudest of all.

"You are the most beautiful of women."

You are the man I want forever.

Seated close to the circle of fire, she noticed the drumbeat changed to a sensual rhythm. Nah-mo placed a glistening bearskin around their shoulders, encasing them as one. While the women danced, the men drank a strong brew made from maize. Their speech became slurred and rowdy...always questioning Clayfoot's sexual prowess. Kah-tay heard them placing bets as to how many times he would mount his bride that night.

"Come," said one of the women, removing the bearskin from their shoulders.

Leaving the circle, women danced around them always channeling them to a new tipi. Drumbeats increased to a heady rhythm.

How quickly they made this home for us.

"Yes, but not quick enough to suit me."

Two women held the flap aside as the mated pair were pushed inside.

"At last."

Impatient man. We have all night.

"And I intend to use it."

He reached for her but she brushed his hands aside.

You will feel better after this.

Kah-tay touched his back, face, and chest, healing his wounds. Fumbling, he pulled the wedding shirt over her shoulders. She curled on the bearskin, tantalizing, a cunning smile on her lips. He stripped the breechcloth from his loins and fell to his knees.

Do not be hasty, my lover. I'm not easily satisfied.

***

Clayfoot dropped beside her. "I have never done this."

"I will give you lessons."

Several times every nerve came ablaze from her power. She had touched his very soul.

Gasping, he said, "It is...much better...as you...promised. Were you...satisfied?"

"If I do not cry out–I need more."

"You spoke!" whispered a surprised Clayfoot

"You bring out my words."

"Each hour I grow deeper into slavery for you, my beautiful Kah-tay. You are with me always."

Much later she nestled in his armpit. He wrapped a protective arm around her shoulders.

"Protect me, my love," she whispered. "I'm vulnerable when I go into deep sleep."

Later, he woke, unmoving, afraid he would wake her. Kah-tay's long hair curled in his armpit, her face against his chest, a gentle smile on her lips. A sudden thought creased his brow. Would he always have to fight to keep her? Through lidded eyes he glimpsed Raven perched above them on a tent pole, blotting out the night sky and brilliant stars. His contented thoughts went to the bird.

Together we will watch over her.

Nestled close to Kah-tay, he heard a rasping whisper. His eyes snapped open.

I always watch over her. Raven cocked its head, its yellow eyes searching the dim interior.

Surprised and fully awake, Clayfoot concentrated on the bird.

You heard my thoughts?

Of course. She asked that power be granted you. More's the pity. Kah-tay will regret that. It's not the first time.

CHAPTER THREE

Kah-tay sat in front of Clayfoot's tipi, pleased she'd suggested he lead a scout party to the grove. A shadow stick later they could see for themselves he was a man of courage and would acknowledge his right to manhood. She could hear the women talking about her, their thoughts drifting like cottonwood silk in a breeze. They were afraid to approach, but were very curious about her flat stones. Round and round they went as she poured grain into the hole in the top stone.

Kah-tay knew they used a large pounding stick after placing the maize in a hollow of a stump. Tedious and inefficient, but they would soon ask her to show how the stones worked.

She'd gone early that morning to the field, long before the sun brought the new day, threading her way among the colorful tipis decorated with individual family totems. She resisted the urge to interpret the symbols. It seemed an intrusion. Most were fecundity symbols, but one leapt out at her. It depicted a saguaro cactus touching a bright sun. A sensual aura came from it leaving no doubt it was a phallic symbol probably added by a hopeful young bride.

In the field beyond, flat stones were there for the taking, and she found wild maize. Now, the smell of fine, stone-ground flour seemed pleasing.

Kah-tay sensed the presence of a small child trying to peer over her shoulder. Ba-chey, the little girl whose foot she had healed, crowded close.

"What are you making?"

"Food. My people, like yours, eat grain they harvest before the snow comes." She tried to sound unconcerned. "It's good to eat with meat and fish. How is your foot?"

"You are a woman of magic. Mother wants to thank you, but she is frightened."

"Everyone is frightened when they don't understand." She poured another handful of maize into the top hole. A grim smile crossed her face.

They would really be frightened if they saw how she made the hole in the top and center stones, but some things were better left unknown.

"I would speak with your mother, Ba-chey. Tell her to sit with me."

Ba-chey ran to her mother. Kah-tay smiled as the youngster pulled the woman's hand, cajoling her to cross the council area. They had much to learn, these people of Clayfoot.

"See, Mother. She makes a powder from wild maize. It looks easier than the pounding stick." The child sat cross-legged beside Kah-tay, snuggling close. Her mother took a place opposite, her eyes filled with fear.

"You're frightened," said Kah-tay. "Why? Because I have power you do not understand? Children should be cared for with love." She continued to work the wheel, trying to calm the girl's mother. "When I was a child I knew great affection from my mother and father."

The child's mother remained silent, her eyes fixed on the whirling stone and the smooth yellow powder spilling from grooves in the stones.

Frightened, the woman trembled as she watched the wheel. Kah-tay decided to enter her mind. Ah. She fears her daughter's healing is temporary and will return in a few days...or if I leave.

To reassure the woman she said, "I am mated to Clayfoot now and will not leave him. Your daughter's healed foot will remain all of her life." She scooped up a bit of maize flour, tasted it, and gave a bit to the little girl.

"It's good when mixed in the pot with meat, or rolled flat and baked then wrapped around fruit or meat. Do you use it this way?"

A relieved look came in the woman's eyes. Kah-tay sensed her curiosity to taste the finely ground flour.

"Here. Taste and see what you can make to please your man."

"I have no man. He was killed by the strange weapons used by the men who wear iron shirts."

"Who provides for you, then?"

"We take the scraps left by others."

Kah-tay's anger surfaced. Soon this woman will have a mate. She has much to give. Her skin is fair and there is love in her heart, but there is an overpowering sense of Ironskin and temptation to feed her child and herself if she gave in to his evil proposal. Little did the woman know Ironskin promised everything and gave nothing. Clayfoot should have killed him.

A shiver went up her back. Someday her husband would regret only maiming Ironskin. Instead of talking to the woman's mind, she planted a seed of well-being, one of love and compassion.

"I am Na-nah. My child's name is Ba-chey." She stood and placed her cheek affectionately to Kah-tay's. "You are a good woman. Especially for Clayfoot. He is fortunate."

"Yes. As long as he realizes it." She gave the wheel a playful spin.

The woman sighed and took Ba-chey's hand.

Kah-tay said after her, "You will soon have a good man and Ba-chey will be accepted by the other children."

"They haven't accepted her yet. They are frightened, but she runs and plays anyway."

Across the clearing two aged, sun-wrinkled crones watched. Kah-tay knew their thoughts. *What right has this outsider to enter our village and heal our people? We accept what The Great One gives us.* Now *they* were coming to see what she was doing. She entered their minds for a closer reading. The feathered one was Ta-nic, Nah-mo's wife; the other, Li-nat, Ra-ton's wife. *Fools*, she thought, then regretted the judgment. They must learn, these simple people, and she had much to teach. They would resent a direct approach. She could not say, 'Do it this way' or 'my people know a better way.' Gentle discoveries would be much better.

"Did Clayfoot give you much pleasure?"

Ta-nic surprised her. *Had they been listening outside the tipi?*

"Clayfoot is a good lover," she replied trying to sound calm.

"He must be. Your shouts of joy kept us awake all night."

An outright lie, of course. They want to make friends with this strange newcomer, she thought, *and Ra-ton's wife had much to be thankful for.* The Chief's desire for peyote had left him. The two women sat and sampled the maize flour.

Ta-nic grimaced. "Need's salt."

Li-nat nodded. "Yes, but it might fill a man's belly if he is hungry."

Of course it needs salt, but her reply was timid. "Do you think so? I'll ask Clayfoot to find some."

"Don't bother. We have plenty and will share."

Yes, you will share. I've known about salt long before you were born, old woman. Kah-tay projected the thought to Raven doing a nervous dance atop the tent pole.

Be at peace my ageless companion. Clayfoot has become one with us, but his people are superstitious. There is much they do not need to know–even Clayfoot.

The bird paced as small noises cackled from its beak. *Phaugh! You go to the Evil place for lying the same as for killing.*

I know. But he pleasures me and it has been a long time. Remember, he promised to care for my little one.

The Raven twittered. *I suppose you want me to befriend him like I did the others.*

Of course.

An awkward silence followed until Ta-nic cleared her throat. She asked how Kah-tay had healed Ba-chey's foot.

"It is a gift from The Great One. I will not see a child suffer."

Both women grew startled when the Raven fluttered to Kah-tay's shoulder.

"This is my friend from the forest." She ran her finger over the bird's head, then motioned him back to his perch atop the tipi.

"Clayfoot said you had strange power over birds." Li-nat dipped her finger in the maize flour for another taste. "He mentioned it when Ra-ton asked him to visit the grove again. The warriors wanted to see where the Noc-Muks lived."

Ta-nic shuddered. "We hope they don't find another one. Their flesh tastes terrible."

"Clayfoot promised he would warn them."

"So, you have seen these beasts before, have you?"

I've fallen into a trap, she thought. To admit she knew about evil-tempered crocodiles would draw her deeper into things they wouldn't understand. Clayfoot would have more problems. The men were still wary of a man with no courage. They had only gone with him this morning because they wanted to confirm their own manhood. She hadn't failed to notice they were armed with every weapon at their command.

"Warriors of my people traveled far in search of food. They discovered strange beasts like these and warned us they were only good for hides."

She hoped the simple explanation would suffice. If not, she would have to enter their minds and...

The Raven cackled. *Your mouth overburdens your...*

Silence! You always poke your beak into unwanted conversations. I have a good mind to send you...

Phaugh! You can't. It is my duty to guard you and you know it.

Dust on the horizon saved her. She pointed at the growing cloud of riders. "The men return," she said to the women.

Li-nat scrambled to her feet. "I must hurry to tell Ra-ton. Since he no longer has strange dreams, he will want to hear every story when the warriors return."

"Nah-mo must hear of it, too. Although I don't see how he can hear with that stinking beast's head over his ears. He looked more handsome with his old buffalo horns."

Kah-tay smiled. He'll not wear it much longer, she thought and entered Ta-nic's mind to see Nah-mo through her eyes. She covered her mouth to avoid laughing. The Shaman looked ridiculous when he emerged from his tipi, wearing the uncured beast's head. The vicious looking crocodile snout bumped against a lodge pole, jamming the foul-smelling thing down to where it covered his mouth and nose. Closing her fist she caused its head to catch him in a tight grip. Nah-mo danced in blind circles, jerking at the long head as he tried to remove his new totem.

"Get it off me, woman. Can't you see its evil power is trying to suffocate me?"

Ta-nic cut the ever-tightening strap to free her husband. Kah-tay felt the woman's pleasure as she sawed very slowly, mumbling how tough the beast's hide was...and that she worked as fast as she could. What wicked pleasure Ta-nic took in prolonging her husband's suffering!

Kah-tay tightened her fist again, causing a bit of rotten flesh to enter Nah-mo's mouth. At last the head came free. The Shaman hurled it as far as he could, gagging on a bit of filthy meat stuck to his teeth. Spitting, he ran to a water skin.

"Get this taste from me, woman."

Ta-nic searched for her bag of salt, knowing all the while where it was, and finally found it.

"Put a large amount in your mouth, Shaman husband. It will help take the taste away."

Kah-tay withdrew from Ta-nic's mind, enjoying the woman's wifely pleasure from an overbearing husband who vented mistakes on his wife. Her thoughts went to Clayfoot as the scout party entered the camp. Had he succeeded? Did the warriors accept him as a one of their own? She resisted the urge to read their thoughts. It seemed only right her husband be the one to tell of his triumph or failure.

Kah-tay marveled at his muscles rippling in the noon sun as he wiped sweat from Mah-ki. A gray-haired brave spoke briefly to Clayfoot across the horse's back then joined his friends.

"What did the old warrior want?" she asked when Clayfoot sat opposite her. He smelled like horse sweat.

"Tato wanted to turn his mare loose with Mah-ki, hoping for another great horse."

He dipped a wet finger in the finely ground maize and tasted it.

"Needs salt."

"Of course it needs salt. Can't you wait until I'm finished with it?" She gave the stone wheel an angry turn. "Ta-nic said it needed salt, too. Wisely, I played the innocent beginner and thanked her. I knew of salt before she was born."

She realized from Clayfoot's amazed look she had made another mistake, but he knew of her powers. What he didn't know about was long life...a gift from The Great One.

Phaugh! You've done it again. Will you ever learn to stop talking?

Kah-tay ignored Raven's admonition.

"There are powers yet unknown to you, husband. You'll learn of them if you have the courage to remain with me"

Clayfoot thrust out his chest and jutted his jaw.

"I have the courage to know fear–and when to run or attack if it's to my advantage." His gaze locked on hers. "I granted you a wish and I will honor it forever."

"You have great courage, Clayfoot. Have no doubt."

"There's still doubt in many warriors. They think it's your doing."

"Then they haven't talked to Ironskin."

"Ironskin is no longer a warrior in their sight. They ignore him." He stood and crossed his arms. "I swam in the pool but only old Tato joined me. They still fear the long-snouts."

"Then they should acknowledge your manhood. There are no more beasts in the pool." She reached for his hand and pulled herself to her feet. Out of the corner of her eye she saw Ta-nic approach carrying a small leather bag. A sense of mirth radiated from the Shaman's wife.

"I bring the salt I promised, although I have no doubt you could make your own." She handed her the pouch.

"I cannot make salt, big sister. Sometimes I can heal the sick or injured. Thank you for sharing."

Ta-nic looked at her knowingly. "I felt you in my mind enjoying Nah-mo's fight with the loathsome snout. You really *are* a Woman of Magic."

The woman is gifted if she felt me probe her mind. I'll have to be very careful.

Raven paced the top poles. *See? I warned you.*

Kah-tay gritted her teeth. *Will you never be quiet?*

"The Shaman did look silly in that snouted beast's head. Every woman in the village enjoyed his outburst."

"Nah-mo is repairing his buffalo horn head dress."

Ever inquisitive, Clayfoot asked, "What did I miss?"

"A lesson in too much pride, man-with-no-courage." Ta-nic patted his shoulder. "My son said you have more courage than all the others. He wished to join you in the water but feared the warriors would scorn him."

"He can join me anytime—or go by himself. There's no danger. The water is clear as the sky."

Ta-nic smiled and invited Kah-tay to visit. "We would know more of your people." Abruptly, she left.

"You must explain, Kah-tay."

"Later. Are you hungry?"

"I'm always hungry...for you." He clasped her hand and drew her into the tipi.

"Wasn't this morning enough?"

"When I think on it, no. And I think of you often."

She sighed. "I think of you, Clayfoot." She loosened the tie on her long shirt. "More often than I should."

"Do not use your powers until the last. I would touch your soul again, my wife."

And he touched her soul...not once, but twice.

Breathless, she gazed at the tent pole, her eyes intent on the ever-present Raven. It cocked its head.

Will you paint a cactus in the sun on his tipi?

Silence. He pleasures me—and it is my right. Watch, now. I'm very tired.

She curled into Clayfoot's armpit and fell into a deep sleep.

***

Raven's caw woke her. *Danger.* She shook Clayfoot awake. *The bird is warning us. Come.*

They dashed from the tipi. At first glance they saw nothing. Clayfoot scanned the horizon.

"I see nothing except a distant rider. Probably one of our scouts searching for game. But he is riding like the wind and the sun glints..."

Kah-tay sensed evil...evil already completed. She heard the horses snort and looked to the high-branched corral.

"Mah-ki!" she shouted and clutched Clayfoot's arm

Clayfoot ran to the corral, leaping over the gate in his hurry to get to his horse. The great beast lay on the ground, his legs flopping. Blood seeped from its pasterns and a deep wound in its chest. His once-speckled white coat was spattered with bright red blood.

"Mah-ki!" Clayfoot cradled the horse's head in his arms. The odor of fresh blood saturated the air. Tears ran down his cheeks. Sobbing, he asked, "Who did this?"

Kah-tay dropped to her knees beside him. She passed her hands over Mah-ki's eyes and the animal calmed.

Who did this, mighty horse?

The man with no hand.

Wrapping her hands around one pastern, she stopped the bleeding. Ligaments and muscles healed. She grasped the next pastern, repeating the healing process until his legs lay still. The chest wound was deep and sucking air.

"I'll try, Clayfoot. But Mah-ki is near death."

"You can heal him. The Great One gave you more power. I saw it the day you came out of the pool. A great light came from the sky."

Kah-tay looked at him quizzically, then placed both hands over the gaping wound until blood ceased to flow. Sucking sounds continued through the wound, whistling around her tightly pressed fingers for several seconds, then stopped.

Are you well?

Mah-ki nickered.

"Ironskin," whispered Clayfoot. "I'll kill him for this."

"It may be more difficult than you think, husband." She lifted Mah-ki's head, urging him to stand. "Ironskin has wickedness in his heart. He may give himself over to the Evil One."

Clayfoot's arms crossed his massive chest. "He can be killed...and I'll be the one who does it."

Raven leaped from its perch, circled once, and followed the distant rider.

CHAPTER FOUR

Distant storm clouds gathered near the horizon. Kah-tay sensed an awesome force growing as it moved toward the village. She knew she had no control over the weather, only the power to escape the deluge. Her adopted tribe of the Horse People would need protection.

Sensations of other beings invaded her mind, pulling her attention from the storm; beings the tribe needed to survive. A strong essence of buffalo came from beyond the hills to the West. She sensed a massive herd stampeding North to escape the violent storm.

"Clayfoot?"

No answer. Kah-tay put aside the tanned crocodile underbelly and searched the area. She found him in the corral with Mah-ki. The old warrior, Tato, lingered there with his young, white mare, talking to her husband.

She wrinkled her nose at the odor of the young mare's heat. Others couldn't detect it, but she could and told Clayfoot the mare was ready two days ago. He had promised Tato that Mah-ki would breed his young mare when it wanted to get to the stallion. Now, his prized horse had leaped the thornbush fence. Kah-tay watched Clayfoot and gray-haired Tato grin as the red-speckled white stallion mounted the mare. Someday she would have to teach Clayfoot the proper method of handling a breeding session. For the present, more important were the approaching buffalo.

I called by mouth and you did not answer. When Mah-ki is finished, gather the hunters. An endless herd of buffalo is coming just beyond the hill in the next canyon. Storm clouds are gathering. I suggest you hurry or there may be hungry bellies if you let this opportunity pass.

Clayfoot glanced at her, the horizon, then the hill. "We cannot leave the breeding. I gave my word."

I don't intend to run from a herd of mindless buffalo because Mah-ki's first breeding is more important than food...and danger if the beasts turn into this valley. They could trample your people to dust.

"But..."

At that moment a strong branch from the thorn bush unwound itself and stabbed a finger-long thorn into Clayfoot's buttocks. He howled and danced away from the bush then fell in the dirt beneath the young mare.

Kah-tay unclenched her fist and laughed.

You are more stubborn than a small horse only two moons old. Have I ever told you something not true?

"No," he said, rubbing his behind.

After Mah-ki dismounted, she nodded her approval. Clayfoot wrapped a braided leather lead-line around the horse's neck and muzzle, but the stallion seemed reluctant to leave the corral.

Clayfoot pointed to the tall hill. Tato followed his bearing then raced to his spotted mare. Evidently her husband mentioned the herd of buffalo.

The old warrior seemed more excited than Clayfoot because he rode through the village, shouting about the approaching buffalo and telling the warriors to hurry. Clayfoot stopped by the tipi to gather his lance and bow.

"Do something about this pain in my ass, woman. You know I can't sit on Mah-ki's back and thrust a lance or pull a bow when I hurt like this."

She touched a finger on the bloody spot, then rubbed her hand affectionately across his muscular buttocks.

"I should let you suffer, husband. Sometimes *you* can be a pain in the ass. Now, return with many dead buffalo."

He held her long moments, his hands sliding down her sides to grasp the firm mounds below her back. She placed her head on his chest, knowing he felt a burst of passion.

Muttered voices drifted across the clearing.

"Clayfoot lies. There are no buffalo. See how he fondles his woman."

"If he says there is buffalo, I believe him. His woman gives him secret signs."

Kah-tay grinned. Reading their thoughts had become easy and knew they'd go if only to prove Clayfoot wrong. Assembled hunters milled through the corral, gathering their horses. Clayfoot grasped his lance, slung his bow and arrows across his shoulders, and raced Mah-ki to the nearby hill.

"Hurry," he shouted. "We must beat the storm."

The warriors raced to join him. Kah-tay sensed they would not let him make the first kill, but knew he would; he was already a distant speck when they charged after him.

***

Women skinned the last carcass when Kah-tay felt a strange fear...an evil, metallic odor. She knew they were jealous because Clayfoot had given her his iron knife to skin and butcher the buffalo.

"Iron knives are for men," one muttered as she cut and scraped with her flint hand knife. Hunters merely dragged their kill to the center of the village then stalked to the talking circle to tell of their hunting prowess. Not one mentioned Clayfoot made the first kill...a kill which turned the stampeding herd and stopped them from entering the valley.

Jealousy from the women didn't bring the fear she felt. Kah-tay perceived something else...something close and sinister. After cutting the last of her share she went to her tipi to rest. The knife lay slack in her fingers as she sat cross-legged, her mind drifting...drifting....

Mother. I'm frightened.

Kah-tay gasped and dropped the knife. She clutched her belly.

Do not fear, little one. You are protected.

Yes. Father will watch over me, but there is danger.

Surprise overcame Kah-tay. The child had progressed much faster than she realized.

Nah-mo's wife appeared, towering over her, a quizzical look on her face. "You feel the child so soon?"

There would be much to explain if they counted days. Every woman knew the number of moons it took before life was felt...most especially the number of moons before a child was born.

"No, Ta-nic. I think it is the thought of food making noises in my belly."

"Humph." Li-nat peered over Ta-nic's shoulder. "It should pass, but please stay down wind from us."

Kah-tay smiled and turned her thoughts inward to the child.

Mother. Are they nice to us?

Yes. They are friends–and will love you.

Where is Father? There is danger.

He is with the men. I will call him. Listen. Clayfoot! If you're through

37

bragging we must talk. NOW!

Clayfoot detached himself from the story circle. He seemed reluctant to leave his new friends. Kah-tay nodded at him to let her visitors know that he was coming. Ta-nic and Li-nat grinned and made excuses to leave. When he reached the tipi Kah-tay placed a hand on her belly.

"The child talked to me. She senses danger."

Dashing outside, he searched the sky and the horizon.

"Are you sure? I see nothing." He placed his hand on her belly. "I find no danger. Nothing will harm the child. I gave my word...and she is *my* child, now."

"Come back inside and listen to my belly. Perhaps you can hear her cry of fear."

Inside the tipi he said, "Remove your clothes."

"Not now. We will do the thing later. Ta-nic and Li-nat have a habit of appearing without warning."

"It wouldn't be something they haven't seen before."

He glowered and she dutifully removed her long-shirt, then lowered her eyes to watch as he pressed his head against her bare belly. Outside, the wind seemed to lull, leaving a peaceful sense of well-being.

Father?

A surge of joy went through Kah-tay when he fell backwards, a surprised look on his face. His eyes were round as two moons.

"She spoke to me! She called me 'father.'"

"Yes, but why does she sense fear?"

A concerned look crossed his face. "Before *you* knew it was there?"

"I rested after butchering buffalo and felt a brief prick of evil, then the child spoke."

"The Great One has given her special power." Clayfoot shook his head. "I wonder what it is? Let me listen again." She noticed a strange look of wonderment cross his face when he pressed his ear to her belly.

Do you love me, father? I need love.

Of course. I've loved you since the day I met your mother. I will protect you forever.

Thank you, father. I love you, too.

"Clayfoot. You spoke to her with your mind."

"Yes, but she is frightened."

Kah-tay watched him go from his off-hand remark to an amazed expression when the shock hit him. He had actually spoken to the child from his mind.

Had The Great One granted him power? A deep rumble shattered her thoughts.

Struggling into her long-shirt, she dashed outside.

A Great Twisting Wind seemed to drop from a dark swirl of cloud. Snake-like, it whipped below the valley, across the lush prairie, rushing toward the village like stampeding buffalo. A very large storm. Small wonder the buffalo ran from it. Nothing could withstand its force. Great pieces of earth and trees were uprooted and sucked into its dark interior.

"Get out of the rain, Kah-tay. It will soon turn to cold rocks and tear the village apart." He pointed across the clearing at Nah-mo. "See. The Shaman begins his dance of protection."

Kah-tay glanced skyward as cool drops of rain spattered her face. Soon, jagged ice would slash from the sky smashing everything in its path, softening the earth and its people for the giant wind-that-sucks-life.

She shot a quick glance at Nah-mo, knowing his show of bravado would do no more than give false hope. Something more would be needed, even if it meant sacrificing all her powers to save the tribe. She pressed a hand to her belly.

"Great One–hear me."

Wind and driving rain ripped the words from her mouth. Kah-tay stood with arms outstretched, facing the darkening sky. In a smooth arc she traced a finger overhead, from East to West, then North to South. Jagged streaks of small lightning crackled between her upraised, widespread fingers. Even if it meant expending all her power, nothing would harm her child...not now...not after her little girl asked for protection. She felt great love emanating from the little one, and from Clayfoot, who'd promised eternal protection.

Out of the corner of her eye she could see Clayfoot's look of awe. Rain splashed against an invisible barrier and ran down its sides. The Twisting Wind flailed against the barrier as she stood, fists clenched, staving off its immense power. After one final attempt to penetrate her shield, the great force moved on to dissipate upward into its murky interior.

***

The drain on her power had been tremendous. Dizziness brought an influx of bright sparks spiraling inward to a black pool of consciousness. Sagging, she felt Clayfoot's arm under her shoulders.

"Great One. Don't let her die," said Clayfoot.

His voice seemed far off, but had a commanding tone. She wondered if her power would return...and she had a child to protect.

Place her upright.

Kah-tay recognized the voice. Barely had Clayfoot stood her, weak and unsteady in the circle of frightened tribesmen, than a huge rainbow appeared in the Southern sky. Clouds parted. Brilliant light streamed down to engulf her. Screams of terror came from children and adults alike. Her power returned. This time, she felt more godlike–as if there were no end to her control. The collar on her long shirt glowed iridescent.

A momentary gleam engulfed Clayfoot.

He'll need it for what lies ahead.

Her heart skipped at The Great One's thunderous voice. Why would she need more power? What lies ahead? She knew the Evil One would tempt her. He always had–often pursuing her, to diminish her into nothingness.

The Enemy wants to steal the child.

Kah-tay shuddered. "I must rest, now."

Clayfoot slipped his arms under her and carried her to the tipi. She drifted into velvet darkness the instant she snuggled into the bearskin.

***

A soft scraping sound woke her. Across the tipi, Clayfoot sat cross-legged, painting a legend on the inside wall. Lazily, she watched the play of muscles across his back and shoulders. He is a powerful man. Who better could protect her? She studied the new story he painted in blue, red and ochre. Others may not be able to read it, but she knew his thoughts. It told of great power from a strange one who saved his people from a Wind of Death...a story of sacrifice and courage when others ran screaming from the twisting evil. At that moment she wanted him more than ever, but she would not interrupt his legend. To watch him at work was joy enough. A smile crossed her lips when he added small ochre dots inside a blue circle. He would not leave the child out of his story as if the little one were part of the rescue, she mused. In a way the child was. Concern for the baby had driven her to risk losing the gift of power.

Clayfoot shoved the paint pots aside. "It is finished."

"A beautiful story, my husband." She held out her arms. "Come. Share it with me."

***

They were no more than finished and cuddling when Ta-nic appeared at the closed flap of the tipi, clearing her throat.

Clayfoot raged. "That woman knows whenever we do this. She never fails to—"

"Hush. She might hear you."

"As if I care. What could she possibly want?"

Kah-tay didn't have to ask. The twinge of wickedness had returned, coming from the East beyond the hill. The same damp, metallic smell like air after a bolt of lightning. Clayfoot clamored into this breech cloth and opened the flap.

"What is it, Ta-nic?"

"Nah-mo said a scout reported a band of warriors coming our way. The Shaman thinks you and your Woman of Magic should be with us when they arrive."

Clayfoot grasped his lance and left. Kah-tay smoothed the wrinkles in her long shirt and invited Ta-nic to enter.

"See the legend Clayfoot painted."

"He is the best artist among the Horse Tribe. His paintings often tell of great battles." She bent to study the bright colors. "He has told of your warding off the Great Twisting Wind. I notice he put the child in his legend."

This woman knows far too much about the interpretation of totems and legends. Someday I'll have to tell her of my people and their power, but she might not believe the truth. It could spell trouble for Clayfoot because he brought a Woman of Magic and her child into the Horse People.

"This is the first I've seen of his paintings," said Kah-tay. "He is very good at telling a picture story. Are you always able to read the legends?"

"Most of the time. Tell me about your—"

"I think we should join the men. Shaman Nah-mo seems to think I may be of help in dealing with the approaching strangers."

"Yes."

Ta-nic seemed disappointed. Kah-tay knew she could not reveal more than they already knew about her.

The Horse People gathered at the ridge of the hill overlooking a swollen stream that once provided their drinking water. Warriors urged their mounts to clear the sharp drop. From there they could race across the valley and the swift-moving foam-topped water.

Stop them, Nah-mo. They don't know what lies over the ridge on the other side of the valley.

Shaman Nah-mo glanced at her, then shouted a command at old Ra-ton and his warriors. The braves cast a disappointed look at the Chief. Apparently they were honed to a sharp edge for battle.

Nah-mo shouted, "Return to the ridge and form a line to protect the village. We don't know who is coming or how many—or what spirits they have to guide them."

Kah-tay nodded approval when he sent Chata, the bowman, to scout across the stream.

"Find where they are and how many," said Nah-mo. "If you can get close try to discover their intentions."

Pleased that only the Shaman and Clayfoot heard her mind-speak, Kah-tay knew it wouldn't do to have the Horse People discover a woman giving instructions for battle. At least Nah-mo seemed intelligent enough to recognize her wisdom. Clayfoot had long since stopped questioning her suggestions, which more often than not sounded like an order.

Surprise registered through the ranks when Chata reached the rim across the valley. He immediately turned his horse and raced back to the milling warriors. Before he reached the battle line, oddly decorated heads of horses and many warriors appeared over the far ridge. Kah-tay counted fifty with a vague retinue bringing up the rear.

A familiar odor floated across the valley...an odor she'd smelled before.

She searched the band of bedraggled, strange warriors rimming the hill. Their Chief struggled to arrange his sodden headdress. The Horse People gripped their weapons and stared across the valley.

Kah-tay skimmed the strange tribe's thoughts. Why hadn't they charged into battle? A sense of subterfuge tugged her mind. The child within her belly squirmed and cried out.

Mother. I am not safe.

Suddenly, the glint of an iron shirt flashed in the sunlight. Kah-tay knew why the child feared.

CHAPTER FIVE

Kah-tay could not restrain a smile. The unkempt Chief straightened his rain-soaked headdress, turned his lance downward, then urged his horse two steps forward.

"I speak for the people of the Badger tribe."

She nodded at Nah-mo.

The Shaman rattled his gourd and shouted across the valley.

"Speak. But know that we see your weapons—and we have a mighty power you know nothing of."

Fool. I told you I would not help you.

Nah-mo jerked his head as if her words clattered his mind.

"We are told you possess a woman of magic," said the leader. "I want her to heal my woman."

"She is not for bargaining. Healing is her decision. Be warned her husband is a mighty warrior."

Clayfoot's chest swelled. He pointed the tip of his lance skyward, showing the strangers where he sat astride Mah-ki in the front row. Kah-tay knew he would fight.

She stepped forward. "I will talk with him, Nah-mo. He has a desperate need."

Clayfoot pointed his iron-tipped lance. "He has other things on his mind, too. See how he grips his lance."

"Do not fear for me, husband." She stepped through the lush, wet grass down to the rain-swollen stream.

The Badger Chief walked his horse toward her, stopping when he was a few feet away. His gaze never left hers. Watching him from across the foaming stream, she could feel his indecision. She detected the smell of cold fear from new sweat oozing down his chest.

Suddenly, a quick jab of heels sent his horse toward the water. He leaned wide to grasp her.

Kah-tay's palm shot out, stopping the horse in mid-charge.

The warrior Chief sailed over the horse's head like a leaf in the wind to land face down in the roiling, muddy water. Just as the enemy warriors started to charge, she gestured. A dense cloud filled the air above them. Their horses bucked and reared, stopping any attempt to reach their leader. The odor of blood seemed to fill the air. She signaled Nah-mo not to interfere, but Clayfoot was already at her side.

"I told you not to intrude, husband."

"I fear for your life," he snarled. "A badger has a reputation for constant anger." He nodded at the top of the ridge. "Look."

Kah-tay found the source of the evil, metallic odor.

Ironskin glared down at them, his horse quiet beneath him. The man held his lance aloft, a bitter expression on curled lips.

"Your tricks do not frighten me or my horse, woman. And I will fight *you,* coward," he shouted at Clayfoot, "with lances from horseback." He leered at Kah-tay. "If your magic squaw will stay out of it."

She felt Clayfoot's rage at the insult and knew he could not be stopped. Perhaps this time he would slay Ironskin. It would be easier to point her finger and send a bolt of jagged blue light at the immoral man...a blue fire that would burn him black like overcooked meat in his cooking pot armor.

But she promised countless winters ago she would never use her power to kill. Others would do it for her if a person needed to meet death. Ironskin was such a person. Someday his blood would spill on the earth, enough blood to put out a fire.

Clayfoot charged Mah-ki forward, meeting Ironskin mid-stream in the swift-running, foamy water. Lances scraped shaft against shaft, sounding like old bones Nah-mo used during his spirit dance to ward off evil. Clayfoot missed a thrust when Ironskin whirled his horse in the muddy water. The armored warrior raised a foot and sent Clayfoot sprawling into the stream. Quickly, he jabbed his lance at Clayfoot, now defenseless and choking on dense foam.

Mah-ki lunged to the bank, pulling Clayfoot to safety, where the warrior could grasp a larger handful of mane and leap astride the powerful horse. Downstream, his lance rushed in the foamy water to snag itself in a tuft of

44

grass. Clayfoot raced after it.

"See how the coward runs." Ironskin threw back his head back and laughed. "Now, I will kill you." He turned his horse toward the fleeing pair.

Across the ridge Badger warriors had their horses under control and watched the battle. Their Chief had his hand raised to hold them in check. Ra-ton motioned a young warrior to put his bow away.

Reading Ra-ton's thoughts, Kah-tay felt his disappointment. Young Chata was the best bowman in the tribe. It would have been wondrous to see an arrow plunge into Ironskin's neck and bury itself up to the feathers. There seemed a silent agreement between the newcomers and the Horse Tribe...let the two men fight to the death.

Clayfoot scooped up his lance and faced his enemy.

"Now comes your defeat, braggart." He tucked the lance under his armpit.

Ironskin charged, a hate-filled leer on his face, his lance high for a swift thrust. He jabbed the weapon just as he had in their last encounter. Clayfoot swerved out of harm's way and grasped Ironskin's arm. A quick tug pulled the armored warrior into the roiling water.

Before his enemy could leap to his feet, Clayfoot grabbed Ironskin's braids. He dragged his enemy toward the bank. Water gushed from the sides and bottom of Ironskin's rusting armor. Once on the grassy bank, Clayfoot pushed his lance through Ironskin's forearm; the one that had no hand. A quick slash shortened the arm again.

Jerking one braid upward, he placed his foot on Ironskin's neck, forcing the man's head sideways. Eyes bulged from heavy pressure as the last of the water spewed from his armor. A quick pull would have broken Ironskin's neck. Kah-tay wondered if he had the will to slay his brother.

"You have challenged me for the last time, braggart. Prepare yourself for the spirit world." Clayfoot eased the pressure allowing his enemy to rise to his knees.

A death chant burst from Ironskin as Clayfoot ripped the knife and sacred medicine bag from his enemy. He hurled them into the storm-filled water. Raising his head for the quick slice of death across his throat, Ironskin closed his eyes for a quick, honorable death. Instead, Clayfoot cut both braids from Ironskin's head and flung them in the water.

Victorious, Clayfoot gave Ironskin the ultimate dishonor. He turned his back and walked away. Leaping atop Mah-ki, he turned the horse to face Ironskin.

"Never return, coward. If you cause more trouble for me or the Horse

People there is no place you can run, no place you can hide, but what my lance will find you. It will turn sharp corners, fly through deep forests, and leap high rocks to pin your spirit to a fiery death. Your iron shirt will not protect you from my anger the next time we meet." The champion turned Mah-ki and rode across the stream to stand beside Kah-tay.

You will regret not killing him, husband. That's the second time you've spared that evil man.

"I cannot kill him. He is my birth brother. Maybe, someday he will anger me enough to spill his blood."

"Perhaps," she whispered, watching Ironskin struggle to his feet.

Together, they watched the dishonored warrior mount his horse and ride from sight.

"He is not much of a warrior," said the Badger Chief from across the slowing stream. "Ironskin promised good fortune and life without sickness or pain if we captured your woman of magic. But know this—he was never accepted as a brother in the Badger Tribe."

Clayfoot grinned. "Do you still think she can be captured?"

"It would be easier to capture the wind," said the Badger chief. He raised his hand in the sign of peace. "I am called Running."

"Running what?"

The young Chief shrugged. "Just—Running. I must have been moving my legs like a charging Wa-e-su-ta To-ga, what you call the buffalo, for my tribe to name me that."

Kah-tay eased closer. "Besides trying to capture me, why did you come?"

"My wife suffers. She cannot bring forth the child in her belly."

"She is with you?"

Running turned his horse and called up the hill. In moments their ranks parted and four men walked their horses slowly down the hillock. Between them lay a woman on a litter.

"A drag hurt her more than the child so her brothers offered to carry her like this."

Kah-tay didn't fail to notice the loving concern when the Chief looked at his wife. Young, with sweat-streaked hair and dusty face, Kah-tay saw she was very beautiful...and much too large in pregnancy.

"Bring her." She turned and marched up the mound to the camp.

***

46

Tipis shimmered in the afternoon sun, their colorful totems weaving among the shadows cast between the white deerskin hides. They rimmed a semi-circle around a large clearing near the ridge. Wisps of smoke drifted from the central fire pit. Running supposed it was the council area which faced the valley and the receding stream.

Everything seemed to undulate, especially the totems on the tipi walls. He could not read the legends, but Ironskin had been truthful about this being a place of Magic. The woman seemed gifted far beyond what that forked-tongue wearer of the iron shirt told him. She must be the source of their power. The storm must have leaped over them, unless....

Running suppressed a stripe of fear trying to weave up his back.

"It is a pity you were caught out in The Great Twisting Wind," said Clayfoot. "My woman gave us protection from–"

Do not brag on me, husband. He may challenge you for me and win.

"The one who led us here said she had great power, but my concern is for Techi. She suffers from the great child in her belly."

"Not for long. Kah-tay will–"

Hush!

Running's thoughts were interrupted by the sudden, ghost-like appearance of women and children peering from the entrance flaps of many tipis.

"Everything seems to move in your camp. Do spirits dwell among you?"

"It's the mid-day sun. From this place on the ridge the village dances for us. It has always been so. That is the reason we stay. Our council fire is many layers deep."

"The Badger People move to follow the buffalo."

"The Tribe of the Horse remains here. We bring the buffalo to us."

Running felt a twinge of magic in the way Clayfoot said it.

"We also have Noc-Muks who visit in the night," said Clayfoot. "We close our tipis very tight to keep them out lest they eat us. Do you know the Noc-Muks?"

"The Tribe of the Badger has never heard of Noc-Muks."

"You will hear of them when the council fire burns high and our bellies are full."

Running urged his horse over the last of the ridge. *These are strange people, but I don't care as long as their Woman Of Magic heals Techi.*

A surge of strange energy came when Clayfoot reached down to the woman walking between them. The huge man lifted her effortlessly to his horse. Something danced between them...something frightening.

***

Only Ta-nic would help. The men sat around a council fire talking and waiting; waiting for food and news of Running's wife. Using mind-power, Kah-tay demanded clean water, asking Clayfoot, who resisted leaving the stories told by the visiting tribe. Tomorrow, he was thinking, they would replenish their supply of buffalo to replace that which they were eating tonight. Tomorrow, tomorrow, she ranted. Angry, she clenched her fist.

Fetch all the clean water in the camp.

Like squirrels running from tree to tree gathering nuts, Clayfoot, Nah-mo, and Li-ton urged the women to forego cooking and gather all the water skins.

"Here is your water, woman," said Clayfoot tossing a half-filled water skin atop the others.

Don't play superior with me, warrior.

Crushed, he inquired about Running's wife.

"News, news, news." She jerked the tie from a water skin. "Like vultures you sit around waiting for news—and something to fill your bellies. Now, go. There may not be news of the kind Running desires."

His fixed look met hers, seeming to beg forgiveness, then he lowered his gaze to the ground and left. Kah-tay knew she had been vicious with him. She would dispel his consternation tonight. Right now, Running's wife seemed dangerously near death.

"She carries two within her, Ta-nic."

"How do you know this? You haven't touched her yet."

"I know." Kah-tay held out her hands and arms. "Wash the dirt from my hands and arms. I must reach inside her and unwind the cord."

"I forget you have power, child." Ta-nic poured water over Kah-tay's hands and arms. "I have never seen this done, reaching inside to remove a baby."

Kah-tay didn't answer. Her thoughts were on Ta-nic and the meager power the woman had. The woman was not afraid when power was used. Ta-nic. Where did her power come from? She was the only woman who volunteered to help. Somehow, the woman knew she would be needed.

"Place your hands here, then here. Feel the two sets of feet poking to get out?" Kah-tay shook the excess water from her hands.

Ta-nic looked up while feeling the twins. "I feel them. It's as if they are

48

fighting each other."

"There is little time. Hold her knees apart."

Kah-tay reached inside the little woman, found the tangled cord, and eased it over the baby's head. Touching the tiny head, she willed life into the child. The boy came out swiftly, crying for life. She tied and cut the cord after the fluid of life coursed through the twisted gristle-like rope. Then she reentered to ease a large girl from the woman's belly. Another loud cry greeted them. Touching the torn flesh, she stopped Techi's bleeding and mended her birth wounds. Ta-nic had already wrapped the babies in new rabbit furs.

Kah-tay leaned against a side pole and closed her eyes. After a deep breath, she wondered if her child would have similar problems. It felt good to bring life into the world.

You are good, Mother. I love you.

Thank you, child. I wish you could see these–

I see them, Mother. Through your eyes.

Kah-tay rubbed a hand over her belly then picked up one of the babies. Ta-nic held the other infant. They were met at the tipi entrance by Running.

After touching each tiny hand, he looked beyond Kah-tay to his wife.

"How is Techi? Will she live?"

"Yes. But she must rest for many days." She noticed him wrinkle his nose at her hands and arms. "I must wash away this part of birthing men rarely see. You have a son and a daughter."

Running dashed from the tipi, whooping his joy.

"Two?" exclaimed the Shaman. "We must hold a ceremony tonight to thank the spirits."

***

The visiting tribe stayed several days, always asking Kah-tay about her power and where it came from. She was happy to see them leave even though they helped replenish the supply of buffalo. Much of the meat had been cut into strips and dried to be divided before the visitors left. Running became a bore with his constant bragging about his twins. Even Techi confided she would be happy when they left. She asked many times if Kah-tay thought he would ever stop bragging about them.

Kah-tay sighed. "I'm afraid not. You may have more of two who are born together and look alike. My people have known this for many years. It is something peculiar to certain people. Ask Running to bring you back if you get with child and feel the presence of two."

"I'm told you can foresee the future."

"No. My power is for the present." A deliberate lie, but it's best not to let the story grow. We'll have enough problems when word of this gets out.

I do not intend to become an oracle like the time....

She gazed past the tent flap and across the clearing. A young brave from the visiting Badger tribe handed a beaver pelt to a maiden of the Horse Tribe. Her thoughts skimmed the young girl's mind.

"It seems your people have made more than friends, Techi." Kah-tay pointed to a tipi almost hidden from view. "See how she tries to appear shy. Her heart is filled with desire for the young brave."

"It is Wagatu, my brother. Many maids have sought his heart." She turned to Kah-tay. "This match would cast our tribes together like two trees from one trunk."

Arms crossed, the maiden's father stood behind her, silent, haughty, until the youth handed the reins of a black stallion to her father. A broad smile creased the old warrior's face.

"I think my people have gained a new member," said Techi.

"Yes. There will be a mating ceremony soon enough."

"I hope it is very soon." Techi opened her milk-sodden shirt. "These hungry look-a-likes need my mother to give me some rest. Suckling them causes a great desire for Running. It has been a long time."

Curious, Kah-tay entered Techi's mind and found something she had never experienced. The strange sensual sensation of nursing pulled at her as Techi nursed one then the other. This is what it's like to feed a child. Kah-tay knew she would enjoy feeding her baby.

***

Running's people had been gone over two moons. Most in the tribe were happy to see them go. Twice-told stories had grown wearisome for the men, but she would miss Techi and her everlasting questions. The young mother envied the attention the Badger Tribe women got from her people. Her brother, Wagatu, and his bride, Niti, took a circuitous route to spend their alone time.

Kah-tay enjoyed another happy event when Chicose, Running's brother, returned. He had become friendly with Clayfoot. The warrior always made sure Ba-chey and her mother, Na-nah, had plenty to eat. Kah-tay smiled at his subterfuge. Chicose desired the young widow. A seed planted in his mind advised him Na-nah was available without a bride cost to her father. That night Clayfoot was all talk about Mah-ki and the black stallion, rambling on and on about their blood lines, crossing them until the tribe would have mighty horses. They would be white with black spots shaped like bear paws and could run like the wind.

Kah-tay pushed him. "You even smell like a horse."

"It is a good smell and I...."

She was about to stop his rambling about horses when Raven fluttered to its perch atop the tent.

Where have you been, dear friend?

I followed evil Ironskin. There is grievous trouble.

What kind of trouble?

He held a dark sacrifice to the Evil One. He made a pledge of faithfulness to the Dark Kingdom.

We knew he was evil. It does not surprise me.

But his pledge was to bring your child for sacrifice soon after it is born.

Frightened, she asked Clayfoot if he heard Raven.

"Yes. Ironskin knows he faces death if he returns. Our child has power, too. Between the three of us, Ironskin is a dead man—brother by birth or not."

***

Long after Clayfoot slept the heavy sleep of gratification, Kah-tay sat cross-legged facing the open flap of the tipi. Her hands rested, palms up, on her knees as she slipped into deep meditation. Had she made the right decision in choosing Clayfoot? His people were backward in so many ways...but so were the others she had known. But no man pleased her more than Clayfoot. Her thoughts slipped to the child.

Mother, I'm frightened.

Do not fear little one. Your father will protect us.

I sense the Dark Kingdom, mother. I do not want to go there.

CHAPTER SIX

Dark Forest. Across the sparkling stream it spread before him; a forbidding wall of dark green and black. Thick-trunked trees grew tall–and it was said they spoke to those who ventured near the ominous place. Hunters who braved the dense foliage never returned.

Ironskin muttered to Dungi, his horse. "Shaman told false stories to hold his power over the tribe."

He rode downstream to the Sacred Pond. Fear touched him when he thought of the Noc-Muks that coward, Clayfoot, and his Woman of Magic brought to the village. The stench of stringy, half-cooked meat still clouded his mouth. Had they killed all of them?

A small ripple glided across the surface of the pond as if responding to the Wind sighing in the trees on the other side of the water. Low-pitched wailing sounds in the trees once brought a kind of joy to his heart. Now he felt uncomfortable, remembering the squaw in the painted tipi. Her story the pond was safe didn't ring true even though warriors had tested it. He didn't care whether Tato, the old warrior, had been swimming with his hated brother. The pond still looked dangerous.

When he was young, his mother told him of Noc-Muks. How they could not be killed. Another movement in the water sent a chill up his spine. Their spirits had come back! They still haunted Sacred Pool. He turned Dungi away. Below the ancient beaver dam the stream dwindled to a narrow strip. It would be safe to cross here and turn his back on the Horse People. They scorned him and now sided with Clayfoot. Since they were children, Clayfoot always bested him in battle. His brother might be stronger, but he was still a coward.

"And now, my right arm is useless from his trickery. I should have goaded the old bull to kill Clayfoot when he was a boy and ran from the crazy buffalo."

He urged a reluctant Dungi across the thin, sparkling strip of water. He paid no attention to the message rippling in the stream. On the other side he paused on a narrow strip of sand and raised his arms.

"I will never return until they are under my power. I give myself to you, Evil One. Grant me power and safe passage. Guide me to your kingdom that I may serve you."

Filled with self-induced courage, he entered Dark Forest. Strange black and light shadows engulfed him, but power from Wa-Ha-Na, the Evil One, would protect him. Dungi stepped precariously on the soft carpet of leaves. The horse shied from the dancing play of light and shadows on the forest floor. Ironskin looked for its source and became awestruck by the strange play of sunlight amid the wind-blown leaves high above. Light came and went while huge leaves whipped across the open spaces in the tips of trees. Voices carried on the wind.

Strange voices in an unknown tongue.

Suddenly, the pull of frolicking light overpowered him. His mind went spinning as it had when he twisted and turned with his childhood playmates until they became dizzy and fell. Ironskin slipped from Dungi's back, his mind as somber as the place he'd entered. It was said a warrior's first and last thoughts were of his horse. Ironskin's thoughts were of a soft voice.

You wish to serve me for power? Only I have the power, frightened warrior. Your wish may be granted, but know this. I am The Master. You are my slave and you will serve me all of your life. There is no turning back from my pleasures and pain. Answer me when you reach the place of Burning Rocks.

How long had he lain, sleeping like an Old One? He rolled to one side, his mind clouded like wind-blown water. Dungi nibbled on sparse blades of grass near a tree whose smooth bark reflected the fast-moving leaves. Bursts of shadowed light splintered his mind. A voice had spoken to him—whose voice?—with words that burned his mind.

Of course he would follow him. That's what he came for; to serve and hope for revenge. No. To *possess* revenge. That is the bargain...and he meant to have it.

***

Pemmican cakes the squaw gave him early that morning were gone. They were given as a bonus, in addition to herself, for the beaver pelt he had stolen from the Badger clan. Fools. They had their chance and bungled it. Running had been warned not to charge Woman of Magic. Instead he should use cunning to obtain her favors. His jaw clenched when he thought of Clayfoot tricking him. Gnawing in his belly told him he must find food and water in this place of dark and light. Strange. He'd not seen any game in Dark Forest, but he hadn't been searching for it, either. Perhaps the stories were true. Nothing lived in Dark Forest...nothing except dank odors and the smell of rotting flesh. It was not wise to search for the source of such odors. The foul smell could be a hapless hunter or a lost tribesman.

Dungi stopped at a bush filled with berries. The horse stripped them from the lower branches, chewing like they were a delicacy. The small fruit must be good for a horse to eat so ravenously. Ironskin plucked a handful.

"Squaw shit," he roared, trying to get the bitter fruit from his mouth. The taste lingered long after he urged Dungi away from the bush. It alternately burned, then tasted like bark from the chinchona tree. He longed for water, his thoughts on the sparkling stream. It tried to give him a message, but like a fool he'd not listened and filled his water skin.

Ironskin raised his arms to the sky. "Is there no water or food in this place?"

"No," the Wind whispered from the tree tops. "You must purify yourself by fasting to prove you are worthy."

"I will die before I reach Burning Rocks."

"Then die you will." The Wind rasped and faded.

"No. I will have my revenge on Clayfoot. I will kill him and take his hair."

His voice died in the confines of the thick trees.

The Wind gusted. "What coward? When I flew across the prairie I saw no cowardice–only a man fighting for his woman. Does not every man have that right?"

"He is a coward," shouted Ironskin. "Since the day he first went hunting he has not been a man. He threw his bow away and ran. Why do you think father named him Clayfoot?"

The Wind did not answer. Forgotten bitterness returned to his mouth. He craved water. Any drink would do as long as it took the bitter taste from his mouth.

Maybe water would be behind the next tree or in the next gully. Two shadow sticks later the forest opened on a broad plain of tall grass rippling in the Wind. On the horizon a tall hill loomed, its top bathed in red. It seemed to shimmer in the sunlight. A black spot stayed motionless near the center of the golden light. Before he could goad Dungi to cross the lush plain, sucking sounds caught his attention. Looking down, he saw Dungi slaking his thirst from a muddy stream. Why hadn't he noticed this water before? Parched, Ironskin slipped to the ground and knelt beside his horse.

"Augh," he coughed, spitting the water from his mouth. "You taste bad!"

Upstream he saw what flavored the water. A dead animal lay from bank to bank across the trickling water. Flies and maggots wove in the flesh making the carcass seem alive. Retching, Ironskin boosted himself atop Dungi.

"You have eaten and drank," he raged at the horse. "Now carry me to the place of Burning Rocks. Go quickly or I'll eat your flesh and slake my thirst with your blood. If I fall you will drag me to the place."

Dungi responded to Ironskin's jabbing heels and galloped across the plain. Though the sky looked clear, cloud shadows drifted across the waving, tall grass. Once, he thought he saw a small animal skitter from view, but when he peered close nothing was there. The horse slowed from the tiring pace in the chest-high grass, refusing to react to Ironskin's harsh heels.

"I do not wish to be caught in the open, you lazy dog for a mother. Can't you see we'd be safer on the hill?"

All at once Dungi stopped, his sides heaving from the fast pace. It refused to move. No amount of urging or loud threats could make it go. Instead, the horse reared and tried to turn away.

"What ails you, stupid horse? You can't be that tired. You can still rear and try to strike. Do it again and I'll slash you like I did Mah-ki."

Foamy sweat covered Dungi's neck and sides. The horse trembled but still refused to move. Confused, Ironskin looked for sign of Noc-Muks or other spirit beasts. He could see nothing.

"You lazy beast." Ironskin lashed at the horse's flank. "Now, be still while I stand on your back." From the added height he could see Dark Forest circled the large plain. Nothing moved.

A familiar sound of stamping hooves startled him. Within easy bow shot a large buck deer stared at him. Moments ago he saw nothing...now there was food. His stomach rumbled at the thought of roasting flesh.

"Thank you, Master of Dark Forest." Using the special loop he had fashioned to hold his bow in the arm with no hand, he nocked an arrow and took aim. "I knew you would provide for your followers."

The arrow flew straight at the buck's heart. There would be food as soon as they reached the edge of the vast plain. He dropped to Dungi's back. Suddenly, the buck shimmered and changed into a huge, angry boar. Its curled tusks struck dread into Ironskin and Dungi. The horse reared and almost lost his rider in its attempt to escape. The uncanny change from deer to wild boar intensified the fright in Ironskin's heart. He let Dungi have his head until they were far back in tall grass. Cloud shadows moved across their path. Again Dungi skidded to a stop and reared, apparently frightened by Noc-Muks from the shy.

"What now, you hard-headed beast? Are you afraid of a shadow?"

Angered, Ironskin jerked Dungi's head away from the swift moving grey shape. "It will be safe to enter Dark Forest if I obey and do not eat or drink." He turned the horse toward the far edge of the plain, but in a different direction from where they had seen the wild boar.

Dungi labored though the high grass. Ironskin thought of his bargain. He had finally obeyed the Evil One's message to fast. The task was very familiar to him. Part of becoming-a-man ceremony was to run five miles with a mouthful of water and not spill or drink a drop. Later, he had to run from daylight to dark without pausing to eat or drink, and most especially not to rest.

Again, Dark Forest loomed near. Beyond it soared the blazing hill. His thoughts were still on his enemy, wondering if Clayfoot could have mastered the becoming-a-man ritual. Had the coward overcome his fear of the charging buffalo? The Wind had whispered it saw no cowardice. Had Clayfoot gained courage? Impossible! It had to be his Woman of Magic. She not only gave him strength but courage as well. Without her his enemy would have nothing. A sharp noise shattered his thoughts.

"Stop," he shouted to Dungi and nocked an arrow. "Perhaps this side of Dark Forest has beasts never seen by men."

Dense, thick trees lay within four man-lengths. A narrow path became visible, but seemed overgrown with vines and fallen limbs. A glance at the tree tops told him he could expect more shadows and spinning lights that played on tree trunks and leaf-strewn clearings. Nothing but the voice had bothered him during the first part of his journey–the time he fell from his horse. Swift moving light and whirling shadows would not catch him unaware again. This time he would avert his eyes and let Dungi have his head.

"Go, horse. Enter the place of many trees and hurry. The sun is already high. I must be at the place of Burning Rocks to give my answer."

Dungi responded to the pressure of Ironskin's heels as if knowing succulent grass grew in clusters around certain trees. The horse unerringly picked out a pathway, pausing to nibble a tidbit of green whenever it could. In minutes Ironskin saw the first play of light and dark.

"You will not fool a warrior." He jutted his jaw, boasting, though the hair on the back of his neck prickled. The sway of light and dark grew intense. It seemed to be all around him. He squeezed his eyes tight. Overhead, voices drifted down to him.

Be good, my son—or the Noc-Muks will come. You have taken the hair of my enemies. I am proud of you.

Ironskin shuddered at the sound of his father before the old warrior's spirit was taken.

A different voice whispered.

My lance will follow wherever you go. You cannot hide nor run fast enough.

Clayfoot's warning angered him. Where did the coward get the idea his lance had special powers?

"Next time we meet, magic lover," he muttered, "my arrows will speak before you can throw your lance. When my power is made great I will hang you from the tallest tree in Dark Forest—and I will cut your flesh once each day until there is nothing left to cut."

Ironskin smiled at the thought of success and power. He still smiled when he woke curled beneath a tree to find Dungi gone.

***

"Fool horse," he growled for the hundredth time. "I'll miss my time at Burning Rocks and have to spend the night in this terrible place. Light is already casting long shadows in front of me."

It seemed he had been running for hours. At times the path would end, covered by dead branches or overgrown with vines or dead leaves. It could only lead in the direction of the light. He continued the pace. Between thoughts of his horse and the half-hidden pathway, he remembered his father's advice about the test of the long run.

Do not be hasty to reach the end, my son. It is better to finish than to fail.

Abruptly, the path ended at the base of the largest tree he had seen in Dark Forest. Ironskin shook his head, wondering if a secret opening could be there—or if he had missed a turn in the obscure, twisting passage. He risked a quick look at the tip of the giant growth.

"Hee-ya," he shouted. "You overlook the world, Old One." For an instant, the urge to soar to its top overcame him–to see where no other could see. He forced his eyes from it, remembering the shadows and light; a swirling mixture of strange power to make him sleep.

"When I receive strength from Wa-Ha-Na, your terrible height will no longer frighten me."

Ironskin stepped around the immense trunk and searched for a pathway. Nothing resembled even a faint outline of a trail that might lay ahead. Scraping leaves and brush aside, he uncovered half-grown sprouts of grass and weeds, but nothing of a path.

The receding light told him to hurry. A night in Dark Forest was not to his liking. Frantic, he worked at the leaves scraping them from the forest floor. Humid new earth assailed his nose and mouth, tasting and smelling like unwashed root-pottage the women made during times of famine.

"Mmugh," he grunted. A trapped feeling descended, pall-like, sending a stab of fear up his spine. No warrior knew what really lived in Dark Forest. A dense thorn bush at the side of the tree made him pause. A tunnel for foxes and rabbits ran beneath its lower branches. Its finger-length thorns were the longest he had seen. The path would be dangerous and painful if he attempted it. Dungi had gotten out. How?

"I'll track you, dog of a horse," he raged and returned to the front of the tree.

A slight depression in the leaves was the only suggestion of his stay. It reminded him of undesired sleep caused by moving shadows. He searched in an ever-widening circle to find Dungi's hoof prints. Minutes later, having found nothing, he glanced back at the tree. How far had he tracked his horse without finding a hoofprint? Overhead, the Wind whipped in the treetops...the place of Sleep. Ironskin felt its tug.

"No! You won't trick me again." He jerked his gaze from the hypnotic Dance of Sleep.

A gust whooshed downward, scattering leaves in a small wind devil, showing him how the pathway was covered. Perhaps the Wind did help. Ironskin renewed his search for Dungi's hoofprints. A grim smile crossed his face when he found a small place of fresh-turned earth. Peering close, he discovered another, then another area of curious, scraped patches of black dirt.

"You were running from something, horse."

In moments Dungi's tracks became numerous, but still placed far apart, sometimes two man lengths. Tracing the horse's route, one thought became clear to him. Dungi found the true path. The clearing had been a sham to make him sleep.

Ahead lay a passage through the trees, clearly the way his horse had taken. Ironskin struck up a man-killing pace. Hunger and thirst plagued him, but he refused to give in. What else could he do? Water was nowhere to be found– to say nothing of food. He kept his mind on the foul tasting Noc-muks Clayfoot brought to the council fire, him and his Woman of Magic. A sharp stab of pain throbbed his arm with no hand. Sometimes he could feel his lost fingers.

"The Evil One will give me a new hand," he chanted.

Often the path seemed to stop, but a new piece of turned, black earth showed where Dungi had stepped. Probably a fear-laden race of terror for the horse. Would he ever find his mount...a horse he had raised from its foaling? Ironskin kept his mind occupied to ward off hunger and thirst and fear. Mostly fear. Darkness would soon be on him. Noc-muks could be anywhere.

***

Gasping for breath, he could see the end of the pathway though the trees and put on a burst of speed. The outline of a horse crossed the light in front of him. It had to be Dungi. Perhaps the horse would be calm and come to his whistle. His hopes plummeted. A bent, dwarfish creature held Dungi with one hand while brandishing a long knife with the other. The small man's skin looked the color of red maple leaves before they die. Dungi pranced around the yellow-eyed man....he was about to think warrior, but no one of this wizened creature's color and size could be a warrior.

"Waugh! All I have is my short knife and a tired left hand. I'm no match for the ugly thing without my bow and lance which are on Dungi's back."

Behind him, the Wind moaned its song of danger. Shadows fluttered across the tunnel. Ahead lay a certain battle for which he was ill equipped.

"It is better to die facing an ugly enemy than the fearsome creatures of Dark Forest." He gripped his knife and stepped from the foliage.

The Red Dwarf smiled wickedly...a smile that went well with its tangled hair and bent shape. Its gaze never wavered from the knife in Ironskin's left hand. Drawing near, it lowered the point of the long knife and widened its smile.

"It wants no fight with a true warrior," boasted Ironskin.

The little man handed the reins to him and stepped back.

"You thought you could escape me, did you?" He rubbed the horse's muzzle playfully. "It is much better to stay with your master, bad horse. You caused me much pain." He turned to thank the Red Dwarf, but the small man had disappeared.

A furious flapping of wings surprised him. From the sky a red hawk swooped low, then soared toward the hills. Wonder filled his mind. The ugly little man caught Dungi then...became a hawk?

"It is better to be gone from this place." He boosted himself on Dungi's back then glanced in the direction the hawk had taken.

"Waugh! It is going to Burning Rocks."

The late afternoon sun set the hillside aflame with the color of a late-night council fire. Burning Rocks! Awestruck, he raced toward the dark orange glow, hoping he would not anger the Evil One by arriving late.

***

Black as a moonless, cloud-filled night the entryway beckoned with a dull orange glow that stayed in front of him to light the way. Figures flitted across the glow, casting misshapen shadows on rocky walls. Renewed fear made him wish he had not been so hasty to make his bargain.

When Dungi had struggled up the last ledge to Burning Rocks, Ironskin saw the mystery of fire. Small flecks of gold in the huge boulders caught the light and hurled it back to the sky. Heat, radiating from the smooth rocks, made them shimmer. How had it happened? No one was there...just the Wind, in a rapid burst, gushing down the hillside. It whispered what was needed before he agreed...and just as quickly left. He'd sworn to serve the Evil One and was drawn to enter the cave. An opening that had been a small dot when he first saw it from the plain became huge. It beckoned him into the bowels of the hill. All at once the glow stopped and he found himself in a large cavern with jagged walls. In its center, fire boiled its rage from a worn hole made smooth from years of intense heat. Ironskin didn't know how he knew about the fire hole; the knowledge just flicked into his mind.

"Are you impressed with my power?"

Ironskin nodded, his mouth agape as he searched for the source of the hollow, raspy voice. Sweat beaded, then ran in rivulets down his face and chest. His moccasins grew hot and he backed away.

"Why are you frightened? You asked to serve me in exchange for power.

Now you are here and you want to change your mind—or is my Kingdom too majestic for your peasant fears? Are you too terrified to speak?"

Ironskin pressed his back against the hot, jagged rocks and found no place to hide. A heavy burning taste smothered his breath. It smelled like Nahmo's yellow powder when the Shaman cast it into the council fire where it boiled with blue flames. Thoughts switched his mind like sparkling leaves from Dark Forest—a sparkle that made him sleep.

"No! I cannot sleep," he shouted, remembering his lost hand and the humiliation of losing his braids. "What must I do? You know this place frightens me?"

"Approach. Walk around my Fire."

Ironskin could only nod and croak, "I'm—I'm—coming to you, Wa-Ha-Na." Master-of-all-that-is-bad was the only name he could think of to address the voice as he scooted the first step. With his back pressed to the wall, he cringed as orange flames belched from the floor.

Slowly, he moved around the intense heat, eyes darting from the fire to the wall in front of him. Courage built as he moved. After all, hadn't the Wind promised?

"Your Kingdom is—" Ironskin caught his breath. Before him a creature sat on a high, black throne. Steam curled around its legs and body, to rise and disappear in the dark space above the Wa-Ha-Na. Its body looked wizened, a dull black, like overcooked meat. Suddenly, a powerful force sent him to his knees.

"Yes. My Kingdom is powerful. You came directly to me, Ironskin. Dark Forest could not discourage you. Therefore, I will grant what you wish."

The Evil One stared down at him with small yellow eyes that seemed to pierce his soul. A sense of immorality pervaded the rock cavern and Ironskin trembled before the mighty creature. Wa-Ha-Na said he would grant his wish. To overcome Clayfoot and kill him would be sweet revenge, indeed. He leaped to his feet with a victory shout.

"At last I will defeat the coward in a fair battle."

"He is no coward. Kah-tay is a mighty force to be reckoned with, but she does not help Clayfoot. Beware of overconfidence, my servant. He could overcome you if she decides to help him."

Ironskin bowed his head, then looked up at Wa-Ha-Na. "What good is your power if I cannot defeat him?"

"I will give you enough magic to fool him. But if he is clever, you will have to fight him again."

"How can I defeat him if I must fight with knives?" He held up his stump of a right arm. "The coward fights with a magic knife."

"Look again."

Ironskin could not believe what he saw. In place of his right hand a mighty paw appeared...large talons shot from its toes. He waved the arm, testing its balance, striking at imaginary enemies in the dark cavern.

"Try it against the wall, my servant."

A ringing, spark-laden blow came when he stuck at the wall. Yes! With this he could defeat Clayfoot. The coward would be cut to shreds...his blood would cover the leaves in Dark Forest...his Woman of Magic would make a fine plaything to do his bidding. Then he could take her to the village along with Clayfoot's hair and the warriors would cheer him for a mighty victory.

A booming laugh brought him to reality. "You must defeat him before you sing of victory."

"What must I do first, Wa-Ha-Na?"

"Become a bird and search the earth for him. Seek him out and take his most precious belonging. He will search for you and you can fight him on your own terms."

"How can I steal Woman of Magic. She is his most precious treasure, but she has power from the Mighty One."

"Are you afraid, again? I do not think of Kah-tay. There are other treasures that are precious to Clayfoot."

"His horse!" exclaimed Ironskin, then looked away, dejected. "But I killed Mah-ki."

"The horse lives. The Woman healed it."

"Good. I will take the horse and ride it in triumph through the tribe."

"What about their child?"

"It is not ready to be born."

An evil laugh echoed in the chamber. "When you return to your village it will have already been born."

"Then I shall bring it instead. Surely it is worth more than a mighty horse."

"Your power will increase tenfold if you bring me the child."

"Clayfoot's child is as good as yours."

Wa-Ha-Na smiled. "Clayfoot only protects the child. Remember, he spared your life two times. The child belongs to Woman of Magic. It is she you must fear."

"I do not fear her. She does not speak in my mind like she does the others."

"Perhaps. Always remember–you are *my* servant. If you fail, your power will be taken from you and you will dwell in the pit with the others."

The Evil One gestured. Flames burst from the great opening in the floor, emphasizing his warning.

Ironskin choked on dry spit. "I will not fail."

CHAPTER SEVEN

Kah-tay woke to the flutter of wings atop the tipi. Raven has been the subject of much talk in the village. Birds never ventured near the other lodges, but the tribe had taken the large bird in stride as part of her collection of strange Noc-Muks and healings.

Clayfoot stirred beside her. Raven's voice rasped her mind.

Phaugh! How long will you keep this one?

Does it matter? I'm particularly fond of him. He is tall and handsome. See how his muscles and flat belly glisten in the morning light? I may keep him forever.

You said that of the others.

Yes, but I was younger then.

You were never young, Kah-tay.

True, but I was never with child either. Clayfoot has great courage, even though he doesn't admit it. And he promised to care for and protect the child as if it were his own. Even now he calls her his daughter.

She poked at the smoldering coals from the night fire, sending a cloud of sparks and smoke upward. The bird beat its wings furiously to ward off the smelly invasion of its perch.

Must you do that? Fire and smoke make me nervous.

Kah-tay smiled. *Then don't chide me for wanting to keep this man. I may ask The Great One to grant him long life and power to be the child's guardian, forever.*

Clayfoot has already been granted power beyond his understanding. Why do you want to keep him forever?

She sat cross-legged, feeling the child stir in her belly. Yes. She wanted Clayfoot for many reasons and she would ask The Great One today.

Looking upward at Raven she projected:

If you are going to be jealous of this good man, I may send you back to The People.

You could–but you won't. You need me.

True. I will never part with you, old friend. But remember my wishes in this matter. From now on there will be three of us–.

If The Great One agrees.

Will you fight me over this, my ageless companion?

When have we ever fought? I want to be sure you understand the consequences of your actions, is all.

Thank you, dear friend. We will always be together, because I need you, too.

Clayfoot stirred awake and pulled her down to the bearskin. He nuzzled her breasts before he felt Raven studying him from his perch.

"I greet you, Black One," he said. "Did you have a good hunt in the early morning light?"

I ate the flesh of a ringtail after a hill cat had its fill. Raven fluttered its wings, then leaped into the early dawn.

Kah-tay entered Clayfoot's mind. Ordinarily he would detect her presence, now that he had Knowledge, but she sensed his mind was still clouded with sleep. Raven's continued thoughts came to them. They caught the scent of morning dew on the glistening, grass-filled valley. For a moment they could see the ground for a day's run in each direction as the bird soared aloft.

"Strange how the Black One sends its thoughts to me," he muttered, returning to Kah-tay's soft breast.

"The bird will be your friend, my husband. Ask of it what you will, for you have been given Power."

"Far different than our first meeting," he whispered against her neck.

"It protected me, then." She nestled closer. "Now, let us release our passion–for the time will soon come when we cannot."

Clayfoot began the rain of kisses she taught him...soft nibbles that brought joy to her soul. Teasing, touching, occasionally growling through bared teeth, they reached a new flight of passion. She delighted running her hands over his tense muscles. Trembling as he caressed her breasts and ran his tender touch down her legs, she murmured, "Now, my love."

He no longer pumped mindlessly, striving for release. Her control slowed him to a higher plane of continued joy as they melded bodies and souls.

***

The sun left no more than a short shadow stick in its morning climb across the sky before she ventured from the tipi. Wisely, she had made the trip to the stream for water when the moon was bright. Now they were ready for the day after a meal of corn cakes and dried buffalo meat.

"I wish to eat our midday meal at the Sacred Grove, husband."

"Why would you want to return to the place of Noc-Muks?"

She felt a suspicious misgiving enter his mind. "There are no evil spirits in the Grove or anywhere near it. You slew the evil ones. Remember?"

A quick swell of his out-thrust chest brought a smile to her face. She remembered how he overcame his fear to protect her, but the strange, long-snouted beasts remained in his memory. To him they would always be the evil water spirits–the Noc-Muks. More fearsome, now, because he and the rest of the tribe had actually seen what had once been a frightening tale to make children behave.

"I'll bring Mah-ki and his white mare you like so much." He left to fetch the horses.

She did prefer the white mare–not so much because of its beauty, but the mare had a rapport with Raven that Mah-ki did not have. Clayfoot's battle horse tolerated the bird, however Kah-tay sensed the stallion became upset by random thoughts from the winged creature entering his mind. The white mare often whinnied at Raven to perch atop its back and walk from withers to rump, scratching the hard-to-reach places a good roll in the dirt did not relieve.

I sense that you also bear a child, White Horse.

A soft nicker came as Kah-tay leaped across its back. Clayfoot would be pleased. Mah-ki's cross with the white mare brought many skins and prizes. While still an outcast he returned to the village from one of his lonely forays, leading a white foal. They no longer called him coward. It was Ironskin who kept the story alive that Clayfoot was never a warrior. Much sought after as a breeder of horses, her husband took his place around the evening council. A story teller of what lay beyond the tribal hunting grounds, and how to slay a Noc-Muk should a warrior happen upon one of the ugly beasts...and he was also a gifted artist.

Kah-tay knew he heard advice from her in his mind. Wisely, he conferred with Nah-mo before speaking, thus giving the impression the Medicine Man agreed with his words. His multi-colored legend paintings decorated many tipis now that he was no longer thought of as a coward.

After riding a few miles toward the Sacred Grove, Clayfoot stopped Mah-ki in a small grove of cedars.

"Tell me, wife. Why do I have this constant urge for you?"

"Mating is new to you. It will wear off in time. Besides, my body smells are pleasing to you–a scent which urges you to mate. Animals have this, too, but in a much larger measure. It is what makes Mah-ki desire a mare when she gives off the scent that she is receptive."

"Then I hope my nose grows long so I never lose your scent. And I don't think it will ever wear out."

"Your nose is quite large enough, Clayfoot. If you are not careful you may smell nothing but the she-cats that roam the hills in search of a mate."

"You would make a stench like that?"

She giggled at his unquenchable yearnings. "Perhaps."

"Come. Let us lay here in the shade of the bushes and consume my desire for you." He encircled an arm around her waist to pull her from the white mare.

A sudden gush of wild cat odor assailed his nose and mouth.

"You did that on purpose! A good wife follows the desires of her husband. Now I must race to the Sacred Pool and wash this stench from my body." He dug his heels into Mah-ki's sides who needed no urging to race for water.

Kah-tay goaded the mare to greater speed, relishing the smell of the hill cat's heat she had created. At each gag from Clayfoot, she burst out laughing.

***

Angrily, Clayfoot splashed from the pool. Water dripped in small rivers from his body. Foam gushed from his nose and mouth. He snorted the heavy odor of the cat's heat onto the waves that surged in front of him by his stomping gait. After climbing the sandy bank, he collapsed on the short grass in the center of the clearing.

"Why did you do that?"

"Because I'm not like Ironskin's squaws who spread their legs in any shady grove just to submit to a man's desire."

"I never meant –"

"I know. Now enjoy the fresh water and rest. I have work to do. We will talk later."

Abruptly, she left so he could nurse his wounded pride. She entered the dense grove of sycamores. It was near this spot Raven had his fill from the remains of the ringtail creature the cat had left. A caw from a high branch signaled the location.

"Thank you, my friend. I need the creature's tail for a medicine stick. It will help foretell the future and calm Clayfoot's people after I fashion the device."

A quick slash of her obsidian blade, she severed the fluffy black and white tail. The blade was a hidden remnant she brought with her in the trip under the Hills of Death. The tail came from a young female in the prime of life. It would make better medicine for her and the women...to intensify her thoughts to The Great One. She could help the tribal women gain new insight into their lives.

Now, she must find a short stick with a hole through its side...a hole large enough to hold the blue stone. It must be a stone of purest turquoise like she saw glistening at the edge of the stream. Clayfoot could help.

Stir from your anger, husband. Help me find a stick the length of your forearm. Slender on each end with a wide section in the middle.

When he started to protest she told him it was a sacred thing he must do. She would teach him many things this day. Ever curious where she was concerned, she knew Clayfoot would exhaust himself searching for what she needed.

A shadow stick later, Clayfoot returned with a widely forked limb from a dead beech tree. Long ago it had been crowded from its place in the sycamore grove.

"Why did you bring a dead branch, husband?"

His voice seemed confident and commanding when he answered. "This is what I saw from your word picture. It will be fashioned to fit your needs."

Kah-tay slipped cross-legged to the ground, unwilling to enter his mind. Fascinated, she watched his dexterity with the iron knife. Grooving a circlet in the forked branch, he broke it from the wrist-thick limb. Her interest intensified when the wood odor kindled ancient memories.

Moments later he had the bark stripped from the limb and each end narrowed to what she had in mind. Where the fork had been a dark, elliptical growth appeared and he used the point of the blade to remove harder wood in the core. Next, he shaped it to an oval opening and carved a groove in the inner surface of the hole.

"Bring your precious stone, Kah-tay."

She bit her tongue to stop the urge to see the picture in his mind. This is a thing he must do alone. After a quick glance to assure herself he was deeply engrossed in the stick, she held her hand over the water. Kah-tay clenched her other fist. The colorful turquoise rose to her grasp with a soft sucking sound, roiling the still water of the pond to a muddy swirl. After a quick dip to cleans it, she caught her breath at its beauty. Brown-streaks formed a word picture on the blue stone of the All Seeing Eye. This will be great magic...in a place filled with enchantment.

"Here is the stone, husband."

Clayfoot grunted. "The wood is about ready. I must heat it to make the wood pliable, then press the stone in place." He put the wooden piece on the ground next to the stone. "I'll gather small, dry twigs and stringy moss to start a fire."

Kah-tay nodded. They were agreed in their minds as to what the medicine stick would look like. While he was gone she piled the dry remnants of the beech wood for the fire. Next she placed the ring tail next to the stone.

"Clayfoot? Have you found the fire starter?"

Silence greeted her and she drew an exasperated breath. It is easy to start a fire...just use the Power. But making fire always gave her a headache. Searching the sandy bank, she found a clear stone. With it, she focused the sun's rays and smiled when smoke curled from the dry wood. What a wonderful odor it made as the small blaze curled through the smoke. Long-forgotten memories of an earlier time when....

No! That was long ago. Raven would take great pleasure in reminding her of it. She called Clayfoot again but heard nothing. Placing the turquoise into the medicine stick would be easy, but Clayfoot was determined to do it his way. It would be much better to allow him this small pleasure in her quest to build strong support for the Horse People.

A sudden burst of air brought a strong cat odor to assail her nostrils. Clayfoot should have washed it away when he rubbed sand over his body. Both horses reared, screaming against the tether holding them to a tree.

"Well, woman. Are you going to stand there and let this she-cat devour me? My lance and bows are next to Mah-ki. Get them."

Kah-tay whirled at the sound of his voice. Clayfoot backed slowly into the clearing his gaze never leaving the intense, unblinking stare of a large mountain lion. She noticed its teats were long and full. The cat must have a den with kits nearby. It would brook no interference from any beast, male or female. Stepping to his side, Kah-tay halted his backward steps. She eased past him to the large cat, knowing Clayfoot could neither hear nor understand what passed between her and the angry lioness. The cat gave a low snarl and abruptly disappeared into the underbrush.

"What did you say to her, wife? She seemed intent on backing me into a corner and then tearing me into small pieces for her kits. I must still smell of stray cat."

"She knew who you were. It is fortunate you were not armed. This way she only had to herd you back to me."

He opened his mouth, apparently to defend his actions, but his gaze went to the fire.

"I see you got a fire started."

"You were gone so long, I decided to rub two dry sticks together." A lie of course, but too much knowledge would only muddle his mind. "Forget the mother cat. Let us finish the medicine stick."

Cross-legged, she sat beside him watching as he warmed the sides of the carved opening. Moments later his upper arms bulged. Using his thumbs, he snapped the blue stone into the inner groove. Kah-tay couldn't resist touching the distended flesh of his upper arms as he strained to push the stone in the opening. A strange surrender of desire surged through her. No other man had his power. Kah-tay warded off the feeling. There would be other times...and other places for....

"Let me fasten the ringtail on the shortest end," she said.

He handed the stick to her. "Will it be done, then?"

"No." The tip of her pink tongue protruded from the corner of her mouth. She concentrated on wrapping the tail. It must dangle free from the end of the stick. "All it needs is the feather of an eagle on the other end to complete the circle."

Solemn, Clayfoot handed her the feather from his right braid. "I climbed a tall peak many years ago to battle an old she eagle for this."

"Thank you, my husband. It requires a feather bought with immense effort. I shall get you an even better feather when Raven returns."

He waved his hand. "I can climb another spire. No bird needs to fight my battles."

"I desire it," she said and went to the stream.

On a promontory overhanging the slow-moving water, she held the medicine stick aloft, offering it to the Great One for blessing. The taste of honey and bitters clouded her nose and mouth as its medicine grew strong.

This totem would foretell the future and strengthen those who believed in the sweetness and acrid distress of life. Now she needed stones from the stream's edge for her amulet bag. They must be stones that would speak to her or leave a message before they dried in the hot sun. Her first attempt to read a stone from this place had been disconcerting. The scent of fetid water and metal rose to greet her reminiscent of the unwelcome battle with Ironskin. She gathered five stones from the bank and washed them, searching for their message. Her stomach knotted when she read the message from the fourth stone.

Beware. He wants the child.

The glyph for 'he' seemed curious. It smelled of iron and looked like a stick man. It could only mean Ironskin. Kah-tay turned a tearful gaze to Clayfoot.

"Read it. You have the Knowledge, my husband."

He towered over her, crushing her to his chest. "Then why do you cry?"

"Read the message of the stones," she said, handing him a damp pebble. She entered his mind to know his thoughts. Would he discover the same warning?

Before he could concentrate on the strange glyphs, they faded in a puff of hot, dry air. He stepped way from her and went to the water's edge. Half-buried in the pale sand lay a large, smooth stone. Anxious, he pried it loose and rubbed a wet hand over a surface that had lain buried for centuries. Her anxiety melded with his. The message started to dry as soon as he brought the stone close. No mistaking this sign. The stench of a sweat-soaked iron shirt made Clayfoot wrinkle his nose.

Next he saw two crossed arrows...the last to fade became the unmistakable image of a newborn child wrapped in the hide of a horse. A child of the Horse People.

"You warned me," he growled through clenched teeth. "I should have killed him the first time." He turned to comfort her but she was gone. "He is no longer my brother, in this world...or the next."

She sensed him searching for her then felt his presence as she stood on the high outcropping over the crystal clear pool. A small dust devil whipped leaves and twigs in circles across water. The ground trembled and Kah-tay bowed in reverence. Moments later she raised her face to the sky and closed her eyes.

Pressing the new medicine stick to her forehead she said, "Protect us from Evil. Bring comfort and knowledge to foresee the future. Guide us to new understanding."

CHAPTER EIGHT

Clayfoot gazed in awe. The small twisting wind hung a hand's breadth above the water, wavering as if talking to her. Small leaves, twigs, and droplets of water twirled in a tight pattern making a strange shape. *Co-wat-ka!* A spirit Noc-Muk? The ground rumbled as though countless buffalo charged across the plain. She did not move, yet he felt a strange energy flowing from her. Was her power being drawn out by an evil force? A ray of sunlight burst from a cloud momentarily outlining her in a glowing flame.

He shrank away in terror. "Kah-tay. Be careful."

His fright was baseless. A soft blue light flowed from the water devil, engulfed her briefly, then danced sideways on the water as it crept toward him. Clayfoot's teeth chattered. Terror crept up his back as if countless centipedes crawled over his body. Unable to turn away, he watched the water twister move closer and felt his legs go weak. The earth shook and he collapsed to his knees on the sandy beach, remembering what he had seen in his youth...a trembling ground that creaked and yawned in a bottomless chasm, swallowing large trees and a herd of buffalo. Nah-mo said the buffalo still searched for a way to get out.

"Kah-tay! Don't let them find you."

Would the Buffalo-Running-Below-The-Earth open the ground and swallow him and Kah-tay? A gust of wind stopped the water and stilled his mind. Even the birds were quiet. His attention riveted to the shape hovering over the water. What did the twisting thing want? His weapons would be useless against...he was about to think Noc-Muk, but this was no beast. It had shined its light on Kah-tay and she seemed transformed.

75

He pleaded at the shape. "I give my life for her. She is needed for the child who I promised to guard. Do not take her, I beg you." Twice he tried a death chant but it would not flow past his swollen throat. Arching his back he spread his arms to force his song of death. Abruptly, a soft blue light engulfed him and his fear was gone, fading like the messages on the stones. The light bathed him, replacing his fear with a pleasing calm. A sound, like a the creaking snap of a falling tree, came. Then it was gone. His thoughts went to his wife.

"Kah-tay!"

She was not on the promontory over the pool. Had the mysterious water-wind taken her despite his pleading? He must tell her of his adventure with the strange wind, but she was gone. Anxious, he dashed up the sand bank to the clearing. He found her collapsed on the soft grass, sobbing.

"What is it, my wife?" He clutched her in his arms and brushed a hand over her braids.

"It was The Great One. He granted me a wish for you but warned me the child is in danger."

"Danger? You mean The Great One cannot even protect his own child? I will keep it safe as I promised."

"It is this land. The Evil One has great power and can seduce men to do his bidding."

"He will not seduce me!"

"No, he cannot make *you* do his will but there are others who are weak or filled with hate."

"Ironskin," mumbled Clayfoot.

"Yes–and it will take much power to defeat that one." She lay on her back, an arm flung over her eyes.

He patted Kah-tay's belly. "Between the three of us Ironskin will die."

"I heard you sever your kinship with him. He is a very dangerous enemy, Clayfoot." She clutched his hand to her cheek. "Promise me you will be careful."

"A warrior must take chances to be successful. But do not fear. That one is as good as dead if we meet again." He put his arm around her shoulders and guided her to the horses. "What is the wish you asked for me?"

"You will find out soon enough, my husband."

Clayfoot tried to probe her mind for the answer but she had blocked him out. He wanted to cajole her, even threaten to leave her at the Sacred Grove, but sensed a coolness pervade her mind and decided she would tell him when she was ready...which may be never.

Rumblings in his belly reminded him why Kah-tay said she wanted to come to the grove.

"You wanted to eat in this Sacred Place. Where is the food?"

She handed him a tightly wrapped deerskin. "What is wrapped in this should fill your belly."

He picked at the small knot, feeling her mirth as the thong refused to loosen. Kah-tay, he'd discovered, was adept at making quick knots only she could undo. Exasperated, he handed the pack to her and watched, fascinated, as she pushed the cords together, then loosened the leather knot. Someday he would learn this trick of hers. She had made his favorite; thin corn cakes wrapped around strips of spiced, dried meat with wild onions.

"Eat slowly. You will choke like a foolish child trying to eat everything in one bite."

"They taste good. What do you put in them that makes me want to eat more than I should?"

"A secret handed down by my people."

He stretched on his belly beside her after swallowing the last cake. Idly, he combed his fingers in the short grass, dividing his thoughts between her and the Sacred Grove. Perhaps she wouldn't detect his presence in her mind if he switched his thoughts.

"You have never told me of your people, Kah-tay. As your husband I should know about them. What if your father and his warriors should appear and overpower me and demand many horses for you. You are most beautiful."

"There is small likelihood of that. I was driven out, remember?"

"Tell of your tribe." Quickly, before she could block him, he asked, "Were there others before me?"

A small parade, visions of men, most dressed like her in white cloth with a golden shoulder cowl and hard-soled moccasins with leg lacings. Others wore loin cloths or colorful shawls and strange, feathered headgear. One was covered in gold and shined like the sun.

The next instant they were gone.

"You closed your mind!"

"You must never search my memory, husband. There is no man for me but you."

"But I saw—"

She pointed her finger at him. "You saw nothing."

Like a fascinating dream that cannot be recalled, they disappeared. Try as he might he could not remember one detail.

He feigned anger. "You wiped the memory of them from my mind."

"Yes. You have no need to think of such things." She caressed his cheek. "I have asked for you, forever."

"And?"

"Forever is a long time, my husband. Will you object?"

"No." He plucked a blade of grass and rolled it between his fingers. After a deep sigh he said, "I, too, wish to grow old with you."

"But we will never grow old."

Clayfoot's mouth went agape. To not grow old meant they could....

"There will be lands to explore, tribes to meet and, most of all, people to heal."

A soft mirth touched his mind. Was she laughing at him? No. She seemed happy to share this wonderful gift with him.

"By 'forever young' will we enjoy each other? Will we have more children? You know how much I desire you."

"Yes. I don't know about children. Whatever The Great One wants. You will have to learn to control your urges for me when we are in the presence of others."

"Waugh!" He pulled her close and slipped a leg over hers. "I know of a large cave. I found it during my wanderings. We can live there. No one will bother us."

"I don't intend to spend forever in a cave, just to satisfy your needs."

"What of the child? Will she grow old?"

She pointed to the rock formation jutting over the pond. "After she is born I will sit with her and hold the divining totem against my forehead. The Great One will guide me about the child. He will tell us many things."

As she talked his fingers worked the ties of her long skirt. She did not resist.

"You know my people live on the other side of The Mountains of White Death. We have lived there countless summers by the shores of a great water one cannot see across.

"A few of our men travel in large canoes we call boats," she said. "They are called 'Journeyers' and go to many lands, always in peace, and exchange knowledge with many tribes."

"Just as you gave my people knowledge." He slipped her skirt apart and caressed her thighs.

"Wait for now, husband. We are alone and I would tell my story." She left her skirt open but held his hand while she continued. "The Great One blessed my people, especially me. I was granted the power to heal.

"We inscribed our knowledge on thin skins called paper and stored them in sealed caves deep in the earth. Once, a tribe of strange white men, with hair and beards the color of red earth, sailed to our shores. Their weapons were crude, long knives and sticks with sharp metal points, which were useless against our power. Theirs was a difficult language to learn. They came from across the great sea to explore and when they promised peace, one of our men guided them North. They soon tired of walking on land and after leaving marks on a rock, they returned to sail on their beloved sea.

"Some of our people lived not far from here in a fertile land. They built mud brick homes high in a canyon wall and became a center of commerce and law. After several hundred summers they, too, returned to the Home. The land had changed and become barren. It was said The Great One was not pleased with them."

She placed his hand atop the moving child in her belly as he thought of their future. Would they always be at peace after the Evil One was put out of their lives?

Are you enjoying the story of our ancestors, little one?

Yes, Mother. Tell how you came here

"The Elders did not want me to heal a woman who desired men. They said she was needed, but she begged me to heal her. They banished me when her desire turned cold.

"We have a large lake high in the hills. When the moon is full during the day it stirs the water in the lake. Faster and faster it turns until the water opens up and sucks anything near its swirling edge down into the blackness at the bottom.

"The next time the moon was full, the Elders put me in a small canoe and pushed me into the twisting water. They didn't know the lake emptied in that waterfall." Kah-tay pointed to the stream of water spouting above headwaters of the pond. "That is how I came here." She smiled at Clayfoot.

"Under the White Mountains of Death, not over them. Raven came with me. My last memory of my people is of the Elders wailing when they saw Raven land on my shoulder. A flock of night birds came with us. I think the Elders knew then they had angered The Great One."

She grew silent until Clayfoot entered her mind, but he spoke aloud.

"How could they overcome your power?"

"They joined their minds to become one great force."

"Do all of your people have Power?"

"Yes. All can mind-speak. Only a few have power beyond that." She plucked a blade of grass, laughing as it floated to Clayfoot's nose and danced.

"Your power has grown far beyond healing, Kah-tay."

"Yes. It seems limitless, but I'm frightened for my people as well as the child."

"They could be gone from the face of the earth for making Him angry. I will protect your little one."

"It is my fear, too, my husband. Someday we will journey to my home land and discover their fate. I hope they still prosper."

She moved his hand to her thigh, indicating she was through talking. In moments they were locked in passion.

***

Kah-tay mind-spoke through her exhaustion, telling him to call Raven to stand watch while she slept...and to find three round, black pebbles, whose messages never die, for her amulet bag. Clayfoot felt her immense trust when she fell asleep.

"Wheeeeet," he whistled. "Come Black One. Your mistress needs you."

You have a way of making her need me, Warrior. No other drained her they way you do.

Startled, Clayfoot looked for the source of the Raven. He found it scratching back and forth across the white mare's back much to her delight from the sound of her low pitched nicker.

"Watch over her while I search for the stones she asked me to find."

Don't I always?

"Hruummmph," muttered Clayfoot. "Who are the others who couldn't make her sleep?"

Did you think you were the first?

"Of course not! The Great One fathered her child."

That was more like planting a kernel of corn. Hardly worth worrying about.

"And the others?"

Haughty, the bird replied. *She will tell you if she decides it is necessary. A word of advice. If you persist in jealous pursuit of her past, she may remove your memory. Take care, mighty lover. You could lose it all.*

Clayfoot sighed. The bird is right, of course. Endless probing about past lovers is dangerous. At least I am the best and that is good enough for me. He went to Mah-ki and swung his leg over the horse's back.

There were no smooth, round pebbles in the stream bed, at least not the kind she pictured to him before she fell asleep. Perhaps they lay on the far side of the stream where it curved near Dark Forest. He gazed at the tree tops swaying in the wind. What danger lay in the dense growth?

Raven entered his mind.

Do I sense fear, mighty Warrior?

Only a fool has no fear of that place.

With your new powers, surely you do not fear a few tall trees. A mighty Warrior with power? I laugh at you. Dark Forest makes you empty your bowels in your loincloth, like the others.

Laugh if you want. I can eat Raven stew when I get back. For your information, I can hold my bowels in any battle. Tell me, are the stones she needs on that side?

Of course. But I doubt you can find them and I cannot leave her. And you may find my flesh less tasty than your Noc-Muks. That is if you're man enough to pluck my feathers. Remember our first encounter?

Clayfoot urged Mah-ki into the stream. Yes, he remembered the endless deep pain the Black Bird raked on his chest during their first encounter. But he enjoyed the banter between them, sensing the bird trying to guide him in his relationship with Kah-tay. Mah-ki surged from the water and shook himself. Clayfoot cocked his head and listened.

Quiet. Stillness became gut rending on the Dark Forest side of the stream. Gone were the songs of birds, the ripple of water, and the faint roar of the distant waterfall. Only when he lifted his gaze to the tree tops did he hear a sound a faint whisper from the wind.

Come. Enter and behold my kingdom.

"I haven't time, Ghost of the Forest. Some other day." He turned Mah-ki to the stream bed and dismounted.

Black pebbles were few and none contained a message like the stones on the Sacred side of the pool. It seemed a fruitless search. The Wind clouded his mind with temptation, but each black stone was pried from its bed as he searched for a message.

"Waugh! They are well hidden, Mah-ki. I wish you could see them and help me."

Moments later the horse stopped and pawed at the edge of the water. Beyond him lay a bed of black stones. Excited, Clayfoot waded into the steam.

"Now, I'll find you!"

His search seemed in vain. Not one message was uncovered.

"You can't see any better than I, mighty horse. Don't play with me like that Black-Assed Bird."

Mah-ki snorted and tossed his head at the water.

"If I go deeper I'll have to dive. Is that what you mean?" He often talked to Mah-ki in their travels, but he had never asked directions of the horse before. Instead of waiting for an answer that may or may not come, he waded beyond the barren bed and dove in waist deep water.

Strange. This side of the stream felt warmer than the cooling waters on the Sacred side of the pool. He swam, open-eyed, searching the bottom. Clustered like rare triplets, three dark pebbles the size of his thumb lay half-buried in the sand, almost as if they were part of the stream bed.

You'll come loose with my knife, sticky ones. You must be the stones she wants for all the trouble you're giving me.

Clayfoot almost dropped them when the strange markings appeared on the under surface of the stones. He surfaced, spouting water, and waved the stones. After a quick rinse he tried to read the message-that-never-changes.

The markings seemed baked in the blackness. What could they mean? His mind reached out to Kay-la.

His thoughts scattered when the bird entered his mind, unbidden.

She sleeps, Warrior. See them, then send the message to me. I know the stones she seeks.

Clayfoot mind-spoke the surface of each stone as he rotated them, one at a time.

The Raven said, *I know the language of The Old People.*

He thought he heard the bird gasp.

They are Stones from the Beginning. The message is very clear. It is Trust–Promise–Compassion. Hurry back, Clayfoot, and show them to the mistress.

Clayfoot smiled. It was the first time the bird referred to him by his given name. Together, they would fight to keep Kah-tay and the child safe.

CHAPTER NINE

Ironskin hugged the walls of the cave, first one side then the other, as he struggled toward the blue glow of the entrance. Patches of dull, flame-colored light reflected from outcroppings, reminding him of the Evil One's throne room. A sudden, bright flash mirrored the pit of fire.

Odd chitterings, groans, and old battle cries echoed in the blackness behind him as if countless wounded and dying warriors warned him of their fate.

"Silence!" he shouted at the din. When he turned to face the entrance his forehead struck a jagged rock. "May a herd of buffalo shit cover your hide," he cursed at the wall of the cave.

Instantly, foul slime oozed from the rocky surface and plopped to the floor. The familiar stench of grazing buffalo filled his nostrils. Gape-mouthed, he dashed from the cave. How could it be? When he wished buffalo droppings on the cave, it happened.

"Power! I have the power." He danced among the gold-flecked rocks, ignoring the bloody wound on his forehead. "Now I can fight Woman of Magic on *her* terms. No longer can she protect Clayfoot."

His foot slipped in the dirty, green slime spreading from the cave to cover the open area around Burning Rocks. An angry glance at the entrance showed a heavy layer of manure tumbling toward him. Waugh! He had cursed the walls for his bruised head and now the spell threatened to engulf him.

"Stop!" He thrust a palm at the slime. "Go back where you came from."

Immediately, the dark green mass withered like grass before a prairie fire and shriveled into the cave. Then it was gone. Gone, too, was the stench. Ironskin shook his balled fist in triumph and again began a victory dance.

Woman of Magic was as good as his. A quick swipe of his hand across his forehead told him the bleeding wound on his head had stopped. He had the power to heal his wounds!

Never again will Clayfoot draw my blood.

Panting from the vigorous dance, he stood on the edge of the high clearing. Far below Dungi grazed on a patch of green, tended by the small wizened red man he had seen before. *Ok-boma-hom.* The man who became a hawk.

"My power is great. I shall raise the horse to this clearing and together we will find Clayfoot and the woman." He extended his hand over the scene below.

"Rise up, horse. Come to the ledge. Together we will fly over Dark Forest to find my coward brother. He will not be successful the next time we meet."

Nothing happened. Dungi seemed content to stay with the little man the color of red leaves. Ironskin clenched his fist as he had seen Kah-tay do whenever she made magic. His eyes rolled upward. Muscles bulged against his iron shirt, straining the leather lacing on each side of the armor.

"Come," he said through clenched teeth.

Dungi continued to graze.

"Curse you, Wa-Ha-Na! You promised great power if I serve you. Is buffalo shit the only thing I can control?"

Wind blew across the cave opening, sending its musical message. The eerie sound scraped terror across his mind.

You were promised great power man-in-the-shirt-of-iron–if you bring the child. What you did was but a small portion of what you will have. But first– the child.

"What, then, *do* I have?"

You can change shape. And you have Cunning to trick your enemies. After a gusty change it echoed down the cave. *You have the power to mind- speak–if you try.*

"It is not enough!"

Test yourself, mighty warrior. Stand at the edge of the cliff. Leap into the air and become a bird. You will think differently once you soar with my friends.

"Leap from a cliff? Do you think I'm stupid like a frightened deer?"

Hollow laughter mocked from the cavern. *Now, who is the coward? Clayfoot, who was never a coward and didn't believe it–or Ironskin who says he is no coward and now questions his bravery?*

Stung by the Wind's taunts, Ironskin strode to the edge and peered down at Dungi. Shadows on the horse made him look up. An eagle soared the wind far above him.

"I will become like you," he shouted at the eagle and leaped from the edge in a graceful dive. His skin tingled. Through blurred vision the world became a silver mirage rushing up to meet him. Wind filled his outstretched arms, now covered with feathers. He swooped low, screeching as he flew over Dungi's back and the grinning, bright-red creature who could become a hawk.

I am an Eagle!

He flew to the soaring bird, who, with a wild screech folded its wings and dropped to the forest.

It knows I may look like an eagle but I'm still a man and its bitter enemy.

Dense, somber greens of Dark Forest lay in a great circle below him, ringing the large enchanted meadow. Burning Rocks formed the end of the prairie-like open space, its rear side engulfed by the dense forest.

A warm gust pushed him higher. Waugh! He could see Sacred Pond...and two horses...and two lovers on the grass-covered mound. Could he dare hope it was Clayfoot and his woman?

Far in the distance, across the rolling prairie, lay the village of the Horse People. How they would envy him if they could see his mighty wings.

Circling aloft he felt his belly cramp. Time to break his fast. The meadow, once bereft of life, except for terrible shape changers, seemed filled with animals. Large and small game roamed through the tall grass. A mother cougar hugged the ground teaching her kits as she stalked a deer.

Rabbits and squirrels scurried across open places among dense tufts of grass.

"That fat rabbit," he screeched and folded his wings to dive on his prey. Ever alert, he noticed his shadow ripple across the meadow, bringing with it memories of Dungi's fright at seeing them.

"Hee-ya," he shouted from the exhilarating dive. His belly would soon be full and he could fly over Dark Forest to good water. No longer would the whirling shadows in the treetops put him to sleep.

The mother cougar gave him a disgusted glance as he soared past the deer, frightening it toward the forest. She urged her cubs to follow the fleeing deer.

"Another lesson," bragged Ironskin. "I might become a rival cougar in my next shaping and steal your cubs. They will know how to catch a good meal when I finish with them." Screeching, he swerved toward his prey and made a final dive.

The rabbit screamed its protest, but the killing blow surprised Ironskin. His taloned foot held the struggling rabbit, but it was his mighty paw, the gift from the Evil One, that raked its throat to a mass of bloody shreds. Elation surged to his mind. Perhaps Clayfoot did him a *ki-ne-ki*, a favor, when he severed his hand during their first battle, then shortened it during their last encounter.

"You are a mighty weapon." Awestruck, he gazed at the terrible thing with its curved bloody talons.

Another swipe at the carcass opened a fur-covered thigh. Savagely, the Eagle tore at the muscles with its beak. The odor of fresh blood increased his desire for food. His belly ached from hunger. Long strips of meat dangled from his beak then disappeared down his gullet.

"Mauk," he choked down the last of the meat. "I will eat your brother when the sun comes up tomorrow."

He hippity-hopped on his eagle foot and paw to a clear place away from the carcass. Slowly, he reverted to his shape as a man, feeling the sensation of many worms beneath his iron shirt, then wiped his blood-covered mouth on the back of the fur paw.

The warrior sat on his haunches, contemplating his kill and the taste of blood. It tasted good. No wonder flesh eaters of the land preferred meat. What surprised him most, he no longer desired salt. Blood was the taste he craved.

"Raw meat is best for warriors in this kingdom," he muttered. "And I will eat my fill–including the flesh of my brother."

He tried to change back to the eagle shape. Nothing. Puzzled, he thought about his first Shaping. He had leaped from the cliff overlooking the small clearing above the meadow where Dungi grazed with *Ok-boma-hom,* the Red-Hawk-Man. The Wind said he must have courage and confidence that a Shaping will happen.

"I will become the Eagle." Shouting the phrase several times, he ran, arms outstretched, and leaped into the air. He flapped at the still air as the sensation of countless thorns tickled his skin. Vision blurred, then cleared. His heart filled with joy for the second time when feathers formed on his arms and lift from powerful wings pushed him aloft. Circling to gain height, he flew over Dark Forest and straight for Sacred Pond. He thirsted for its cool water.

***

Ironskin circled twice over the beautiful grove and the green clearing. Was it safe to land and drink? Clayfoot and his Woman-of-Magic were there, doing what they usually did when they thought no one was watching. In a jealous rage, he swooped low determined to stop them, but when he entered Clayfoot's mind he found it closed to everything except the woman riding his hips.

"They don't even know I'm here. After my thirst is gone I will show my new power. Then she will be mine and the child in her belly will belong to Wa-Ha-Na."

He fluttered to a pebbled beach just beyond the rocky promontory and dipped his beak. Ah! Sacred Pond had the best water. He drank his fill, absorbed in the wonders that had now become his.

***

They cried out together, clutching each other for long moments.

"You become better each time, wife," panted Clayfoot. "When we close our minds to the world we become one and for that small instant it is more glorious than life itself."

"Yes. For me, too. That is why I have asked for long life for you. To stay forever in your arms."

Raven hopped from the mare's back.

If you are finished with this foolish nonsense of humans, I suggest you look at the intruder who drinks beyond the high rock. Danger. It is not what it seems.

The bird's mind-speak startled them. Thinking it was one of the Horse People, Kah-tay tugged the long shirt over her bulging belly then glanced at the rippling stream. An eagle drank from the pond.

Strange.

They never come this close to humans...and this is a very large eagle. Raven was right. There was something strange about the bird. Could it possibly be sick? Before she could warn him Clayfoot was already beyond her, an arrow nocked in his taut bow. Her husband must have seen the thought-picture of the large bird.

Ziippp.

The arrow sounded angry in its flight to its victim, followed by another...then another.

The eagle screamed when the first arrow found its mark. It leaped into the pond. Two remaining arrows struck the beach where it had just been. Startled, she saw it change shape into a large mountain trout just as it cut the water. Her gaze followed the ripple on Sacred Pond to the opposite bank.

A Shape Changer! Here? In this land? But how...?

"I hit it with a killing blow but it did not fall."

"No, husband. We are dealing with a different force. It can change shape at will. It is very dangerous." She sniffed the air. "Do you smell the iron? He is very close."

"Who? Ironskin? He is as good as dead if he gets within bow shot." He took a deep breath then smacked his lips. "I smell it, too–and taste it. It is him."

Across the pond a large trout flopped to the bank, shimmered, then slowly emerged as a man. Protruding from his iron shirt was an arrow.

Slowly, with deliberation, the man pulled the arrow from his chest and snapped it across his leg.

Ironskin mind-spoke. *You cannot win against my power.*

The Shaping spread his arms and leaped into the woods. She saw a surprised look on his face when he disappeared into Dark Forest.

"Clayfoot! Did you hear him?"

"Yes, but how?"

"He has reached the Evil One and made a bargain for power." She clutched her husband's arm. "He is just learning the Shaping. I touched his mind when he fled. The eagle Shape would not come."

A shudder ran across her shoulders. What kind of bargain? How much power? Unconsciously, she rubbed a protective hand across her belly.

"How many shapes can he take?" Clayfoot waded into the water and retrieved his remaining arrows.

"Have you no fear, my husband?"

"Not of him. He must do battle in human form or there is no honor. But Ironskin does not care about...." His voice trailed off.

"Quick! We must make a seal he cannot break. If he has been given power to take a different *human* shape he can fool us into believing what we are not."

"You mean he can become you?"

"He may look like me, my husband, and mind-speak like me, but you will know instantly the shaping is not me."

"What about you? What if tries to become me?"

"Come to the water."

She mind-spoke to the Raven.

Search for the evil Ironskin and report. He must not see what we do.

She clung to Clayfoot until the bird returned. All her power must protect her husband if Ironskin returned before her defense would work.

He sleeps beneath a large tree. His bloody shirt of iron lays beside him, but the bleeding from his wound has stopped. Unfortunately, he will live.

Kah-tay searched Clayfoot's face. "You heard?"

"Yes. But how can you prevent him from—?"

She held out her hand. "Give me your knife."

Kah-tay led him to the water and holding his hand in a tight grasp, walked on the sandy bottom until the water became two man-lengths over their heads. Sunlight filtered down to amplify their actions. She felt Clayfoot's amazement they were able to stay submerged...and they no longer needed to breathe. Her power often surprised him.

She opened her shirt and cut a deep gash in her chest. Another slash and Clayfoot's chest lay open. Pulling him close, she pressed the wounds together.

As our blood is mingled so are our souls. You will always know it is me, my husband, when you mind-speak. The bond can never be broken. Do you swear to believe this?

I swear to always know it is you.

They clung together as blood flowed from heart to heart. Small, eerie bubbles rose from their pressed lips as they held each other.

Even the Evil One cannot penetrate this bond made under Sacred Water.

She drew back and traced her finger along his deep knife cut. Instantly the wound healed. Her open chest showed no sign of a cut when she drew back for him to see. He touched her face and pushed to the surface. Hand in hand they waded from the pool.

Raven paced along the upper ridge above the pool.

Phaugh! It's about time. I thought you made a pact to die together.

Not quite yet, Black-Ass. Now catch a fish of bright color for your mistress to cook. All this has made us hungry.

You wouldn't be hungry if you would keep your loin cloth fastened up, Man-of-Muscles.

Kah-tay smiled. In the face of grave danger these two would argue...and become close friends. She sensed the bond between them tightening. They would depend on each other a great deal to protect her and the child. But a sinister question nagged her mind. How much power had the Evil One given the rogue warrior?

CHAPTER TEN

"You sit in the shade many hours every morning." Ta-nic crossed her ankles and lowered herself to the ground. "Don't your legs become tired and cramped?"

Kah-tay withdrew from her trance. It seemed useless. The Great One would not hear her plea; neither for protection for the child nor strength beyond measure for Clayfoot. The Evil One held sway in this land and they would have to battle his creatures on their footing for the safety of her child.

"Your child is active this morning. Not many days before it cries out for its first food, eh?" Ta-nic drew her legs up and rested her chin on her knees "Ah, to suckle a child again. What sweet pain to feel a little mouth and toothless gums pull at my nipples. It has been a long time." She gazed across the prairie dreamily.

Kah-tay smiled when she joined her thoughts with the Shaman's wife. Yes, she thought, I've shared the joy before...but somehow it is not the same one's own. She rubbed a hand across her belly and let her thoughts drift with Ta-nic.

I'm coming, soon, mother. Will you be happy to see me?

Of course, little one. You will bring much joy to both me and your father.

But you are troubled, mother, and I'm afraid.

Hush, child. There is no reason to fear. Clayfoot has become strong. He will protect us.

Then why do you cry out to my real father for protection?

Astonished, Kah-tay covered her mouth. The child knows! But how? If she knows about the Great One...she knows about the Evil One...and

91

Ironskin...everything.

Do not fear. Clayfoot has great power.

If the Evil One or Ironskin try to hurt me I will burn them in the pit.

"Do you often talk to your child?" Ta-nic rolled to her knees, a knowing smile across her face.

"But how–?"

"You broadcast your thoughts, child. Even one who is not gifted could hear them."

Not true, of course, but Kah-tay wondered where and how Ta-nic received the mind-speak. She decided to ask.

"My father came to us many years ago," said Ta-nic. "He looked much like you–light skin and dressed in a short tunic with a wide golden collar. He said he was driven out after a fight with the Elders.

"He married my mother after she defended him in council–one of the rare times a woman spoke at the evening fire. Some wanted to drive him out or kill him because he had strange powers.

"I remember how handsome he was and how good he was to me. 'Concentrate,' he would say and I would listen to the voice in my head when he spoke. Until you came it had been a long time since I heard a voice in my head or knew of someone else's feelings."

"What happened to him? You're not so old but what he could still be alive."

"I was told he was killed in a war with the Snake People. I don't believe it. Our men were jealous because he never grew old. Mother always had her young lover who was good to her–and to me. But mother grew old and wrinkled as I became older. One day he never returned."

Kah-tay realized Ta-nic's father was from the Home. No one ever left the Home except the Journeyers and they always returned with knowledge, and seeds for new trees and plants...especially food plants. She was the only citizen of the Home to be driven out except....

"What was your father's name?"

"Lomat." She ducked her head to peer in Kah-tay's eyes. "Was–he from your people?"

A quick skip of her heart was all she allowed. Lomat. This is where he came? Her mind filled with visions of the rejected lover. At the time she was married to...her mind flipped though the index of years she'd had husbands...never lovers. She was a faithful wife, but Lomat wouldn't take "no" for an answer, persisting in his efforts to woo her away from Gamin, until the Elders heard her cry for help.

"Yes. He was a good man–a–a Journeyer. We wondered what became of him." It was pointless to tell this woman-who-would-be-her-friend, her father had been forced to leave the Home, never to return. At least he'd become a good father...but like Ta-nic she wondered if he really died in battle.

The Shaman's wife glanced beyond Kah-tay.

"Li-nat comes. She must not hear us speak of these things. Especially of talking in the mind." She leaned close to Kah-tay's ear. "She is a good woman, but her tongue is loose. She loves to be the center of attention with a good story–especially if it's about others."

"She should be content to have her husband free of peyote. He would have died from it."

Ta-nic nodded and glanced at the corral. "Your husband comes. Does he know of your people?"

"Yes." She thought how easily Clayfoot had accepted her story...and her. Men often told her she was beautiful, and she supposed she was, but they were frightened away when they felt her powers. Not Clayfoot...at least not after their first encounter.

"I'll leave. Perhaps we can speak of these things again."

Kah-tay did not answer. Instead, she went to Clayfoot, hoping Ta-nic would forget their conversation. She sensed there was little chance of her forgetting now that the woman discovered Lomat was known to her.

"How is the new foal?"

"Tato is pleased as am I. It will make a fine mare when she is ready to breed." He dropped to the ground under the Oak tree and reached for her hand. "I heard some of the words you said to the Great One this morning. You must feel desperation to let your thoughts scatter."

"Yes. Even Ta-nic heard me. Did you know her father came from the Home? That he was one of my people?"

"I do now. I remember him. Lomat was his name, I believe. The Horse People often called him a liar when he spoke of strange lands and people beyond the hills–and of a great water where waves became taller than a man." Clayfoot plucked a blade of grass and rolled it between his fingers. His eyes closed. "Ta-nic was thirteen winters when her father went with the hunting party and never returned.

"He told wonderful stories to fill young boys heads with dreams of wandering the hills in search of adventure." Snorting a laugh, he sat up. "I was the only one from the Horse People to see what lies beyond the horizon.

Like Lomat, I too, was driven out. And that damnable Raven enjoys teasing me about it." ·

Kah-tay cast her gaze toward the corral. "Where is my friend?"

"Probably pacing the mare's back. He pestered me all morning, asking about humans and the fascination they have for laying atop one another...and why they don't breed like horses and other animals."

"What did you tell him?"

"That we prefer to look at each other when we breed." He tossed the blade of grass aside and plucked another.

The play of muscles cross his belly and chest brought a longing Kah-tay knew she could not risk and quickly suppressed it. Patience, she reminded herself.

"He must have found that amusing."

"No," said Clayfoot. "The Black One stopped pacing and gave me some peace instead of his constant questions and then asking, 'why' after each answer. It grows very difficult to talk with Tato and carry on a different conversation with Raven at the same time. I could not reach his mind when we finished teaching the foal to lead. After Tato left Raven seemed to be in deep thought."

Kah-tay frowned. "Very odd—but the bird has been acting withdrawn since our return from the pond."

"Odd is a small word for his behavior. Crazy is more like it."

Kah-tay sent her mind-probe to the corral. Raven was not there and she fanned her thoughts to the horizons. Nothing. A furrow crossed her brow. It was not like the bird to leave...and it had never strayed out of range from her mind.

***

A large eagle circled high above the village of the Horse People, its mind a jumble of mind-speak. Too many talked at the same time. Ironskin's Shaping tried to concentrate on Kah-tay's mind, her thoughts were very powerful. He heard his name mentioned along with the Evil One in loud bursts that nearly cracked his mind.

"I'll worry about her later. It's the other voice I need to hear."

Ironskin cocked his eagle head to better concentrate on Raven's chatter. "What nonsense! The bird asks questions about what it already knows."

He dropped lower, about the span of one hundred men, careful not to send his shadow across the village. It would not do to be discovered as it would only delay his plan: A plan he discovered near Dark Forest while recovering from Clayfoot's arrow. Cursed brother. It was a lucky bow shot.

The Wind pushed a sudden upward gust and whispered.

Why do you persist in thoughts that Clayfoot is inept? He is one of the best bowman in the plain. You must use Cunning. Your brother has great power and more can be given him when he needs it most. Remember his warning that you would flee from his lance.

Ironskin circled from the Wind. *I have a plan.*

Then use it!

The Wind pushed outward tilting the eagle on its side.

Yes. But first....

Thoughts of a band of crows mating in Dark Forest beneath the trees in the circle of light returned. Could Raven be tempted? Its mind-speak with Clayfoot had been nothing more than questions about mating. It was the season for mating, too. The females gave off a scent as they flitted among the males, selecting a strong provider...one who could find the best carrion.

"I have what you need, Raven. In the bag around my neck. A foul odor you will find most pleasing."

Ironskin's screech echoed from the clouds as he veered to prevent his shadow from crossing the corral. Tato would consider it a bad omen and could influence Clayfoot. Now, he must be very careful.

"Wind," he called, "help me. I will fly low and empty the mating odor. Carry the scent of the lovely, black-feathered maidens to Raven. Let us hope he detects the desire he finds so interesting."

Upwind, Ironskin dropped lower until he was out of sight of the village. The Bag of Tempting he had so laboriously made hung around his neck while he was still in his man shape. It would not come loose with a talon and a paw; a major impediment when he was in a Shaping. He had to return to his body in order to do manual tasks.

"I cannot fight Clayfoot as one of the Evil One's beasts," he muttered and dropped out of sight in a clump of chaparral. "Just as well. It will be more pleasurable to spill his belly when I'm in my true shape."

Ironskin scanned the horizon for intruders. It would not do to be seen this close to camp and his only escape would be a Shaping. Something that would surprise and frighten any warrior. Silent, he closed his eyes and prayed to the Wind. "Be my friend and carry the scent where Raven perches atop the mare's back."

A chilling tingle started as his shape changed. He opened the pouch at arm's length letting the blue-black tainted wisp of fragrance drift toward the corral. The small cloud seemed to roil as it flowed, pushed by the evil current, skipping over brush and stones on its way to Raven. Grinning, he watched it ooze through the thorn bush corral and settle around his quarry. It swirled once as if enticing, then drifted to the East: A place known only to Ironskin...and the Wind.

"Now," he whispered. "We'll see if you really *are* interested in mating."

He watched Raven pace atop the horse's back, stop and glanced at Kahtay and Clayfoot lounging beneath the tree, then leaped from his perch.

"You will follow, stupid bird, but you will never catch the scent until you are deep in Dark Forest."

Ironskin vaulted from his hiding place and took his eagle shape. Plenty of time, he thought, before it reaches the forest. Circling high, he took one last, longing look at the village, then followed, keeping a safe, high distance from the Raven.

***

So intent was Raven on the heady scent that drove man and beast to foolishness, he failed to notice the dark shape winging its way above him. As the enticing odor fell through an opening in the tree tops, he plunged after it, expecting a Raven paradise. And it was there, dancing in the interwoven play of light and shadow on the forest floor. Comely maidens circled the edge of light as the mating lust drained what was left of his mind.

"*Clayfoot is right.*" Gleeful, he dropped to the center of passion. "*Who will be first?*"

Light and Dark joined in the mating dance, reinforcing his loss of reason. Dark Forest's magic sleep overcame him before the first maiden hopped toward the center.

***

In the orange glow of sunset, light glinted and changed. A fearsome shimmer caught his eye, but he was unable to escape it. Stout bands of vine formed a net over his body...his wings would not spread. There was no room to pace and think and it hurt his mind. He focused on the orange glow. Where had he seen it before? Scenes of the council fire and the bloody fight between

Clayfoot and....

Ironskin!

Yes, stupid bird. You succumbed to the greatest weakness of all. Now you are mine.

It will do you no good, you stench of Evil. She has the power to overcome you and your evil master.

But now there is one less to help her. Soon there will be others who will desert her and I will win.

Phaugh! You fail to know Clayfoot's love for her. He will guard her and the child with his life. Look at what remains of your hand. He will not be so generous when you challenge him again.

Ironskin shimmered in the growing darkness. Soon, a mock Raven paced the ground in front of the netting, mimicking his every move.

What do you think, Black-Ass. Will they follow me?

Raven's heart sank. After several frantic attempts to peck his way through the net he said, *Don't get too close, Evil One. Your stink will give you away. She is not easily fooled.*

We'll see.

With that, Ironskin took flight and disappeared in the waning sunlight.

CHAPTER ELEVEN

Clayfoot clasped his hands behind his head and snuggled into the bearskin. Sleep had become elusive these last few nights with Kah-tay demanding this or demanding that–and fear for her precious Raven.

He thought about what Ta-nic said earlier.

"She is near her time–and this is her first child. You must expect small angers from her. She is weary from the weight of the child."

"Not small angers, Ta-nic. Eight moons ago she made my life miserable with her demands for wild onions...or...or...fresh berries. Now, almost every night something irritates her. If I move too slow to meet her demands she acts like a she-cat with a thorn in its paw."

"It will pass. In a few days–or one shadow stick it will be over. Then we will have to endure her endless claims she has the most beautiful child ever born."

"Today she acted like one touched by *Ka-Wa-Co*, the crazy spirit, with her dragging everything out of the tipi and cleaning as if each speck was her bitter enemy. Then she cooked a haunch of buffalo...enough to feed a war party. I'll be sick of nothing to eat but the old *Wa-e-su-ta* before the haunch is gone."

"If she cooked that old bull the warriors killed yesterday you'll need new teeth long before you finish the haunch."

Ta-nic had laughed but then she said something disturbing.

"Kah-tay is under great stress. Not only from the birth of her first child...it's as if something is about to happen over which she has no control. I can see it in her eyes–you must have heard her cries to the Great One, and now her lifelong friend is gone."

Ta-nic had seemed to search his eyes for an answer, but he wasn't going to reveal what he knew about the Home or any thing Kah-tay had told him. Ironskin's sudden appearance and strange powers bothered him, too. Wisely, they decided not to disclose what had happened at the Sacred Pond.

"I do my best, Ta-nic. You know I love her. I just want her to get well. I'm sworn to guard her and the child. She heals others, but herself she cannot...."

That wasn't true either. He thought of the secret seal they formed at the bottom of the pond. She healed the deep wound she cut in her chest at the blood-joining.

Sleep stayed elusive. Kah-tay could wake any moment and tell him to get the women...her time was near. Ta-nic's parting words made him nervous.

"If she had the energy of a quick storm come upon her, she may call the women experienced in these matters sooner than we thought. The child could come anytime."

Clayfoot unclasped his hands. Kah-tay mumbled something in her sleep. It was in the language of the Home, which she had been teaching him, but much too low and fast for him to understand.

She woke with a start. "Clayfoot. My time is near. The first pain came and went. The child will not talk to me except to say she is busy."

"I'll call the—"

"No. I wish the child to be born in the Sacred Grove. The place where we first met."

"But—"

"Please?"

"I know nothing of birthing a child. You must have one of the women who—"

"What is there to know? I'm the one who has to do everything." She threw off the thin blanket, a gift from the Weaver Clan, and reached for her long tunic. "Now get Mah-ki and the mare ready. We must reach the Grove before sunrise." She stretched for her ever-present totem stick.

Clayfoot shrugged. It was useless to argue with her when she was *lo-ma-te*, in one of her spirit moods. He brought the horses as ordered.

"Lift me to the mare's back. I cannot sit astride for obvious reasons." She handed him a wrapped bundle. "Put this food on Mah-ki's back. We may be gone one day or many days." She tucked another bundle under her arm.

He made a show of grunting from her weight, oofing and groaning as he settled her on the mare, feet dangling off one side.

"Don't act as though you're lifting a bull buffalo, husband. You could easily lift twice my weight with one arm."

"You are not the maiden I captured in the grove that first day, woman." He gave a tender brush at the mare's mane and handed her the reins.

She reverted to the language of the Home. "I think we could argue about who captured whom."

"Waugh! That's true. Let us get this over with. My thoughts are on other things."

"And I know what *that* is," she retorted, turning the mare's head toward the distant grove.

He gritted his teeth. Mating was farthest from his mind. Hunger gnawed his gut, but he would eat when she suggested it. And he intended to keep the thought uppermost in his mind so that when she mind-probed, his longing for food would ride like leaves in the wind direct to her consciousness.

Clayfoot urged Mah-ki ahead at a faster pace, pausing to look back after he reached the top of the hill across the stream. His breath caught when he saw them. Kah-tay and the mare, reflected in the silver light of a full moon, looked like ghosts gliding across the meadow. She must have mind-spoke to the horse because it picked its way around small mounds and across hidden runnels where rain had gouged its way down to the stream. There seemed to be a sense of urgency in neither Kah-tay nor the mare. He waited, filled with awe at the sight of her and the horse.

"Any sign of the child's progression?" he asked when they drew abreast. "No."

As soon as she said it he noticed a quick clenching of teeth, then her lips pressed tight when she urged the mare to move on.

"I think we should move faster," he said.

"Patience. The pains are far apart. It may be several days before the child decides to come into the world."

She became silent for much of the journey, asking once if he brought his bow and lance.

"I'm never without them since that day when my evil brother appeared at the Pond." He squeezed Mah-ki to walk faster so he could scout the area ahead of them.

Never had he seen the night so clear. Every bush and tree seemed aglow as if dipped in silver and then stuck back in the ground.

"Stay with me, husband. A Shaping could swoop down any time and–"

"It will be a dead shape no matter what kind it is."

He unleashed his bow and nocked an arrow.

***

Sacred Grove seemed a place of magic. Countless drops of morning dew sparkled the ground and lower leaves of the sycamore trees. Droplets reflected a waning moonlight to spread like a welcoming carpet before them. It seemed like stars had come down to earth and were reluctant to go back to the heavens when the soft, orange glow appeared in the East. A broad beam of light swathed across the pond in a breath-taking moonglade.

"Waugh!" Never had he seen magic so strong.

Kah-tay whispered, "Can you hear the voices?"

Cocking his head, he glided across the small dew-filled meadow, his mind set for probing thoughts. Soft, unintelligible sounds drifted in the dim light, sounding like prayer song, then council talk. All were foreign...voices he should know and understand.

They were from the spirit world, he decided, and returned to Kah-tay.

"How is the child?"

"Crying to be born. The pain is much greater, now. I wish Raven were here to comfort me."

Crestfallen, Clayfoot sulked. "I am here to comfort you, wife. Tell me what you need. Wild onions? Sweet berries?"

Her gentle touch rested on his arm. "I know you are with me, husband. But Raven has been my constant companion for many years and now I–"

"I understand, wife. That fool bird picks the worst time to be doing...whatever it is he's doing."

"I have called him many times, but no answer. I fear for his safety."

"Surely the old bird is too intelligent to be taken in by Ironskin–or the Evil who dwells in *that*," he said, nodding across the pond at the blackness of Dark Forest.

Kah-tay shuddered against his arm. Where is her power, he wondered. It was not like her to cower in fear.

"It is the child I fear for," she said.

"But your power is great, wife. Nothing can harm you or the child."

"The baby is vulnerable until I perform the Rite of the Seal so that it cannot be caught or duplicated in a Shaping."

"Then go to the water."

"Not until the sun makes the water clear."

"It should be clear, now, Kah-tay. This is the brightest night I have ever seen. Even *cha-ta,* the water-that-gathers-in-the-night, glows brightly."

She nodded. "Yes. I have seen it through your eyes, husband. My mind was joined with yours, and when we arrived I caught the beauty as you see it. I, too, find it majestic to behold."

At that moment a cloud drifted across the moon plunging the grove in darkness. She clutched his arm, groaning at what must have been a sharp pain.

"When?"

"As I told you, the sun must be high enough to light the water." She reached for the bundle of food. "Fill your belly, Clayfoot. This may be the only time you have."

"How can I see to eat in this dark? My eyes are filled with stars left from the brightness of the moon."

In the dim light he thought he saw her gesture at the grove. In moments the cloud drifted away and the *cha-ta* returned, lighting the meadow around them. How could she bring the light-of-life back, but not be able to protect the child? Who or what had she become?

Wary, he bit into a chunk of the old *Wa-e-su-ta's* haunch followed by a large piece of *tse-ast-ti* bread. Strange. The meat tasted tender...or did she make him think it was tender? The bread was excellent as always. Her mother taught her well. Her mother...how long ago was that? He suppressed a tingle of fear trying to snake up his spine. Kah-tay was his woman. She asked him to care for the child and it followed that she would not harm him. Nevertheless, she became a source of wonder.

"You make good food, wife. I am ready for the day...if it ever gets here."

"Not any more ready than I am, husband. The pains are very close." She refused his offer of the remaining meat. "See?" She pointed to the orange glow in the East. "The sun will be here–and not a moment too soon."

Clayfoot yawned. "Now I'm sleepy."

"You wouldn't be sleepy if you felt what I feel." She grasped his hand and placed it on the bulge in her lower belly.

Pain wracked his guts as she mind-spoke her agony.

"Waugh! It's like many winds trying to tear my belly apart. It won't go down...or up. It stays there like too much *ban-at* root and hurts like a mighty gut wind."

She gave him a wan smile and pointed to the sun. "It clears the trees, husband. Do not interfere."

He stole a glance at the glistening dew. It had changed its points of light from the West to face Eastward and the light from the morning sun. In one shadow stick it would be gone, disappearing where ever *cha-ta* goes when the warmth of the sun takes it away.

"I breath deep of your life, water-of-the-morning," he whispered to the dew. He sucked in huge gulps of humid air. "You brought me much beauty on this day. A good omen my child will come into the world safely."

He did not see or feel Kah-tay when she left, but now he saw her standing on the promontory overlooking the Sacred Pond. She raised her arms just as a ray of light burst through a cloud.

"Waugh! She glows like the morning dew."

Huge-bellied, she stood in her usual method of a supplication he had seen her do many times, unwavering as the sun rose above her. Accustomed to her gestures and strange words that he'd seen her perform so many times, he still felt prickles up his back at her magic.

He sat, chin on knees, and watched, occasionally feeling the warmth of the sun. Beside him lay his bow and arrows ready to defend her against any Shaping or beast from the Evil Kingdom.

Suddenly, water gushed down her legs. She leaped into the Pond, which seemed to open and swallow her. The wind sighed in the sycamore grove as he vaulted to his feet. He rushed down the beach to the water's edge, an arrow nocked and ready.

"Kah-tay!" His voice echoed across the rippling pond. No answer. His heart raced. She had been under the water longer than the best swimmer could hold his breath. Panic-stricken, he plunged into the water; his bow and arrows left on the beach, her underwater magic forgotten.

Sunlight sparkled on the bottom sand highlighting pebbles that speckled the floor of the pond. Ahead loomed a dark cloud of water, roiling as it came toward him. His heart raced at the sight. Another Noc-Muk? If so, it would meet death. A strange taste entered his mouth.

You will not get the child or my wife!

Slipping his knife from its sheath, he swam to the murky haze of water. Kah-tay was not there. He pushed himself further into the dark mass, his eyes darting as he searched every direction for his wife.

He raged against the water. *By the Great One you will not stop me until I find her.*   .

His arm bumped against something in the murk and he swirled, hoping it was Kah-tay. It was not her. Disappointment changed to surprise when he saw a baby, its umbilical cord still attached to a bloody glob that seemed to pull it down to the bottom of the pond. Frantic, he slashed at the cord, missed, and felt the blade bite deep in his leg. Blood spurted adding to the brown fog of water. Ignoring the pain, he thought only of his mission. Save the child. Another swipe of his knife severed the cord and freed the infant. He grasped it and pushed for the surface, his lungs burning for air.

"Waugh! What must Kah-tay be thinking? Drown you as you were being born?" Holding her aloft, Clayfoot gasped and staggered up the beach to the clearing. "Your cries of birth are not heard and I know nothing of what women do when a child is born. I have failed my sworn duty to protect you.

"The Great One would not be pleased. He has granted me many wishes...and now I have failed him."

The baby lay on the grass, motionless. Perhaps if he offered it to the Great One he will grant it life. Clayfoot slipped a hand under its back to lift it high, crying out, pleading that this link to his beloved Kah-tay would not be taken from him. No sooner had he raised her aloft than she slipped from his hands and rolled down his arms. She struck his chest with a low thud and he clasped her in a tight grasp to his chest. Immediately, a loud cry burst from the infant.

"Thank you, Great One. I didn't know the women hugged them to make them cry, but how will I feed her?"

Panic gripped him as he clutched his daughter. What could he do? Kah-tay was gone. No one could live under water as long as this. A Shaping could come any moment and challenge him for the little one. No! The Evil One would not get her. He clasped her to his chest and looked for his knife. It lay on the grass where he dropped it when he laid the baby....she squirmed, bellowing for-the-spirits-knows-what, then he realized it needed milk from Kah-tay's breasts. His thoughts roiled. Perhaps Ta-nic or Na-nah, Ba-chey's mother would know what to do. He must hurry to the village, but Na-nah had left with Running.

The infant's oozing cord frightened him until he remembered the colored cords women tied around it. A tight thong from Mah-ki's braids stopped the flow.

Noises from the pond drew his attention. Noc-muk! They didn't waste any time, but by the Great One, they would not get the child. Now it became more than his duty to protect her. The infant was flesh and blood and...alive. Warmth expanded in his chest as he realized he was the child's father. His knife went across them, chest high, protective and poised to meet the challenge. He would fight to the death.

His mouth gaped when Kah-tay strode through knee-high water, foamy waves surging ahead with each step toward the beach. Her white cloth clung to her much as he remembered her that first day, its wide golden collar reflecting the brilliant sun. Even the leg lacings of her sandals amplified her strength. Determination molded her mouth as she came toward him, water draining from her waist-length hair.

This was no Shaping. After the Sealing of the Water she could not be mimicked...nor could he.

"Give me my child." She snatched the baby from his arms and held it to her chest, undoing the front lacing of her tunic. Grinning, Clayfoot knew his worry about feeding the infant was over.

***

Kah-tay felt the tug at her womb as the child's greedy mouth and lips sucked at her swollen breasts. She had known the feeling before when she mind-searched Techi nursing her newborns. But this was different. Something deep within her, almost sexual, as her womb collapsed.

Tenderly, she let the child drink its fill, switching to the other breast when needed and languidly enjoyed the feeling in her abdomen.

"Waugh! She sucks like one of Mah-ki's foals."

She reached for Clayfoot's hand. "She is hungry, my husband." Nodding to the white mare she added, "Bring the rabbit skins I sewed to wrap her in."

After the infant fell asleep Clayfoot cleared his throat. "I feared you drowned. When you didn't appear after that foolish leap into the pond I went in and found the child in a cloud of muddy water. I cut my leg when I tried to free her from a cord pulling her to the bottom."

"That was blood. It was a Sealing ceremony. You were needed to rescue our child and shed your blood to mingle with mine and the babe's. Now she is Sealed against a Shaping just as you and I are. Let me heal your leg."

"I might know you had some magic to scare a turd out of me. Can't you tell me your plans so I won't think the worst. I feared you were dead." Mouth agape, he watched the ragged cut on his leg grow together.

"I can sleep a long time in water such as this, husband. Do not fear for me. It is the child–"

"I know where my duties are. My life is pledged." He handed her the rabbit skins. "I will call her Alua-Te-Te."

"It is the wife's right to name—"

His hand went out from his side in a flat-palmed gesture of finality. "I have named her."

"I'm pleased you used the language of the Home. It means—"

"Born of water!" Calm, his voice almost reverent, he said, "Like all children she will have a play-name. I will call her Te-Te."

Her jaw jutted. "I prefer Alua."

She glanced up from her seated position and studied this man she had come to love. His muscled body thrilled her. His strength seemed beyond compare. Plus he was handsome with long braids that hung to his waist. She smiled, knowing he would always protect her...and a child who was not his. But first, she must consult the totem.

Was Clayfoot's name for the child the correct one? Would his strength hold against the evil forces she knew would tempt her again? The Totem slipped from the well worn deerskin pouch and she pressed it against her forehead. Concentrating as she held Alua to her breast with one arm, she felt the cool turquoise when she entered its stream of apparitions. A smile creased her mouth. The name was acceptable. Clayfoot would remain true to his promise to guard her and the child.

The vision changed.

Sun glinted off a wing far in the sky. At first she thought it might be Raven, but her heart seemed to skip when she saw an eagle. Ordinarily, an eagle would be a good omen, but the soaring bird sent a shudder up her back. She held Alua protectively and put the totem back in its pouch.

"See what threatens," she said, pointing skyward.

"Yes. I didn't want to frighten you. I've been watching it for almost a shadow stick."

Kah-tay noticed Clayfoot's bow with a nocked arrow grasped in one hand, his knife in the other.

"Is it—?"

"Yes. I called for it to come closer, but it just laughed. It's Ironskin. Can't you smell him?"

Anger tinged her voice. "You should have killed him that first time." She clutched Alua-Te-Te close.

His voice became a grim whisper. "I know that, now."

CHAPTER TWELVE

Kah-tay unfolded the deerskin from Alua-Te-Te and slipped her finger in the child's fist. A tingle of joy went through her when the child gripped her finger.

"I've counted on both hands the number of times you looked to see if she is healthy," said Clayfoot.

"Aren't you proud of her, husband?"

"Of course I'm proud of her. She came at a great price and is my ward to guard with my life." He stopped Mah-ki beside her and leaned over.

"Let's see how tight she grips a man's finger." He stuffed his forefinger in her other hand.

Kah-tay watched his silly grin turn to surprise, then to open-eyed amazement. His hand and arm shook as beads of sweat formed on his brow and coursed down his cheeks.

"What is it, husband. Is something wrong?"

"Get out of her mind, Kah-tay. No child has this kind of strength. You are making her do it."

"Do what?"

"She's crushing my finger!"

"I'm not the cause."

Kah-tay entered the infant's mind.

See how strong he is, Mother? He will not cry out in pain or try to shake me off. He will be a good protector.

Why do you test him, Alua? You knew his vow before you were born.

It is something I must do, Mother. His words are one thing...his actions are another. He holds still for the pain. He will be a patient father.

Kah-tay smiled, reassuring her daughter Clayfoot would indeed be a good father. She had selected him for just that reason.

Now, release him, Alua. He has held still for your foolishness long enough.

It is not foolishness, Mother. I must know these things for myself. You can see and feel firsthand while I could only see through your eyes. Now I see for myself.

How can you see? You haven't opened your eyes, little one

Kah-tay shifted Alua-Te-Te, grimacing at the added weight of Clayfoot's hand still held in a bone-crushing grip by her daughter. At that moment the infant's eyes opened.

I see you, Mother

Kah-tay gasped. A flood of emotion washed over her, like a summer sun-shower, as she felt the child's love. She had experienced it through others, but it wasn't the same. Her very own child made a difference. Their gaze locked for an instant, sharing the moment, then Alua shifted her gaze to Clayfoot.

Yes, Mother. He is handsome–and very strong. Much more than the others. He has Truth in his eyes mixed with the pain.

She drew a sharp breath. The others? Scanning the infant's mind, she saw the succession of her previous mates unfold before her.

"Clayfoot! She was born with all my memories. Alua knows everything about the Home and my other–"

"Ask her if she can remember how to release my finger. I may never pull a bow again."

"Thank you," she whispered. For once she felt pleased her husband was occasionally slow to comprehend.

"Alua. Would you release the grip on your father's finger? I think he has passed your test." *And I would appreciate your not telling him of my past life. He caught me unaware and saw his predecessors and I had to wipe them from his mind.*

Father will learn nothing from me. On the other hand you must tell him about long life and what it means.

He knows. You must have been sleeping when we talked of the Home and my friends...and enemies. He has been given the gift, Alua. We will be together until the End.

And me?

Kah-tay's mind clouded as she shut out all but her private thoughts. There was much to worry about in this land where evil dwelt. The Home was different. All children were safe. But then, some adults were foolish to the point of exasperation. In her case, their senseless anger over healing a wanton woman almost caused her death. Not much difference where men are concerned, she decided.

"Waugh! The child had the grip of many she bears defending her cubs."

Clayfoot shook his swollen finger when Kah-tay broke from her reverie. His finger had an ugly bruise and, probing his mind, she felt the pain and shock over Alua's amazing strength.

"Hold out your hand, husband."

Moments later he smiled. The tight grip that caused so much misery apparently forgotten. He hadn't realized the crushing strength came from the child's mind, not her hand.

"Is the father allowed to hold his daughter?"

As she handed the bundle to Clayfoot, Kah-tay sensed an instant surge of laughter that she quickly suppressed. Was Alua laughing at her protector? Or was she pleased to have him hold her? Before closing her mind, she grimaced at the unmanly words coming from Clayfoot's mouth. Cooing and clucking. True, they were sounds of endearment, but aloof warriors of the Horse People seldom expressed their feelings about an infant. That became apparent at their disgust over Badger chief Running's constant bragging about his twins. However, Clayfoot was not a haughty warrior. He enjoyed being common; and the company of new friends.

Her husband was different. A smile creased her lips when she thought how Raven and Clayfoot would fuss over the baby like two sun-wrinkled grandmothers, each trying to outdo the other expressing concern for the child.

Raven!

How he would enjoy the moment! Would he and Clayfoot try to outdo each other? Suppressing a surge of panic, she knew she must search for her friend. After an anxious touch on the soft deerskin covering the totem, she stopped the white mare.

"Husband. Watch the child. I must go to the Sumac thicket. We will be in the village, soon, and I—"

Clayfoot dismissed her with a nod at the clump of man-high, slender trees, never removing his gaze from Alua. Once inside the thicket she removed the totem from its sheath. Despite the heat, the turquoise stone felt cool to her touch...almost cold when she pressed it to her forehead.

"Great One. Let me see Raven, the friend you gave me from The

Beginning."

Thoughts rolled like waves on the sea, whipped by a fierce wind. A slight taste of salt air made her think of the Home. Had Raven gone there? Deserting her in a time of need? Never. His ancient vow was forever.

She saw a small, dark cloud rolling over the ground, skipping brush, flowing in and out of thickets so dense she could not see through them. Voices. Dim, mocking as if they knew she were listening and daring her to find their hiding place.

"You'll never find us, Kah-tay."

"Your power is useless, Kah-tay."

She felt her knees grow weak. "I'll find you. Nothing can withstand the power granted by the Great One."

She redoubled her concentration, watching the dark cloud, occasionally catching its odor as it sailed over the trees. Birds! A large flock of...a feather taste filled her mouth. Wild, but still the unmistakable odor of ravens. Then a faint odor of rusting metal....

Where was he? Suddenly, she saw him. Pacing. Heavy vines formed a net that entrapped him. She entered his mind.

You will never fool her. She has power such as you've never seen.

We'll see, Black-Ass.

Had Raven gone mad? He was talking to himself.

The vision faded. Her thoughts rushed back, a sudden storm pelting her mind like gusts of wind-driven rain. Who...or what had entrapped Raven? She must save him.

"But I can't go. It will be too dangerous for Alua," she whispered. "And Clayfoot must stay to watch over us. Who can I send?"

Tears flooded her eyes. All she could do was pray and use the totem. Through it she could see the present. Perhaps the future...or at least guidance for the future.

"Come, husband," she said emerging from the thicket. "We must hurry to the village. Raven is missing and I fear for his life."

If Clayfoot heard her he showed no reaction. She willed herself the strength to climb up on the white mare's back, puzzled by Clayfoot's preoccupation with Alua.

"Give me the child, husband. It's time to feed her."

***

They paused at the top of the rise overlooking the stream and the village atop the next hill. Ornate designs seemed to dance on brightly painted tipis clustered around a well-beaten council and dance area. Alua-Te-Te gave a final pull on her nipple and Kah-tay forced a smile as she tucked her empty breast back in her tunic. With Raven missing, and constant reminders of danger, she tried to suppress the apprehension welling in her mind. Surely they would be safe when they reached the village.

"See, Alua. This is our home." She turned the sleepy-eyed infant toward the view. "We are in the land of the Horse People."

"Waugh!" Clayfoot grinned. "She has the appetite of Mah-ki. In one moon she will be full grown."

"I hope she lives to—"

Clayfoot rubbed his hand along the shaft of his lance. "I swear this lance will pierce Ironskin's heart if he tries to claim my little Te-Te. He has been warned there is no place he can hide but what my lance will follow and destroy him."

Kah-tay gave him a wan smile knowing Clayfoot had no fear of the evil pervading them. She knew he thought only of Ironskin, believing he was the source of evil. Her husband had no concept of the Evil One.

Just because a man turns to evil deeds, because it is his nature, does not mean there is not an Evil presence to urge him from the right path. She had known of the war that raged between The Great One and The Evil One since The Beginning. Now, little Alua-Te-Te had become a pawn in the battle. Oh, how she wished for Raven.

Voices scattered her thoughts.

"Clayfoot and Kah-tay! They're back...they're back! And they bring their baby."

Children who had been swimming or playing in the water rushed up the embankment to greet them. Upstream, women were cleansing what few pots they used...and at the water- gathering place young girls filled water skins. Soon, most of the Horse People stood in the clearing waiting for them to approach. Ta-nic greeted them.

"Wait for the blessing of the Shaman. Nah-mo will ward off the evil spirits so the child will grow strong."

Kah-tay smiled, grateful for her concern. They needed all the help they could get, but she doubted the Shaman's power went little farther than impressing the villagers.

Rescue Raven from his web, she thought. Then I'll believe in your power.

Nah-mo rattled his gourd then danced around her and the child, mumbling strange words that grew louder with each circle. Suddenly, he stopped and with a final shout tossed a handful of white powder in the air.

A wry smile creased Kah-tay's lips. She could enhance his efforts to impress the tribe but what good would it do? With Raven gone she had lost her eyes to the outside world. The totem was her only.... No! She had forgotten the three pebbles in the amulet bag. The pebbles with messages from The Beginning. They, too, had power.

"Come, husband. We must go to your tipi. There is much to be done."

Ta-nic touched her arm. "Let us see your child, Kah-tay. She must be as beautiful as you. Did you have a difficult time in the birthing?"

"No." Kah-tay uncovered Alua's face and upper body, then held her up for all to see.

A few shrank away in fright when the infant opened its eyes. Only Ta-nic stayed by her side.

"She has your eyes, woman of Clayfoot. Black as night. Does she have *your* mind strength—or is she like her father—fearless and strong as a bull buffalo?"

"She is like her father," said Kah-tay.

They know nothing of your real father, little one. You have strength beyond their understanding. I hope you have a chance to use it wisely.

They seem frightened, mother. Am I in danger?

Not from them. It is the...

Clayfoot entered their minds.

Come. Let us go to the tipi. There is much to plan if we are to find Raven.

Kah-tay smirked. So. He *had* been listening when she returned from the Sumac thicket. What plan would he suggest? A quiet desperation settled over her as they went to the tipi, followed by a small gathering of curious children asking again to see the infant.

The elders remained in the council circle, collected in small groups. Much hand waving accompanied the warrior's animated conversation, their words coming to her in a cloud like locusts, demanding food for their fear. Alua-Te-Te. Had she...? A quick probe of the child's mind revealed nothing, but Kah-tay sensed a barrier. Not the complete block she was used to...more like a dense undergrowth...a jumble of thoughts. Had Alua deliberately hid a power she barely understood?

"See how the elders talk, wondering what to make of our child." She nodded at the suspicious group.

"They always do that when they are confused," said Clayfoot. "I saw little Te-Te's eyes dart over the people and they acted like a snake had just measured them for its belly. She has a–a–demanding look about her. But I discovered, while you were in the thicket, she searches for love. The Tribe mistook her stare for something else." He held the flap back for her to enter the tipi. "Give them time. They only just met her."

When Kah-tay entered the shelter she glanced first to see the totem Clayfoot had painted on the wall opposite the entryway. Instead she found a grinning Ba-chey blocking her view.

The first of her healings! A child who brought her much joy during her first trying days after Clayfoot brought her to the Horse People.

"Ba-chey! What a wonderful surprise. I thought you would be happy playing with the children of the Badger tribe."

"Running let Chicose bring us home for a short visit. The Badger People hunt nearby."

Strange. Running would never enter the Horse People's hunting grounds without first paying a visit and asking permission. Perhaps they were coming later...or had encountered a large herd of buffalo and would hunt first and ask for consent later while they shared a feast.

"How is your mother?"

"She is well and happy to have a husband to provide for her."

Ba-chey stepped close and watched while she opened her tunic to feed Alua. The little girl put her finger in the baby's hand while the infant nursed. Kah-tay noticed Alua pull away, apparently more interested in filling her belly than attention from their inquisitive visitor.

"I'm going to put the horses in the corral," said Clayfoot and left.

When Alua had drained both her breasts, Kah-tay put her in the cradle board Clayfoot and she had painstakingly made. A large handful of silkweed cotton went in to absorb Alua's wastes before the lacing was snugged.

"May I hold her, Kah-tay? She is such a beautiful child."

Smiling, Kah-tay handed the cradle board to Ba-chey.

"Gently...gently. She is still very small."

"I know."

Ba-chey rocked her arms and sang a song in a language Kah-tay had never heard before. The youngster danced slowly around the tipi, humming as she moved. Before Kah-tay realized what was happening, Ba-chey ducked out the entry.

"Ba-chey! No!" Kah-tay leaped to her feet to stop the little girl. She emerged in time to see a large eagle spring into the air, the cradle board clutched in one talon, the other foot a large paw swinging free.

She pointed her finger to send a bolt of lightning, then stopped. Killing the bird would send Alua hurtling to her death on the ground below.

"Clayfoot!" Hysterical, she ran to the corral. "They've taken the baby."

The eagle faded to a small speck when Clayfoot joined her. She collapsed in his arms, sobbing.

Sniffing the air he raged, "Ironskin! The stench of his shirt fills the air. He will burn in the unending fire for this. Come. I'll get the horses."

CHAPTER THIRTEEN

The eagle fluttered its wings to slow the headlong rush to Burning Rocks. An urge to return to the man-shape grew strong, but Ironskin willed himself to wait.

"Not yet," it screeched and spread its wings, dumping the precious bundle against a large boulder. "Good. The child still sleeps. Wa-Ha-Na didn't say whether he wanted it dead or alive. Better dead than face the fate the Evil One doubtless has planned."

He hippity-hopped toward the entrance. Would it be torture? Or perhaps to raise the infant in the ways of Evil? That will be an unpleasant surprise for the *tu-ba-se*, the Always-Good, Kah-tay. She would be pleased to come under his control to save the life of this spawn of Clayfoot.

"With my new power, Clayfoot will be very dead and Kah-tay will be mine."

If Eagles could laugh it tried very hard. The best he could manage came as a low cackle. A slight, tingling shimmer and the eagle Shaping faded. In its place stood Ironskin, triumphant, laughing in anticipation of new power that would soon be his. Snatching up the cradle board, he raced down the dull, flame-reflected corridors of the Evil Kingdom to reach the room of the fire pit. Shadows layered the orange glow pointing the way to the lower room of Wa-Ha-Na.

He shivered. "Waugh! Two days ago the shadows were little Red Men, slaves of...."

A loud shout scattered his thoughts. Battle cries of old enemies. Wild-eyed, he crept close expecting to see a warrior leap from behind the next bend in the cave, war club raised high to smash his brains against the rocks. He raised the cradle to fend off any blows from his enemies.

Coward!

Ironskin searched the dim area. Who called him a coward? A hidden force drew his gaze to the cradle board. He had used a child as a shield.

What difference did that make?

Thrusting the cradle board further into the dim light, he eased around the corner. Shadows flickered, orange and black, denying the existence of an enemy. He snarled to overcome his pounding heart. Who, in this world, cared if he used the infant as a shield? He would win at any cost. A small advantage, the slightest delay by a foe, would be the edge he needed to win, no matter the price.

"Show yourself," he shouted, tucking the cradle board under his paw arm. He drew his knife. "I'll show you how a warrior's death becomes easy. Your pain will last but a moment."

Ironskin scanned the walls, searching for life. Voices and old battle cries faded. Silence pervaded the shadowy gloom.

Why does your heart pound, mighty warrior? Is it because you are frightened of the dark? Is there a Noc-Muk ready to eat you?

He glanced at the infant.

"No. It can't be you. Babies can only cry. Someone has found the cave and is trying to stop me. Maybe Wa-Ha-Na is testing me." The knife went back in its sheath. "I have passed his test. Woman Of Magic actually gave her child to me. Me–Ironskin. Her sworn enemy, thinking I was Ba-chey, her first healing. Kah-tay is not as powerful as she thinks. She is easily fooled. Soon, I will be the most powerful."

He gave a leap of success in the darkness and thought of his reward. Before one moon he would command many warriors and have all the women he could....

Grasping the cradle board, he dashed for the place of the fire pit–the dwelling of the Evil One.

***

The dim room glinted in flames of colored light cast from the open pit. Its walls must have been melted from solid rock by an age-old fire and looked more frightening than his first visit. Yellow powder Nah-mo often used in his rituals clung to his mouth and nose as it dusted from the rock walls. With each step or brush of his hand on the wall he stirred more of the smelly dust that hung like fog on a lake. It was not there during his first visit.

"Smells like eggs left too long in the sun," he whispered as he clung to the hot walls.

Easing along the wall, he paid no heed to the cradle board as it bumped along behind him. His thoughts centered on the Evil One. Surely Wa-Ha-Na would be pleased.

"Wa-Ha-Na? I have brought the child."

Echos of his voice rumbled around the room, matching the glowing shadows. "Child–child–child–child...."

The echo seemed to wake the voices of old raiding parties; enemies from the past he had slain in battle. He couldn't see them, but their sounds brought memories flooding to his mind.

"Go away. You're dead. I have already counted coup on you."

Do voices from the past frighten you? Surely a fearless warrior would not be alarmed at little voices.

Ironskin dropped the cradle board against the wall.

"It *was* you!"

A deep voice came from the soot-covered throne.

"Yes. She was born with the gift. Now *you* will have to remove her from the board and bring her to me."

Ironskin's mouth gaped. Wa-Ha-Na had not been there a moment ago. Their last encounter he came in a blaze of flame from the pit followed by heavy, dark smoke.

"But–"

"You have been chosen, Ironskin. Do as you are told."

I must not let my mind dwell on why, he thought. The Evil One does what he does...but with his power why does he want me to remove the child from her cradle board? He went to the wall and placed the cradle upright.

The infant's eyes opened and stared at him with intense blackness. When he reached to undo the top lacing a jagged blue streak crackled from the board. "Waugh!" he cried, shaking the tingling numbness in his hand and arm. "You have burned my good hand. I should have dropped you in Dark Forest when I had the chance."

You never had a chance, coward. The power you seek will soon become a burden you cannot bear. A pawn is what you are. A pawn in a game of power that will take you to a nowhere place.

He saw her gaze flick to the black figure seated in the throne.

Mother will never–

"Silence!"

Ironskin felt the Evil One's voice boom in the place of the fire pit, down all its corridors, coming back to them in torrents of anger.

How can I be more silent? I'm unable to speak. Do what you will. It will be to no avail. I was born with all the memories and power of my mother. Soon, she will come and–

"She will never find you. My power is greater than Kah-tay's." He gestured at a cloud of smoke. "Look!"

Sooty mist cleared from the smoke. Woman of Magic appeared, Clayfoot behind her, holding Mah-ki's reins. The totem was pressed to her forehead. Voices came.

"I see her!" said Kah-tay. "She is in a dark place fighting with–"

Ironskin felt like a corralled horse. If they discovered the hiding place where he had taken the infant...but Wa-Ha-Na....

Clayfoot's voice shattered his thoughts.

"We will find her, wife." His hand slipped up and down a large lance, the weapon Ironskin heard him promise would follow wherever he fled.

"Now see the picture I send to her totem," Wa-Ha-Na snickered. He flicked his fire-blackened fingers at the cloud of smoke.

Alua Te-Te lay in a sunlit meadow. Dazzling birds of many colors hovered over her, bringing berries and gifts of food.

Kah-tay gasped. "Now I see her in–"

The vision disappeared.

"She will see what I want her to see." The Evil One turned to Ironskin. "And you will make sure she does not find Burning Rocks."

"How must I do that, Wa-Ha-Na? Her power is great."

"You have been given Cleverness. Think of something."

Unbidden, thoughts of Raven entered his mind. Kah-tay would follow her friend and not even know who it was. Originally, he had planned to use Raven's shaping to capture the child, but using Ba-chey had been a better ploy. How astute he had been! Now, he could use the bird's shape to lead Clayfoot and his woman far into the desert while Wa-Ha-Na planned his battle with the child. How strange the infant had such power. He moved away from her, fearing another jolt of her strange, numbing lighting.

"They will leave the village very soon to search for her child," said Wa-Ha-Na.

"I will be there to guide them. They will not find her."

"Then go!"

Baffled by Wa-Ha-Na's lack of explanation, he trotted to the opening and spread his arms.

***

Alua-Te-Te kept her eyes riveted to the Evil One. He had other plans than to lead her mother astray. Memories poured over her bringing with them battles fought long ago with this creature. Kah-tay had always won, but his power seemed very great. Her plans to resist him were interrupted.

"You may think your defense will keep you safe, little Alua–but you don't have my experience in dealing with people. They always succumb in the end."

Mother has resisted you since the Beginning. She will not change, and you will fall back into your pit of fire.

"I will win this time. She never had to protect her own child from my pit of fire."

How do you propose to put me in the pit? You cannot even touch me. Mother will not sacrifice me to your evil kingdom.

"She will do my bidding. Remember, she has little power once she enters the cave."

You sent Ironskin on a foolish mission. Is he another sacrifice to bring mother under your influence? What fools your servants are!

"Of course! They all discover that it's a ruse, sooner or later, and come under my influence. It's not so bad. They enjoy the pleasures of my kingdom– as will your mother. She will do my bidding to save you."

Never! You will find she has more power than you dreamed possible. The worst that could happen is an impasse. If memory serves me, you were never good at impasses. Don't forget she has Clayfoot. He is a–

"Clayfoot is a dolt. He had nothing until she gave it to him. Once he sees...." Wa-Ha-Na stopped talking.

Alua, strapped in her cradle board, floated away from the wall. She rose to the jagged ceiling, circled its extremities, then dropped to hover close to the soot-covered creature.

See? I have power in this evil place. What makes you think mother will lose hers?

Wa-Ha-Na glared and fell silent. She matched him stare for stare. What hidden evil had this creature planned? She could not enter his mind, and she had closed hers.

As I said. We are at an impasse. And you will lose.

"No! You will lose. I will keep Kah-tay and Clayfoot searching in the desert just long enough for you to become weak from hunger. How long can you last, little Alua? Not more than a day without your mother's milk." He gestured at the walls. "Not even I can make food from these rocks. Can you suck one of them and find your mother's milk?"

I have other powers. We shall see who wins.

Alua floated to the wall. Wa-Ha-Na had a point. Already hunger gnawed her belly. How she longed for.... No! She must not succumb. Turning inward, she shut down her senses. It was up to mother, now...and Clayfoot. She could last longer than a day, but in this mind-state she grew vulnerable. Before darkness clouded her thoughts, she set a shield wall around her. Nothing could penetrate its protection while she was alive.

Mother, hurry.

CHAPTER FOURTEEN

Kah-tay brushed at the tear-streaked dust on her cheeks. They had ridden many shadow sticks at full gallop; the horses seeming to sense the urgency of their mission. Clayfoot called a halt near a towering oak tree to let Mah-ki and the white mare rest, saying he wanted to reconnoiter and make plans for continuing the search.

Poor little Alua-Te-Te, she thought. Just starting life only to be captured by my carelessness. Her eyes had gone dry from the last tears and now she grew angry. Angry at herself for allowing the Shaping to fool her. Angry at this place for its evil. Most of all—angry that an innocent baby would suffer at the whim of a demon.

"I think we should search in a different direction."

Clayfoot's dry croak startled her. He'd been silent during the search, apparently to allow her self-recrimination to fester and heal. She closed her mind to outside thoughts, especially from Clayfoot, fearing his anger would boil and blame her for losing Alua. He remained silent until now.

"Yes, husband. Where you lead I will follow."

"Use your totem while we rest the horses. If you can get a vision of where she might be it would help."

His voice sounded harsh, but she resisted the urge to mind-speak–to discover his true feelings. Could she chance a question about his anger? If he was embittered at her they would have a dilemma that could affect little Alua and the future of their mating. There were evil forces at work he might never understand.

"Are you furious with me for allowing the Shaping, which I thought was

Ba-chey, to hold the child?"

"No! The form Ironskin took would fool anyone." He rubbed Ma-ki's nose with a wet fur then went to her mare. "I'm angry at the Horse People for refusing to help us. They could have sent a small war party to help search."

"They are frightened, husband. Alua's longing for acceptance and love was not understood. They are terrified by what they think is magic–even a healing."

"Magic is a frightening experience, wife. Even I stand in fear when you change things. They still talk about your altering the course of the twisting wind and how you protected the village."

"You should not blame them. It was my fault Alua was taken. I should never have let Ba-chey–"

"It was *not* Ba-chey, wife." He offered her the water skin. After they drank, he tied the water skin on Mah-ki's back.

She touched his arm in a gesture of reproach. "Remember, Ta-nic wanted to help search, but she is old and Nah-mo forced her to remain with the others."

Kah-tay sensed rejection when he pulled away. She entered his mind but found it blocked. Tears that had dried up sprung to life.

"Do not reject me, husband. This is more than I can bear."

"It is my anger, Kah-tay. Not at you, but at the Horse People for their stupidity. Most of all, at Ironskin." He clasped his hand around the lance in a tight grip. "How he will pay when we meet. All these winters he called me *co-wat-ka,* a coward. He is the coward. Stealing his blood kin's children for revenge."

She stepped close and placed her head on his chest. "Comfort me, husband–and pray we will find Alua in a safe place."

His strong arms pulled her tight. For a brief instant they were one, then he drew back.

"Use the totem."

She removed it from its sheath and sat cross-legged, the totem in her lap. Her mind drifted to the Abode of The Great One, invoking his help.

Voices cried out in her stream of consciousness. Shrieks from the past came and went like wind-blown rain. Gamin smiled at her. Gamin. Her previous husband. He had understanding in his smile. At last he realized he did not have long life. And Lomat was never more than an annoyance the Elders dealt with. A calm settled over her and she placed the totem against her forehead.

See? Your child is safe in a meadow with birds tending its needs.

Alua lay in on a soft bed of short grass. Bright colored birds flitted about her, some dropping close to place tiny morsels and droplets of milk in her mouth. Kah-tay's smile turned downward. That Voice! She'd heard it before. Always tempting with its lies. The vision of Alua was not true, but an illusion. Her child seemed half hidden behind a murky shadow.

Agonizing surges of power from her mind could not break through the strange barrier. Without help, they could search forever and never find her baby

I'll not succumb, Evil One. You will be destroyed.

Before the laughter she knew would come, Kah-tay withdrew to her quiet place. A place known only to her where she could regain her strength. Perhaps more strength to fight the inevitable battle with Wa-Ha-Na, as the Horse People called him. But first, they must find Alua and protect her from the Evil One.

So. We do battle again. What have you done with my child?

She sleeps in the meadow. Did you not see her?

Lair! She clenched her fist to amplify her power.

Hollow laughter echoed and died. The vision faded and she fought to regain the power of the totem. Closing her fist in white-knuckled tightness, she saw Alua in her cradle board. The child was asleep.

Alua! Wake! Tell me where you are.

She saw her baby stir, then return to its sleep. Kah-tay felt warmth and the odd smell of sulphur. The child is in a hot, dry place–asleep in the shade. In a desert? Perhaps near the place where Nah-mo digs his yellow powder? "I can't seem to waken her," she murmured.

She dropped the totem in her lap and looked up at Clayfoot, knowing he would see the pain in her eyes. "She is asleep in a warm place. I cannot break through the strange barrier that surrounds her."

"You must have had a mighty battle. Your fist turned white from the struggle." Clayfoot dropped beside her. "Tell me which way to go now that you've seen her."

"I don't know."

"Then I think we should go to Sacred Pond. Your power seems greater in that place."

He sunk his teeth into a piece of pemmican, bit off a portion, then offered the spiced meat and grain to her. She shook her head. Food was furthest from her mind, but she was pleased Ta-nic had thrust the food package to Clayfoot before they left the village.

"Eat!" he said. "You must keep your strength. Even Woman of Magic must remain strong. Besides," he grinned, "you will need to have full breasts when we find her. My little Te-Te will be very hungry."

Kah-tay knew she could last several moons before needing food, but to please him she accepted the compacted nourishment. As she chewed, she watched Clayfoot. Though his eyes were closed she could see his jaw muscles pulse. Perhaps his defenses were down and she could probe his mind.

Kah-tay shuddered at the brief vision of his thoughts. Bits of Ironskin's flesh and broken bones were pounded into a blood-soaked rocky soil. She had never seen such anger! If her hatred for *wa-ka-tona,* a stealer-of-children, was not so great, she almost felt sorrow for the wicked man. Hatred seemed to be all Clayfoot felt...so overpowering she withdrew in haste.

How he had changed these last few moons! Going from her would-be captor, to slave...and now a forceful father bent on rescuing his child. He'd commanded her to eat! She...a woman of power...a woman blessed by the Great One for long life...and to bear his child: Alua-Te-Te was destined for greatness with power beyond measure. That is if this warrior she induced to be her mate lived up to his rage-filled purpose. To rescue Alua, the child he called his own.

Not one of her previous mates had commanded her thus. She comforted herself with thoughts of him finding Alua.

"Look." He pointed to a cloud of dust rising from the trail they had just ridden.

Her thoughts flew with her vision. An old man followed them on a young, white stallion that had black spots shaped like bear paws.

"Tato!" they said together.

Clayfoot frowned. "The old fool. He'll slow our search."

"A man is offering his service," retorted Kah-tay. "If he can ride a horse that has Mah-ki's blood, and the strength to pull a bow, his help should be welcomed."

"He will get himself killed."

"Tato has cunning—and can track like a she-cat after a deer in tall grass." She turned to face her husband. "He looks on you as a son. Are you aware of that?"

Clayfoot lowered his head. "Yes. And I—I consider him my father. That is why he should stay in the village. I wanted him to see a granddaughter he has never had."

Kah-tay patted his arm. "He will see her. Little Alua will be back with us soon." She hoped her words of encouragement were more than just words. If anyone could find her child it would be Clayfoot.

Kah-tay knew her power had been weakened by the Evil One. Perhaps if she kept Wa-Ha-Na occupied in a battle of wits her husband could kill him. Clayfoot's gaze never left the incoming rider. She entered his mind and found a small joy that the sage warrior had broken with the Horse People and chose to join them in the search. However, a small doubt seemed to linger in Clayfoot's thoughts. Was this another Shaping come to distract them? They would soon know.

"I see you, Tato," said Clayfoot.

"I see you, man of courage. I was at the corral giving Bear Paw his first experience with a man on his back when I heard wailing from village. Witless idiots! They are frightened of their own shadows."

Clayfoot crossed his arms. "Yes. They refused to come to our aid when they saw the eagle fly away with our daughter in its claw."

"Someone...Ta-nic I think, said it was not an eagle, but a Noc-Muk. Is this true?"

"Yes," said Kah-tay. "It was what my people call a Shaping. Something an evil person learns to do to follow the one you call Wa-Ha-Na."

"Ironskin," said Clayfoot. "When I find him his bones will join his blood in the ground. There will be no honor in his death."

"It is true, then. Ironskin has become a *wa-ka-tona*?"

"Worse," snarled Clayfoot. "He has evil power–*and* my daughter."

Kah-tay grimaced. Alua was her daughter, too. Surprise crossed her face when she heard Tato next words.

"Some men need a good killing." The old man sat and reached for the pemmican. "I will join you in the search for your child. Ironskin's spirit will not rest while I can still pull a bow."

She had never considered Tato a savage warrior. For some reason she'd never tried to enter the old sage's mind. He was just...Tato, Clayfoot's elder companion.

"Tato? Why did you follow us. You know the danger." She pulled the water skin from Mah-ki's back and offered it to him. "Has Clayfoot told you about me...about my people?"

The old man nodded. "He told me."

"And?"

"I told him he was fortunate to have a woman of magic in his tipi." Tato washed down the pemmican and added, "He needed magic in his life, and you brought it."

"It wasn't enough magic to save Alua from the your Wa-Ha-Na. There is evil in this land, Tato. Clayfoot knows it...but anger covers his fear."

"There is more to fear in life than to love. Evil always hides behind the nearest and dearest."

Clayfoot put down the blade of grass he had been rolling. "I think we should hurry to Sacred Pond. Her power is stronger in that place." He rose to gather Mah-ki's reins, then turned to face her. "Use the totem again, Kah-tay. The barrier might not be as strong.

She reached for it and relaxed. Before her thoughts entered the mind-stream she heard him ask if he held it to her forehead could she use both fists for power. How observant of him! But did she dare? The last time.... She nodded. After all, what good is power if you don't use it. And there was never a better need than now.

The vision was brief. Alua had placed a shield around herself. Where had she learned...? Of course! While still in her belly, Alua must have experienced the power of the shield against the Great Twisting Wind when she protected the village. What else could the infant do? Kah-tay knew the answer, but Alua could do nothing while she slept behind her protective cover.

It is up to us, husband. We must battle the Evil One and Ironskin together.

***

Tato broke the silence of their journey. "Sacred Pond is just beyond the next hill."

It had been a hard ride, pushing the horses as much as they dared. Kah-tay felt torn between relief to be able to stop and rest and the need to push on. Clayfoot provided the answer.

"We will quench our thirst and rest the horses. After we've eaten it will be time to renew the search."

"It will be dark, soon," said Tato.

"Kah-tay can see in the dark. Her magic is strong. She will guide us."

Kah-tay smiled grimly. Clayfoot relied too much on her power. While it was true she could go with ease in the dark, because her friends, the Night Birds, provided sight she did not possess. To them she owed a debt of gratitude. They came with her and Raven when they entered the churning lake waters near the Home. What a sight that had been–the Elder's fear when they saw a gathering of birds flitting about her, forming a protective shield!

Her thoughts turned to Raven. "I could do better if Raven were here."

"That Black Ass is no better than Ironskin. He deserted you when we need him most."

"Don't say that! He has been with me since...."

Her voice went silent. They wouldn't understand the span of years she dwelt in the Home–and other lands. Raven was her long-lived companion; one she could consult or pass the span of days with. He was precious to her. Almost as precious as Alua. Many winters would pass before Clayfoot would grasp the concept of the Home, and the knowledge that would some day be his. Kah-tay's thoughts turned to family. Her husband had already demonstrated his love for a little girl he hardly knew. They would be happy if they found Alua in time to.... Remorse and pain stabbed her heart.

"Halt!" She raised her flat-palmed hand. "There are others in the Grove. I sense them lying in wait. No. They are resting in the meadow."

Clayfoot and Tato had their bows unsheathed, strung, and arrows nocked before she finished her warning. Ready for battle, they preceded her down the slope toward the sycamore grove.

Kah-tay sensed a curious force emanating from the meadow inside the grove. Birds usually sang their joyful songs but now were silent or no longer in the grove. The power she sensed seemed weak, but not evil, which meant she and her companions were safe. Better to inform her husband now than after he'd killed....

Husband. They mean us no harm. Look before you loose your arrows.

I sense danger in every corner of the earth. It will remain until Ironskin is dead and my little Te-Te in safe in my tipi.

Please. Obey me in this, my husband.

As you wish. I hope you won't shed tears over my butchered body if you are wrong. Remember, Ironskin will give no warning in our next battle.

Relieved, she saw him release tension on the arrow and turn to warn Tato. What waited in the meadow was....

"Tato is gone! Did you send him to the other side?"

He frowned. "No. Did you see where he went?"

"No." Kah-tay pursed her lips. "I fear more for the old warrior than whatever waits in the meadow. He is not accustomed to power–especially when it is directed at him."

"Are you seeing the future?"

She nodded, then placed a finger over her lips in a gesture of silence.

They had reached the bush behind which Clayfoot had first seen her. She motioned him to dismount.

"See who is in the meadow?" she whispered, pointing at two figures standing with their backs to them. They seemed intent on whatever lay in the grove across the meadow.

Clayfoot placed his lips close to her ear. "Are they men from the Home? They look like it in short tunics with gold collars. Notice they have the same sandals as you wear with lacing up their legs. They don't carry weapons, either. One seems older. The other looks to be...not yet a man."

"They are from the Home–a man and a boy. The question is–what are they doing here...and how did they get here?"

Kah-tay was about to step from their hiding place when Tato startled her. Across the meadow, he burst from the grove, his bow ready. Shouting a war cry, Tato loosed an arrow.

As swift as it came toward the man, she heard its deadly whine. Swifter yet, the man stepped aside and reached up. The arrow stopped in mid-flight, held in his tight grasp. The boy's hand shot out, palm forward. Bear Paw's hooves appeared to have been rooted to the ground.

"Eee-yah!" Tato sailed over his horse like a leaf tumbled in the wind.

"I know how that feels," snorted Clayfoot. "Let's find out what they're doing in this Sacred Place."

"I will be interested to learn that, myself." Kah-tay stepped into the clearing, hoping to find Alua. She called a greeting in the language of the Home. "See to Tato," she added. "He may require healing for broken bones."

"Waugh! He may never ride again, the old fool."

"I don't think he is hurt that bad. Only his pride will require mending if I'm any guess of character."

"He'll get over it. I'm more interested in how the man stopped an arrow that should have pierced his heart."

"Ask him," she said over her shoulder. "But remember, we cannot tarry. My child is in danger."

"Our child, wife."

She felt his indignant pride as he followed her to the strangers from the Home. Clayfoot was right. She'd been amiss in claiming sole rights as Alua's parent. He had sworn to protect the infant while it was still in her womb. Clayfoot mind-spoke with Alua to establish a fatherly bond. Most of all Alua had, in the few hours they had known each other, called him "father" even though she knew who her real father was. The youth surprised her when he rushed forward and knelt, grasping her hand.

"I am overjoyed to find you well, Princess." He kissed her hand.

She gave a shy grin to Clayfoot. The title had long been outmoded. The Elders resented it after the Home became a Republic. Her husband's astonished expression demanded an explanation. Perhaps later, after they rescued Alua-Te-Te, she would tell the story.

It happened long ago. She'd have to be very careful. Clayfoot, though he hated to admit it, could be jealous of her past husbands. His occasional probing seemed more than a quest for information. Some details were better left untold until he was well entrenched in their mating.

Princess?

That was long ago, husband.

You are still a princess to me, wife. After my little Te-Te, of course. Remember, we cannot remain here. I have a task to prove my worthiness. These strangers could be Shapings. His hand still gripped the iron-tipped lance.

The man stepped forward, a wide smile on his face. A Journeyer medallion hung from a gold chain around his neck.

"Yes. We are most pleased, Princess Kah-tay. I am Ortig. The boy is sixteen. His name is Squi. We were caught in the lake when the waters churned, sucking us to the bottom." He motioned a thumb at the waterfall. "It has an exhilarating exit as you already discovered."

Excited, Squi said, "We were searching for you."

"Is this true?" It had been forbidden, she thought, but after the Elders frightful expression, before she disappeared in the depths of the lake, they may have relented.

Ortig lowered his gaze. "The boy wanted to become a Journeyer. I, too, felt the pull of the unknown. While the Elders were otherwise occupied, we took my fishing boat to the lake when the day moon was full."

"This is where it comes out, Ortig. A land of great contrast; of malevolence and goodness. It is one of the abodes of the Evil One. He has stolen my...our child." She nodded at Clayfoot who supported Tato, half dragging him to her. "I will have to heal the old warrior. He insists on joining us in the search for little Alua-Te-Te."

Ortig's expression changed when she mentioned Alua's name.

"It became necessary to birth her in water...the rite of the Seal. Shapings lurk in this land. One stole my day-old infant. We have also been Sealed to prevent a Shaping from emulating one of us.

"Clayfoot has sworn a blood oath to rescue our daughter and slay Ironskin who has given himself to the Evil One. Ironskin can become a Shaping at will, and has been given power by the Evil One."

She knelt where Clayfoot deposited Tato. A touch of her hand healed the warrior, then she channeled her thoughts to her countryman.

Be warned, Ortig. Clayfoot suspects you and the boy may be Shapings. He will slip his knife between your ribs at the slightest inclination you may not be what you say.

We serve you, milady. However, I doubt he can slip a knife between my ribs.

He has been given power, Ortig. Do not give him cause for suspicion. His thoughts are mind speak when he desires. Even I do not know the extent of what the Great One has given him.

Your husband has nothing to fear. Nor will we give him reason to suspect we are what we are not.

Ortig turned to Clayfoot. "We would join you in the search for your daughter, husband of Milady Kah-tay. We are sworn to serve her–and now you. We will give our lives for her."

"How do I know you are not a–?"

"Put your knife in my heart, husband of Kah-tay. No Shaping can survive a mortal wound." He nodded at Kah-tay. "She will heal us to prove our words."

"Ironskin did not die when my arrow pierced his iron shirt. Raven told us he slept in *that,*" he nodded at Dark Forest, "and regained his strength."

"Then your arrow did not pierce his heart."

"I never miss."

"You did that time."

Kah-tay stepped between them. "It did not appear to be a miss, husband, but his armor could have stopped the full force of the arrow."

Clayfoot nodded. "You ride behind me, Ortig. Maki will carry both of us. We will talk as we search. The boy will ride behind Tato."

"Agreed. Which direction do you search?"

"She will use her totem to discover the way."

"No need," said Tato. "Here comes her Raven. It will show us the way. That damn bird knows everything."

Kah-tay's heart filled with love. Her friend returned! She held her arms out to the bird.

"Come, dear friend. I have missed you."

There is no time, Kah-tay. Follow me if want to see your child alive.

132

CHAPTER FIFTEEN

They stopped to rest the horses at the top of a small knoll. Kah-tay scanned the area. Below lay an arid, cactus and mesquite strewn desert. Giant saguaro popped up occasionally to break the monotony of the scene. Clayfoot slipped to the ground.

"Walk the horses. They're tired, especially the ones carrying double."

Kah-tay felt torn emotionally. She had to keep going if her deduction about Alua being in a warm, dry place was true. Caked salt streaked the horses' skin to match her own dried tears. She felt the white mare probe for Raven. Tato scattered her thoughts.

"Tell me, Ortig. How did you catch my arrow? Never have I seen a warrior do that."

Squi started a muffled laugh, but squelched it at a glance from Ortig.

"It is learned from practice, Tato. Imagine the arrow traveling like a turtle–very slow as it flies toward you. Then step aside and reach for it."

"Impossible. No arrow flies like a turtle."

"Did you stay on a horse the first time you got on it's back?"

Tato scratched his chest. "No. I fell off a few times before I learned to become one with a horse."

"Just so. It takes many hours of practice."

"Hours? What is that?"

Ortig glanced across the open space.

What do I tell him, milady? I did not realize they have no concept of counting time.

Tell him it is a way the people of the Home mark the passing of time–from one shadow stick to the next. She drew a mental picture for him. *The Horse People have a different way of marking time. Each day is a new sun.*

There is much we could teach them.

Grim-faced, he walked faster as he explained to Tato. She glanced at Clayfoot. He accepted her explanation of everything, and she felt relieved. The ways of the Home were advanced far beyond his knowledge, but he learned more with the passing of each day. His new found power was.... Her brow wrinkled. How much power had the Great One granted her husband? She grimaced at her questioning thoughts. If we find Alua... No! *When* we find Alua I'll ask him. Longing flooded her mind. Please hurry...please.

Squi asked for a drink of water. Clayfoot shook his head and she knew the impatient youth was not used to going without. Probably from a wealthy trading family according to the silver-threaded pattern woven into his wide collar. Why had he joined Ortig? Something else she would discover when their search for her–*their* daughter was over. Her husband resented the parental slip she made earlier.

Clayfoot stopped the search party. "Ask Raven if there is water close by. He won't talk to me."

Kah-tay channeled her thoughts to the bird. She needed water to relieve her parched throat as badly as the others.

Dear friend. Is there water nearby? We are thirsty.

Yes. In the arroyo beyond the next rise.

Thank you. Please come to me and rest. Ortig and Squi are here. Do you remember them from the Home?

Waugh! They will slow your search with their wild tales. I must stay high to see where your child is hidden.

Kah-tay frowned and brushed at the dust on her cheeks. Neither Ortig or Squi had reason to slow their search. In fact, she felt pleased the two were helping. Their power, added to hers and Clayfoot's, would be helpful if they had to battle the Evil One. But there was no reason Raven could not comfort her. Perhaps he is just as eager to find little Alua as she and Clayfoot.

"What did he say?" croaked Clayfoot.

She pointed in the direction the bird indicated. "There is water beyond that rise."

"Then let's hurry. We can't survive much longer without water–especially the horses." He flung a leg over Mah-ki's back and pulled himself upright.

Fuming, she watched him ride down the steep slope, dodging and turning with Mah-ki's stiff-legged steps down the sandy soil. He could have at least helped her up on the white mare. Apparently he *was* angry at her despite his words to the contrary. Until she could enter his mind there would be no way to tell his true feelings about the loss of Alua–and Clayfoot stubbornly refused to open his mind.

"Here, milady. Let me help you." Ortig offered his hands as a stirrup.

"Thank you, Ortig. Tell Squi to be careful. Staying behind Tato might be difficult. The old warrior still thinks he can keep up with Clayfoot."

"Your husband is very strong, milady. As is Tato. They are a handsome clan, these Horse People. I detect the presence of power in your husband. If I may speak boldly, you made an excellent choice for this mating."

"Be careful, Ortig." She projected her feelings that it was none of his business, and she didn't know the extent of her husband's power. "The Great One gave him much, but Clayfoot hasn't been able to penetrate my mind about my past life. I had to erase it from his memory, once. He probed when my guard was down. He questioned Raven...and he'll soon ask you and Squi about the Home and sneak in a thought about my past life."

"Thank you, milady. I am warned."

She felt his acquiescence to her warning and said, "And please stop referring to me as 'milady.' The monarchy ceased to exist many years ago."

"There are several who wish it returned, Kah-tay. Privately, of course. We were much more content under an enlightened monarchy."

"Father didn't think so. But after mother wished for an end to her long life–and father terminated his soon after she died, the Elders decided to accede to his wishes and form a republic."

"There are many who still visit the mausoleum where your parents are buried. It is said some channel private meetings to determine how to deal with the unrest."

"It still goes on, then?"

"Yes. The moral climate is in decay. The Elders fear your power and the concern you might return from the dead. They are ashamed of the trumped up charge regarding your healing of the prostitute."

She drew a deep breath. Returning to the Home would present a new set of problems. Clayfoot had long life, now, and the people may not understand an outsider as their ruler–even as her consort. And there was Alua, when we find her. The child's parentage and power could complicate an already fragile political situation. But it was not an immediate problem. Alua-Te-Te must be found...for her sanity as well as Clayfoot's. There was no telling what he would do if anything happened to *his* daughter. He would kill without mercy...including her if.... She shook her head to clear the evil cobweb. Panic returned to her thoughts. They *would* find Alua.

"I'll tell Squi to clasp Tato's waist. Are we in a race to see who gets to water first?"

"I don't think so, Ortig. Clayfoot understands the need to hurry. This desert is no place for an infant."

She settled her aching hips and thighs then urged the white mare down the loose sand and rocks. Ortig rode behind her now that Clayfoot had raced ahead. His hands were light on her hips. She thought not of Ortig, but of her husband. Try as she might to suppress the thought of Clayfoot's hands caressing her body, they crept though like the scent of flowers in the night. She shook her head. Now was not the time. But after they found Alua....

***

Tato's horse drew along side her. Squi shifted his weight and joined Ortig already standing beside her on the rocky peak. Clayfoot was a small dot in the arid valley below them.

"I thought there was water," Squi whined.

"So did we." Ortig rested his hand on the white mare's neck, then glanced up at her.

Tato growled an epithet. "That cursed bird is no more than a piece of buffalo shit. Where is the water it promised?"

"I imagine Clayfoot is thinking the same thing," she muttered.

Hurry–hurry. Alua is near. I can sense her presence.

Raven's mind-speak floated clear although the bird was a mere speck in the distance.

Clayfoot's thoughts channeled to her.

The damn bird lied, wife. We need water. It knows but it insists we continue. We can't go on without rest and water.

I don't understand. Why would Raven lie? It wants to rescue Alua as much as we do.

No answer. He had closed his mind again and stood, not looking at the bird, but surveying the desert. His thoughts came after a long wait.

See the tall saguaro in the distance? Ride along the ridge and meet me there. I know this place.

Why? Raven wants us to hurry. It says....

Do it! Raven lies.

His mind-speak became the strongest she had ever felt, almost rocking her from the mare's back. Ortig's hand slipped to her leg to steady her.

"What is it, milady?"

After she recovered from the shock and force of his command she said, "Clayfoot wants us to meet him by the tall saguaro."

Tato followed her pointing finger. "What's there beside more of this place-of-buffalo-turds?"

"He says he knows this place."

Without waiting for their reply, she rode the mare at a walk along the ridge. Ortig trotted beside her.

"If anyone knows this place it would be Clayfoot," Tato grumbled. "He wandered to the corners of the world."

"Not all, my friend," snorted Squi. "He has never seen the Home."

"No outsider has," muttered Ortig.

Kah-tay kept pace with Clayfoot, who walked Mah-ki, weaving among mesquite and sage, silent in his rage. She tried again.

Speak to me, husband. My heart breaks for the child. There is no one to comfort me. I need your strong arms to hold me—to keep me from succumbing to the Evil One.

Wa-Ha-Na hasn't a chance against you, wife. I long to hold you—even more. But I have sworn to protect the child—and you. The child comes first. After we find her, and have no doubts we will, you will get more than comfort.

She drew a deep breath of hot, dry air. The sun was already high. They had been on the trail of the evil Ironskin for more than a half day, and she sensed a small humor, probably to console her, from Clayfoot. Yes. She had chosen wisely. When the time came, she would tell Ortig how and why she made him her choice.

"The tall saguaro stands in the valley below," Tato grunted. "Now what?"

"We join Clayfoot there." She pointed to a dark shape weaving through the mesquite. "Clayfoot will be at the tall cactus when we descend from this hill."

"Waugh! I thought that was a she-cat tracking him." Tato unstrung his bow.

How quickly the old warrior armed himself! She never noticed him slip the bow from its sheath, and drew comfort from his presence. Someday she would inquire about his personal life.

***

"See the round cactus shaped like a bear cub standing on its hind legs?" Clayfoot pointed at spiny, green bulbous plant. "It stores water. The secret is to open it without getting stuck on its painful spines."

"See. Raven was right. There is water in this place."

"Are we in the valley?" Clayfoot stabbed his lance in he ground and stared up at her.

She stiffened her back. "No." No man had ever addressed her in such a fashion.

"Then the damn bird lied. Water is not in the valley, but in a place where the desert keeps its secrets."

Ortig pursed his lips, and she felt his mind channel to hers.

How dare he talk to you in this manner. I've a good mind to–

You wouldn't stand a chance, Ortig. It's but one of the many reasons I chose him. He may address me in any manner he chooses. I am his wife. After we find Alua, he will be my gentle lover, again. You will see.

And if he doesn't?

I am his other weakness.

She shot a short, triumphant smile at Ortig then turned her attention to the cactus. "Tell me, husband. How does one get water from a desert plant?"

"I remember these plants." Tato gave a considerate look at Clayfoot. "Not that I doubted you, my son, but the desert does not give up without a fight."

"Watch." Clayfoot handed Mah-ki's reins to Squi and took his lance to the large plant. After several stabs at its base, working in circular manner, he toppled the cactus on its side. Next, he used the sharp lance to cut a gash down its length. Deeper and deeper he cut until it lay in two pieces.

"The pulp is more than half water. Scoop it out and suck." He wedged out a large chunk with his knife and urged it on Mah-ki. The horse munched and sucked greedily. After the horses had their fill, they searched for more of the bulbous plants. Four fell to Clayfoot's lance before they were satisfied and the water skins filled.

"Call Raven and see if the bird wants water," said Clayfoot.

"I already have," she said. "It keeps urging us to hurry."

"No bird in its right mind would fly over the desert unless it knows where there is water." He leaned against Mah-ki and searched her eyes. "The bird speaks with *to-ka-te*, on both sides of its tongue." With a gesture of his flat palm, he indicated he no longer trusted the bird.

"But, husband. It urges me to hurry. Our child is very near." Frantic, she cast an imploring glance at Ortig, hoping he would help persuade Clayfoot.

If they stopped now Alua would be lost forever. The Evil One would have his way, finally, and her age-old battle with the Beast would be lost.

"You and Raven were becoming such good friends," she pleaded. "Can't we look a little while longer? We are so close. Raven says—"

"The bird is *cow-at-te*, crazy in the mind. He has never been the same since our visit to Sacred Pond." His jaw muscles pulsed. "My daughter is not something for him to play a child's game with."

"*Our* daughter," she said. Her husband was becoming too arrogant.

A lifelong friend would not lie—not about little Alua-Te-Te.

Ortig stepped between them. "This is no time to quarrel. It is strange for her friend to stray and keep urging her onward with mind-speak."

At her sharp gesture, and glance at Tato, he stopped speaking.

The old warrior does not know of such things. He is curious enough as it is. I fear he might make the Horse People more frightened than they already are.

Ortig nodded, adding she had not channeled her thoughts.

Clayfoot lifted his gaze to hers and used the language of the Home.

What difference does it make if we find our child? If I tell Tato to keep something close to his heart, he will do so.

The four looked at Tato who leaned against Bear Paw, apparently following their intense gaze at each other.

"All of you seem *cow-at-te* to me—making angry she-cat faces at each other." He pointed to a speck in the distance haze. "Call the Raven. Ask the wise one again where the child is."

"Thank you, Tato," said Kah-tay nodding her appreciation.

Desperation tinged her mind as she projected to the bird.

Dear friend, we have come so far. Where is my child?

The others joined her gaze as the bird stopped in mid-flight and circled low.

It projected louder, its mind-speak shuddering her spine. *Your child is near. Just beyond the next hills. Hurry. Leave them if they won't follow. Have I ever failed you?*

No. But I cannot survive in this desert without Clayfoot.

The fool is trying to keep you away from your infant. He is jealous. Now hurry. The little one needs its mother's milk.

"Did you hear?" she asked the others.

All shook their heads. The bird seemed adamant in speaking only to her. She bit her lip to quell the churning in her stomach. Why was Raven doing this?

"Raven says Alua is beyond the next hills."

"The bird is crazy. I will not follow it." Clayfoot pointed across the desert. "Many times I have traveled this path. I do not lie. Those are the next hills."

Kah-tay's heart sank. The mind-picture her husband projected showed the haze-covered mountains were many days in the distance. But her baby needed mother's milk...milk already leaking from her swollen breasts.

She jutted her jaw. "I will go alone if you will not help. My child cries for me."

She pulled herself up on the white mare's back and turned its head toward the hills. Clayfoot's voice echoed after her.

"Ortig. We must stop her. The bird will not come to her or to the white mare which he is so fond of. The pain in my stomach tells me," he pointed with his lance. "*That* is not Raven."

Squi leaped on Tato's horse. "Milady, wait. I'll come with you."

CHAPTER SIXTEEN

Raven paced the small space inside the gloomy web that confined him to the forest floor. Gone was the odor of comely maids-of-mating that enticed him to Dark Forest. Instead, the acrid stench of man and rusting metal clouded his senses.

Damn Clayfoot! It was his fault; him and his everlasting talk of mating. He, Raven, was never to mate. Kah-tay was his companion–his ward set by the Great One. And he had failed his duty.

However, she asked for special favors for this man and curiosity stirred his memories. What was it like to have a mate? Sometimes it seemed a joyous drudgery, considering the conversations and mating practices he observed in the past. So much mating with so little results. Except this time, Kah-tay would give birth, a gift from the Great One.

Perhaps she has already had the child. If he hadn't listened to Clayfoot's vivid descriptions, his curiosity would not have led him to this foolish predicament, and he would be listening to a child's wails of hunger.

Voices from the past crept into his mind, telling him who was at fault. His breast beat with the realization Clayfoot had not succumbed to temptation. *He* had.

Angry, he pecked at the strand of netting that vexed him most, that foul piece immediately in front of his beak. As usual it sealed over when he stopped. Often it sent streaks of pale lightning to keep him at bay.

The shimmering field had been effective in confining his mind probes to Mistress Kah-tay. Try as he might, he could not get through the barrier. There would be great danger if she followed the servant of Evil.

Cursed Ironskin! Cursed Evil One! How dare they restrain a winged companion sent by the Great One. When Kah-tay discovers what they have done she would....

He stopped pacing. What could she do? Nothing if she thought the evil she could be following was her friend. That's what Ironskin had in mind! An instant mind-probe, while the Shaping had paraded in front of the confinement, revealed the iron-shirted warrior's plan. He bragged Kah-tay would not recognize that her dear friend was not what she thought. Surely, she would discover the ruse and turn away.

Clayfoot! Would he discover the truth? He had the power if he would just keep his mind out of the....

Raven calmed his anger. Kah-tay's husband was not at fault. It was useless to place blame, he reminded himself. That would be fuel for council-fire talk after they defeated the Evil One and exacted revenge on Ironskin. There must be a way to outwit the shape changer.

Raven stopped in the center of the cage of vines and nestled on the small pile of leaves scraped up when he raged at his captor. His body went limp, almost lifeless, as he let his mind drift. The net could not hold his stream of consciousness, but he had no power. A solution could come from his subconscious. From a remembrance of an ancient dream, perchance. Then he could fly to her rescue.

***

Get out of here, nestling.

His clutch-mates shoved him aside. The carrion smell grew so heady he almost fainted and he had to content himself with a grub scratched up from the soil. It was deep in the earth, but not deep enough to hide from his keen senses. He hopped away, knowing when they had their fill he would get the leavings.

I'll not always be small.

***

What passed for a raven's smile crossed his beak. If they could see him now.... Except they were gone, centuries ago. He was the one given long life and chosen as the appointed companion to the darling of the Great One. Small wonder. She always pleased him. Kah-tay. What a friend she had become! And he had been sworn to her service from the moment of her conception.

As a child she insisted on digging furrows in the soil to expose worms and grubs for his sometime friends, the other birds. She became particularly fond of robins who enjoyed her efforts, and she would scrape deeper, begging him to help. He, a carrion eater! Well, dig he did, often plunging from his perch on her padded shoulder to claw a stone out of the way to expose a fat worm or grub.

Why don't you make a device to dig with instead of your sandals? he'd asked soon after she had learned to mind-speak. She couldn't have been more than three or four. Or was it two? So long ago. It seemed he'd been digging her blessed worms forever.

Of course, she asked him to help with her other duties, but always to serve the Great One. He owed much to them for his happiness once he realized he would never be more than just a companion. How often he had plumbed her mind when she became a woman—and mated.

What passed for another smile split his beak.

He *would* have to make a smart remark about mating and she learned to close her mind. But the men...rutting animals...all of them, including Clayfoot whom she decided to stay with...forever.

She'd been digging for worms when he came charging through the grove on his horse, his mind between his legs like all the others.

What a fight that could have been until she called out and stopped me from raking the poor, over-muscled horseman to death.

Clayfoot. How quickly he learned to mind-speak. And his power! Even he didn't know the depth of it.

Phaugh! Why am I dreaming of earth worms and Clayfoot's power. Raven ruffled his feathers and looked for something to eat. *That cursed Ironskin left nothing. Probably meant for me to die.*

His belly longed for its fill of a long-dead carcass, any kind would do. Perhaps he could worry a she-cat over its kill. Instead, he raked a talon in the soft earth hoping for a grub, anything to stave off his growing hunger pangs.

Dig!

That is what voices from the past were saying. Would Ironskin's evil spell extend below the earth? Badger-like, he clawed at the edge of his entrapment. The smell of old earth filled his nostrils. As soon as he had an opening large enough to crawl through, a vine dropped into the hole, stopping his progress. It seemed as if the strands were alive.

Phaugh! I'll outwit you, web of corruption.

Spurred by anger, he rolled out of the hole and surveyed the net. A small place between the lower strands spawned an idea. If he dug a longer trench he might be able to squeeze between the earth and webs. Raven attacked the dirt with determination born of fear for his mistress. Mindless of the tight pressure, he forced himself into the opening and wiggled forward. A fat grub lay in his way. The tempting morsel made him pause, but it smelled of evil– an odor made in dark marshes by creatures that dwelt in its midst. He had been there before.

No time to stop.

After eyeing the small strand above him, he urged himself further into the hole.

Ouch!

The small strand of net touched his back, sending a jagged shock through his nerves. Instead of stopping him it served to drive him forward. He flopped unceremoniously to the ground outside the web. Haughty, he fluffed the smelly crumbs of dirt from his feathers and cocked his head. With a semblance of pride more than accomplishment, he paraded in front of net.

There! This is what happens to nets that try to contain an emissary of the Great One. We always break free.

He paid little heed to long-forgotten voices that had been showing him how to overcome his predicament and winged his way to the top of the trees.

"Stay with us," they whispered.

"I know a way to bring fire to your invitation," he cawed. "Should I give you a sample?"

Small limbs in the highest tips shrank from his threat.

"No? Then I'll be on my way," he cawed and circled high above Dark Forest.

The freedom of flight felt wonderful after his long confinement, but there was little time. A sense of urgency propelled him. Raven didn't know why, other than Ironskin's shaping was making a mockery of his friendship with the Mistress. An inner feeling told him to hurry. But where were they? The village of the Horse People? Or by their favorite place of enchantment– the meadow by Sacred Pond?

***

Raven flew higher than he had ever gone, always circling to ride the wind. A distant glint at the far end of Dark Forest caught his eye. Even from his great height, he could sense Evil. But there was something else...a feeling of Kah-tay—but not Kah-tay.

By the Great One! I hope she hasn't given herself over to Evil—not after all we have been through.

The urge to fly there grew strong, but he had no power to combat what might lay in the confines of the rocks-that-seemed-to-burn. He turned toward the village.

"Are you frightened, Black One?" whispered the Wind.

Only a fool is never afraid. Do not bother me, tool of evil. My power against you is strong enough.

"True. But you do not know where to go." Candor flavored its tone. "I do, and can carry you on my breath for a small favor."

I do not bargain with wickedness. Kah-tay can reach me whenever she needs my service.

"True. I will give what help I can. Where will you go first?"

Follow and see, you carrier of all that is bad.

"I also carry good things, Raven. You never pause to observe. Always think the worst—that's you."

The Wind was not going to cease temptations. It never had, vexing Journeyers and shop keepers alike. He decided to search the village before casting a mind probe for his mistress, then beat his wings against a wrathful gust.

***

An empty tipi greeted him. Raven perched atop the pole to survey the floor and walls. Smells of human life felt pleasing. Missing was the child's cradle board Kah-tay labored over for several weeks, refusing all offers of help. Since it was gone she must have decided to have the child away from the village. His friend, the white mare was gone, too, as well as Mah-ki.

Strange. All the women were either in the village or working by the valley stream.

He could ask what the villagers knew, but considering their fear of him, it was not wise. They could panic and shoot their arrows. If one should strike him the process of rebirth would be long and laborious...at times, painful. He had little time for delay.

Ah! Ta-nic detached herself from the circle of women. She came toward

145

the tipi. Once inside she pulled the flap tight.

"Kah-tay is not here, Black Wing. I do not want the others to know I can speak to you. She had the baby at Sacred Pond and brought her here. An eagle came and stole the child...at least it was an eagle when it left."

A Shaping. Which direction did the thing go?

The old woman looked surprised. He decided she was not used to hearing voices in her head.

Ta-nic pointed. "Toward Dark Forest. Clayfoot and Kah-tay pursued. I don't know where."

She is surprised I can mind-speak. How much does she know? What had Kah-tay taught her?

I know where the child is. He thought of the presence he felt at the place-that- glints-in-the-sun. Kah-tay's child! Small wonder he sensed the mistress.

"Then you must hurry, Black Wing. I fear for the child."

I, too, fear for the child, woman-who-can-mind-speak.

Raven left her gape-mouthed as he flew to the refuse area. After tearing loose a few pieces of rotting flesh, he choked them down, then leaped into the air.

***

A familiar odor touched his nostrils when he landed in the meadow by Sacred Pool.

Others from the Home have been here.

Hopping to the edge of the circle of grass, he caught a lingering odor of his friend, White Mare. Gone, but a strand of precious white hair lingered on a low branch of sycamore. How he longed to pace her back, bringing relief to her itch and a satisfying stretch to his talons.

Enough! Where had they...?

Kah-tay's scent seemed strong, as did Clayfoot's...and two others.

Nothing more to be gained here. The sky will show the way.

Raven sprang into the air, his wings beating a swift rhythm to gain altitude. Circling, he could see overturned rocks and torn tufts of grass pointing the way.

Why would they think the child was in the desert?

Wind murmured close to his ear. "Do you want my help?"

The Evil One will take his revenge if you do.

"I do not always follow his orders. I go where I will. See?"

146

Raven felt a strong upward current. He flew higher than he had been since his youth...over one hundred man lengths. In the distance he could see ant-like figures atop a hill, move, then stop. White Mare glistened in the afternoon sun; a beacon urging him to hurry.

"I can help or hinder, friend Raven. A favor? Or should I call for rain? Or any of countless ways I have to hinder men?"

A stiff head wind, sudden, filled with gusts, rocked his struggling wings. It brought a familiar stench, faint but recognizable.

Why do you persist? When you hinder my quest, something good comes. When you help, disaster follows.

"What good comes from a strong head wind? Wind at your back is always an advantage."

Your wind of hindrance brought a hint of rusting metal. Ironskin flies ahead of me—and I can hear Kah-tay's pleas for help. Her anger is strong.

"The first battle for the child begins. For a small favor I will give you favorable winds."

Favor? When have you ever returned a favor?

"Many times. You fail to remember the good times I blew your Journeyers to distant lands. I witnessed the Beginning because I existed before your time."

What favor, then, if I should need your help?

"I'll think of something."

No. I will not fly in a dark hole to satisfy your whim. And that is all you are...a whim.

"Very well, obstinate One."

Raven felt the push of an onrushing storm. It tumbled him toward the figures on the hill. In a brief instant, he saw Kah-tay ride down the hill. Her anger at Clayfoot for not going with her seemed strong. For a moment, a sense of abandonment clouded his mind, then lost in a tumble of wind and feathers.

Kah-tay could not be his priority. Her anger would subside when the false raven was destroyed. But where was the evil Shaping? Perhaps he should have offered Wind a small favor. What harm could come from helping a sometimes friend?

The wind stopped. Raven plummeted from the sky where he soared higher than he had ever been. Below, winging toward the distant hills came a metallic stench, then a glint of his stolen shape. Clayfoot's plea, begging her not to follow the bird, came as a pleasing surprise. For once the muscled learner of the Home had it right. Raven's swift mind-probe saw Clayfoot's suspicion that the false raven was a Shaping to lead them further and further from the stolen infant. Beneath Clayfoot's proud exterior, he felt the sorrow pervading the warrior's heart. Raven turned his concentration to the mission.

His enemy winged below, broadcasting an enticing, urgent message.

Hurry–hurry. The child cries for its mother.

Raven's beak opened to scream a war cry. No, he decided. The element of surprise would be to his advantage. He folded his wings to plunge at the Shaping. His wings stayed furled until he landed atop the man-turned-bird. Instead of falling, he clutched his beak around the Shaping's neck and raked his talons down its back. A scream of terror cawed from his enemy.

Wail your death, evil spirit. You will soon join your ancestors.

A quick release on the Shaping's neck, to peck at its eyes, brought disappointment. They fell to the desert floor in a flurry of feathers, dust, and loud cries of anger. Raven blinked to clear his vision. The Shaping's mind-speak jolted his senses.

You will not succeed, Raven. I don't know how you escaped, but you will not live another moment.

Phaugh! What do you know of moments...or success. You are born of evil and will return to evil.

We shall see.

A huge paw swiped at him, missing. Another blow, this time with the taloned leg, cast a net.

Your spell worked but once, Raven said as he artfully dodged the enchanted web.

They leaped at each other, claws extended.

Now you will taste the pain of death, said Raven.

Ironskin dropped low but not fast enough. A red slash gushed below his neck, exposing flesh and tendon.

My strength will overcome you, pet of Kah-tay.

A shimmer brushed the dust cloud. Ironskin's raven shape took the appearance of an eagle.

Undaunted, and ready to give his life, Raven flung himself at the bleeding wound in the eagle's chest. Pecking and clawing his way into flesh and bone, he reared to strike a killing blow.

Not yet, Raven. We will meet another day–in my home–and on my terms. The eagle screamed and leaped into the air. Its powerful wings slashed the air lifting it above the desert.

Raven followed, swept by a vigorous gust of wind.

"See," came a soft whisper. "I told you I would help. Observe where he goes."

From his vantage, high above the desert, Raven watched the crippled eagle flapping toward Dark Forest.

Kah-tay! I know where the infant sleeps...and where the next battle with Ironskin will take place.

CHAPTER SEVENTEEN

Kah-tay's lips tightened to a grim smile. *Only a boy to help? What kind of men are you?*

Clayfoot frowned. *Men who are tired of following a liar. That Raven has not spoken a true word since he found us at Sacred Pond. He is co-wat-ka, crazy in the head."*

Waving his palm sideways in a gesture of finality, he crossed his arms. She knew that gesture very well! The only way he would follow was if she forced him. His voice came again.

"Tell the bird to come to you. We will go no further until it becomes your pa-na-te, a true friend. It will not speak to me, Kah-tay–or anyone but you. That is not like the Raven I know."

She motioned Squi to return to the others at the crest of the hill. Clayfoot was right. Raven had never refused to come to her call...even when she had been ordered to sacrifice her living heart by Quetzal, the Golden King of the Azteca...a man of strange power from the Evil One. In a quick dive, the bird had plucked out the king's eye and rescued her from the jealous rage of her husband. Plus it saved her from losing power by not having to plunge him from the steep temple. How long ago...?

She cleared her thoughts and called Raven but the bird's only answer came as always.

Hurry–hurry. The child is beyond the hills.

Tato appeared beside Clayfoot. The old warrior was angry at Squi for taking Bear Paw without permission. She left his mind and found Ortig had closed his thoughts.

I will return, husband. Tell Tato not to be angry with the boy. He is headstrong and eager to serve me.

Clayfoot nodded. She felt his intense gaze on her as she urged the white mare upward. There was sorrow in his heart...for her and the child. And something else. Love, such as she had never known.

"We will find Alua-Te-Te, my husband," she said drawing abreast of the waiting band. Her attention went to Tato and Squi. The old warrior seemed furious.

"Get off my horse, boy-with-snot-on-his-lip."

"Can you make me, old man?"

Tato's lance tapped the youth's chest. "If I have to."

"Squi!" Ortig gestured at the arrogant boy. "You are not serving the Great One. Do your mantra of forgiveness."

Crestfallen, Squi slipped from the spotted horse. All at once, Kah-tay felt the white mare stiffen, then glance to the East. The horse lifted its head, ears pricked forward, to a movement only a keen-eyed horse would detect. Mah-ki emulated the white mare. She sensed Clayfoot's gaze following hers. Something the horses could see, or detected, lay beyond her vision. Just as she decided to invoke far-look, the white mare bowed its back almost throwing her to the ground. Grasping a handful of mane, Kah-tay perceived the horse's antics. White Mare tossed its head, as she often did, when calling to Raven.

"There is movement nearby," said Clayfoot. "It is a friend, else the mare would tremble."

"Yes. It is closer now, but I cannot see it."

Astride Bear Paw, Tato reined in to join them. "Horses have more brains than men," he said and squinted at the cloudless sky. He pointed his lance. "That is not a mating in the sky, if I know ravens."

Kah-tay invoked far-look, amazed the warrior could see that distance with his rheumy old eyes. One raven was atop the other's back, its beak tight around the bottom raven's neck. Claws on the upper bird raked vicious, blood-filled streaks down its victim's back. A sudden down draft forced the fighting birds lower, bringing with them a familiar stench of rust. The birds struck the ground in a dust-filled cloud, claws raised to strike death.

"Ironskin!" she and Clayfoot shouted together. His lance went up in a protective gesture. She was grateful for his concern. The stealer-of-children was too dangerous if he won this battle. Clayfoot would do the killing for her after they discovered where the evil man had Alua. A death-struggle ensued between Ironskin's Shaping and Raven. Both minds were closed to their shouts of encouragement, but she screamed anyway, hoping her true friend would be the successor.

In a brief moment, one bird pulled back. A mirage-like shimmer revealed an eagle with one talon. The other foot ended in a sharp claw. Raven cawed an unintelligible sound and charged. Its beak plunged deep in the eagle's chest.

"Kill it, Raven. It is evil." Her shout went unheeded as the two struggled.

Out of the corner of her eye she saw Tato jab his heels in Bear Paw's sides and level his lance.

"Hee-ya. I want your feathers, one-who-changes."

The eagle leaped in the air, escaping Tato's lance by scant finger widths. Its flapping wings seemed slow as it gained height.

"I hoped we could capture it," said Clayfoot.

"Yes, husband. It could tell where it has taken my—our child."

She felt his arms slip around her shoulders. "We will find little Te-Te," he said. Brushing her cheek against his hand, she knew he would never give up the search for Alua. Raven hopped to her shoulder, accepting her loving pat as he preened his tousled, blood-streaked feathers. When he finished, Kah-tay cast her gaze at the ground.

"I'm sorry, husband. I felt so sure the Shaping was Raven that I made us follow—"

"We all followed the stealer-of-children." He shot an angry glance at Raven. "If Black-Ass, here, hadn't left us we might be in the place where our Te-Te is sleeping, instead of this land the Great One forgot, with saguaro needles in our ass."

Is it my fault you can't tell the difference? The Shaping's stink gave it away. Wind told me after I escaped from Ironskin's barrier. He has much power now that he has accepted Evil.

Kah-tay arched her eyebrows. "What barrier?"

It tempted me with maiden-scent...and I followed, curious to discover what keeps Clayfoot so entranced. Then it trapped me in a magic net.

"Raven! If you wanted to know about—"

I know. I should have asked you, but your precious Clayfoot...he is so descriptive—

"How dare you!" She faced her husband. Fury tinged her voice. "Talk about our intimate pleasures."

"It's nothing he hasn't perched on the top pole of my tipi and seen. Our minds probably broadcast that pleasure to the world."

She sniffed and extended her jaw. Even so, he had no business provoking

Raven to experience on his own that which he had forsaken to be her companion.

"We wouldn't be in this predicament," said Clayfoot in the language of the Home, "if you had taken the Sealing of Blood in Sacred Pond."

I hate water on my feathers, man of many muscles. You know that. Even White Mare couldn't drag me under its surface. Water is for drinking.

Squi cleared his throat.

"Is there water nearby?" he croaked, acquiescing to Raven's aversion to the liquid. "I'm thirsty."

Tato nodded and placed his hand on the boy's shoulder. "The lad has a nose for first things first...when he gets the snot out of it." He shook Squi's shoulder.

Water is by that outcropping, said Raven. *I noticed it when I was chasing that Caster-of-Nets. It weeps into a shallow depression of rock which lies in the shade.*

Bird droppings covered the rim. Squi rushed to the small pool. Kah-tay expected him to plunge his face in the wetness. Instead, the youth extended his hands over the water and mumbled a phrase in the language of the Home.

"What's he doing, now?" Tato charged forward, but was stopped by Ortig.

"He is purifying the water."

"He can pray after we drink."

"No, "said Ortig. "I mean he is really purifying it. The boy senses a poison, probably from the bird droppings. He has power from the Great One to do the rite. One of the few granted him."

"You are a strange tribe. Too much magic to suit me." He sat on his haunches, Bear Paw's slack reins in his hands. "Tell him to hurry. My throat is so dry if I could spit it would be dirt."

Squi lowered his hands and plunged his face in the water. Moments later, he backed away. "It is safe." He gestured at Kah-tay. "Milady?"

Kah-tay smiled at the boy, grateful for his power...and testing it before offering the precious liquid to the others. She drank sparingly, then stepped back.

"Clayfoot?"

"No. Let Mah-ki and the mare drink. Not too much at first. It could give them sickness of the foot."

Clayfoot, she thought. Always considerate of his horses. But then why not? He was of the Horse People and well known across the land as one who is ready to trade his precious commodity for the goods and services of another tribe. After her second drink, she unpacked the last of the pemmican and divided it. The horses nibbled at spare grasses and weeds growing near the spilled-over water.

***

Sitting by White Mare, her thoughts went to Alua-Te-Te. How were they going to find the gift from the Great One? A gift she had longed for all her life. The promise came true when she gave herself to the All Powerful. And the joy she felt when Clayfoot, even though his first intentions were less than honorable, consented to mate her and care for her and the child...even swore an oath to protect them with his life. She knew then he was a man like no other, and made her decision. Tears curved down her cheeks. With all her power, she had no control over the evil in this land. A place where they steal babies to.... Raven hopped to her shoulder and rubbed his head against her wet cheek.

Why do you weep, Kah-tay?

She touched a finger to his beak. *My child is lost to the Evil One. I fear she will not survive if her protective shield fails. She will starve.*

Clayfoot joined their mind-speak. *We will find Te-Te.*

Ortig sat beside them. *Do not fear the power in this place, Kah-tay. It was fated that we meet and join our power with yours. Have faith.*

Squi joined his thoughts with theirs. *What little I have is yours, milady.*

"Thank you," she said aloud.

"For what?" Tato asked. "You sit in a circle making strange faces then say thank you? What kind of *co-wat-ka* is this?"

"I should have known it was a Shaping," said Kah-tay, ignoring the old man's questions.

"How could any of us know." Clayfoot, relaxed, shifted his weight. "It wasn't until the wind brought the scent of wet, rusting metal that we knew it was Ironskin."

"You suspected long before that, husband."

"Only because the bird would not come to you."

Squi leaned forward. "The smell of metal? I've been tasting and smelling metal since we entered this place."

Clayfoot groaned, seemed about to speak, than clamped his jaws. She reached out to touch him. "There was no way Squi could know it was Ironskin."

"I know, wife. But it was so close we never realized. Now we don't know which way to search."

Raven sailed from White Mare's back where he had been scratching his friend.

Your babe is alive, Kah-tay.

"Yes, we know. The totem gave us a vision of her. She sleeps behind a protective barrier. We–I thought it was in this desert because it showed a warm, dry place. The vision grew dark, so I thought she must be in the shade. We followed the Shaping. I was wrong."

No. The vision was the right one but misinterpreted. I know where she is. I sensed what I thought was your presence when I flew over Dark Forest. Now, I know it was your child.

"Well, tell us, buffalo turd." Angry, Clayfoot towered over her and Raven.

She is in a place that shines like fire. It is at the far end of a strange meadow encircled by Dark Forest. Raven paced nervously across her shoulders.

"Don't threaten Raven, Clayfoot. He is helping the only way he knows." She stroked the bird's back. "Thank you, my friend."

"Place that shines like fire?" Clayfoot collapsed beside her. "There is an ancient story about such a thing. Before Dark Forest became a place where no hunter or warrior went...it is called...." He pressed his lips together accentuating his furrowed brow. "Burning Rocks," he murmured.

That is what it looked like, man of muscles. It will take all your strength to get there. Dark Forest is not a friendly place.

"I will use all my strength to find little Alua-Te-Te."

Raven fluttered atop Kah-tay's shoulder. *Born of Water. What a quaint name. Your doing, I suppose. Did you think the language of the Home would give her special power?*

"Her power may be limitless, considering her parentage, Black Ass. She hasn't lived long enough to learn to use it. If you kept your mind out of what's under your feathers we could have been there long before now."

Kah-tay's heart seemed to skip. At last they knew where Alua was.

"Stop it, you two."

Tato disrupted the argument. "I know of Burning Rocks. Never been there, but Great Grandfather told us stories. It should be an interesting battle before we rescue your child." He handed her the white mare's reins.

"It may be more battle than you care for, Tato."

"Wife of Clayfoot, know this. There is no battle too great for an old warrior.

156

Especially one from the Horse People." He flung a leg over Bear Paw and reached for Ortig's hand to pull him up behind. "I will either tell lies to your daughter about how Clayfoot rescued her–or my spirit will roam Dark Forest to frighten little children."

Kah-tay, with Squi behind her, followed them down the hill. As soon as Clayfoot reached the bottom of the hill he had Mah-ki at full gallop. A cloud of dust settled around her, its grit drying her throat and scraping between her teeth. At the ravine, she dug her heels into the mare's sides. Her fears redoubled. Would they reach Alua in time? She wished they had waited to let her consult the totem.

CHAPTER EIGHTEEN

Exhaustion and anxiety gnawed her. They had pushed hard to reach Sacred Pond which lay beyond the next hill. Kah-tay longed to use the totem. A vision of Alua-Te-Te resting in safety would lift her spirits, but she feared Ironskin would seek revenge by harming her child.

Their ride had been a silent one, except for an occasional mind-probe to comfort and support her. Now, she longed for a cleansing swim to wash the stickiness from her heavy, leaking breasts. Sweat, joined with milk, stained a shirt which clung to her like dirty bark on an old tree. Drawing comfort from the thought of cool water, she thanked the Great One for Raven's appearance. Otherwise, obstinate and frightened, she would have followed the Shaping far into the desert.

She turned for a final look. The last of the giant saguaro mocked with its spiny arms pointed to the sky. It reminded her of a foolish chase following a devil-man, that could mean the death of her child. When the white mare reached the top of the rise, her gaze followed Clayfoot's pointing finger.

"See," he said. "The stream below Falling Water goes swiftly at the bottom of this hill. Sacred Pond is two shadow sticks away."

"More like three," Tato muttered.

They goaded their horses to the narrow strip of white-capped water.

***

"I will meet you at Sacred Pond." She handed the totem to Clayfoot after wiping water from her chin.

159

"Why must you do this, Kah-tay? It is dangerous to swim in swift water."

"It is something I must do, husband." She waded into the rapids, Clayfoot's last words and Ortig's answer echoing in her mind.

"She acts *co-wat-ka*."

"*Co-wat-ka?* What is that?" said Ortig.

"Her mind is mixed like the pemmican she makes."

"Ah! She will be safe, Clayfoot. It is something she has to do."

"She told you?"

"No, but I sense her need to be in the water."

Kah-tay did not turn to wave. She waded out as far as the roiling stream would let her, then went with the rush of water. Brushing sand and rocks, she let the stream pound away her feelings of guilt as it tumbled her against its sides and bottom. With her mind closed to the need for air, she rode the current, feeling a rebirth of faith.

She had failed to recognize Evil: Failed to realize her husband was right about the false Raven. She would have insisted crossing the cursed desert, eventually killing her companions. Worse, she would have killed her daughter...her precious gift from the Great One.

Tumbling, she clutched her amulet bag, sensing the life-giving force of the Three-Stones-From-The-Beginning. Truth coursed through her veins, reminding her *she* was also a gift–a Healer. And she would remain in this kingdom until needed elsewhere.

What of Clayfoot? she wondered

He will be your companion. Or do you retract your wish for long life for him?

Never! He is a mixture of the best of those who came before. I love him.

Be at peace. Stop punishing yourself for the sins of others.

Will she live?

Only you can answer your question, Kah-tay.

She rubbed the last of recrimination for her actions against rough pebbles lining the bottom of the stream. Force from the rushing water had diminished to a fast pace and soon gave way to a swirling pressure in the curve above Sacred Pond.

I am united with my pa-na-teta. She used the Horse People's word for friends. *They will be hungry.*

Clenching her fist, she called a large fish and slipped her fingers in its gills. They would have food for the evening meal and the journey through Dark Forest.

160

***

The first to notice her was Clayfoot, smiling as he had many times when she emerged from the water. "I feared for you, wife. It is my right, even though you have strange power to live under water."

"I needed—"

"Ortig explained. I felt the same need when I was a wandering outcast before you claimed me." He eyed the huge fish, then seemed to marvel at her strength. "I hope it tastes better than a Noc-Muk."

"You will find this more to your liking, husband."

Ortig watched her through lidded eyes. She entered his mind only to find emptiness. What was he thinking? The man appeared old, but did not have long life. Those who did seemed to recognize it in each other.

Sometime during the dreaded journey through Dark Forest she decided to question him. For now, they needed to fill their bellies. At a nod from her, Squi began gathering dry brush.

***

Clayfoot belched. "The only food needed with the many-colored fish was more of your bread."

"Fish from your pond is excellent." Ortig finished the last of the meal and smiled at Clayfoot. "You are fortunate to have milady—er—Kah-tay to find them." He motioned Squi to put out the fire, then asked, "Tell me, why do you call this place sacred?"

Clayfoot looked wistful. "Many years ago the Horse People used this meadow and pond for the rite of admission to the tribe. After I returned from one of my wanderings, I discovered Ra-ton, the old chief, had declared Sacred Pond and these woods to be filled with demon spirits. He had a vision during one of his peyote dreams that said we should stay away.

"After the Horse People humiliated me for my cowardice, this place became my comfort."

"You, a coward?" Ortig glanced at Kah-tay.

"Something Ironskin belittled him about," she said, hoping Clayfoot had cleansed the memory of fear from his mind. A charging buffalo would make any child run for his life.

"I ran away during the becoming-a-man-ceremony. The old *wa-e-su-ta* looked bigger than a mountain." Smiling, he rolled toward Kah-tay. "Your princess convinced me it was wise to run, or I wouldn't be here to tell of it."

She pressed her lips in a tight grimace. Princess. The title had no place in their life. She grew irritated when Squi addressed her by the old ways. The youth insisted on referring to her as "milady."

I'm no longer a princess, she projected to Clayfoot.

You are to me. What does that make little Te-Te?

Anxiety clouded her thoughts mixed with annoying smoke from the cook fire. Her stomach knotted when the image of Alua's quandary crossed her mind. *I can suppress the vision, but I don't want to.*

By focusing her mind on the child she could retain and enjoy the smallest detail of Alua's body...her baby smell...and her mind. How much power did Alua-Te-Te have? Clasping her hands around her knees, Kah-tay rocked from side to side, her mind engrossed in conversations she and her daughter had while the child was still in her womb. Power had been given the babe long before she was born. Her mind drifted to an earlier battle with the Evil One. So long ago, she thought. She had won that time, when Quetzal went berserk and wanted to sacrifice her to the.... What was the name of the strange god her golden husband had embraced? But the Evil One, in a monster form, promised to return saying, "The next time I will win."

Had Alua become a culmination of the Evil One's promise to prevail? She glanced across the pond at Dark Forest. Gloom crept back at her in the light from the setting sun. Soon they would enter its dense growth and forge their way to the place Clayfoot called Burning Rocks. Would the men hold fast to their vow to help her? Would Alua be strong enough to withstand the lack of milk she desperately needs?

Pain stabbed her swollen breasts. They must hurry–not because of her pain, but Alua was in a very dangerous predicament. The child could be powerless from lack of nourishment which would weaken her defensive barrier. Ironskin could shape himself into anything...even a rock behind Alua. She shuddered at the thought. Grasping the totem, she went to the promontory overlooking Sacred Pond, fearing to look at what may be her child's future. A night bug flitting around a council fire, drawn to see what lay ahead?

Watchful eyes and support of her companions flooded her mind as she trudged to the rocky point.

Cross-legged, she sank to the hard surface. Gurgling water grew fainter when the totem's first shimmering visions engulfed her mind. Now that she knew Alua was not in the desert, Kah-tay concentrated on Burning Rocks. Out of a sulphurous mist, Alua appeared, still in her cradle board and behind a protective barrier. Kah-tay marveled. What power it must have taken for Alua to wrap herself in a shield against the Evil One!

Alua! Wake! Speak to me.

She saw the child give a reluctant stir and felt her refusal to lower the shield. Kah-tay projected her love. Suddenly, the Evil One grinned at her.

I will win, Kah-tay. My power is great in this land of slaves to pleasure.

Not everyone, Evil.

Name one who I cannot tempt.

Besides me, Clayfoot. Tempting is one thing. Winning is quite another. My husband has power hidden even from me.

It will be my pleasure to see him fall after I wrest power from him.

Irritated, she flung her mind-probe like a striking snake. *Begone!*

Of course, milady. Grinning, the Evil One gave her a ceremonial bow. *We will meet soon enough.*

A centipede of shivers crept up her back. Did Clayfoot have the power to win this battle?

***

"We will wait until the moon stands high."

Clayfoot's authoritative voice reverberated in her mind long after he issued the command to cross the stream. It irritated her. Delay after delay had hampered their search. Even though she knew they had lost most of the day searching on the false lead from Ironskin's Shaping, and that it was mostly her fault, she felt the loss of another moment a victory for her enemy.

Kah-tay grew aware of fear gripping her companions. Dark Forest was a place of black enchantment...a pall of death descending on warriors and Journeyers alike. She knew hapless warriors who dared enter its presence never returned. They were lost in a dark web of evil confusion. She began a litany to offset the spine-tingling essence of Evil.

> *I will keep my mind ever on the goal*
> *Though evil pervades my very soul*
> *I will not waver from my path*
> *The Great One's light will be my bath*
> *Grant me succor through the coming fray*
> *Keep me safe through night and day.*

She broadcast the mantra to her comrades, repeating it until they appeared calm. All except Tato. Squi, from his seat behind Tato, covered his mouth and pointed at the old warrior's back.

Milady. Tato is filled with fear. His trembling almost shakes me from the horse.

Squi's giggle irritated her. Apparently Dark Forest did not frighten the youth. Why? What strange, new power had been given the youth? Or was his age a factor in not having fear? Clayfoot was right. Only a fool does not show fear.

Squi, I forgot. He does not mind-speak, and it is not a pleasant journey for old warriors steeped in tales of terror. Do not laugh at him. Dark Forest is a place made by the Evil One. Until we are safely beyond its power, we can be influenced in our decisions. Already, I sense a pull from its black environs.

Ortig cast a frown at Squi. "There is a song for your mantra, lady. I know enough of the Horse People's language to sing it in their tongue. Perhaps it will calm the wise old warrior."

"Teach it."

The song had a lusty overtone she suspected Ortig adapted from his many journeys. It sounded familiar but she refused to probe her memory. She should, she knew, to help take her mind off her child—and this place of demonic terror. But it served its purpose. Tato's voice surprised her. He had been silent during most of the council ceremonies before Alua's birth. Now, he sang louder than the others. Probably from fright, she thought.

Squi grimaced at her. *See how the old man's eyes roll in fear—even as he bellows to ward off the spirits he thinks live in this place.*

Squi! Have respect for your elders. She gave him a sharp mind-pain. *Just because you are unable to show fear doesn't mean others...*

No—no. I'm sorry, milady. Forgive me. He squirmed behind Ortig, obviously uncomfortable. *I fear to say this, but Clayfoot is going in the wrong direction.*

Then tell him.

I heard. Clayfoot gave a slight tug on Mah-ki's reins. *What makes you think I can't follow the star that never moves?*

Sir. You are following the star...whenever you can see it. I—er—but the direction we should be taking is on the other side of that big tree. The boy pointed at a large oak tree straddling the path.

Clayfoot glanced at her as if wondering what to do. He did not mind-speak or answer her probe. His reply to Squi shocked her when he spoke aloud for all to hear. Especially Tato.

"We followed one Shaping today and it almost cost us our lives." His lance glinted in a shaft of moonlight when he pointed at the tree. "We will take your advice, but know this, *wo-ta-kay*...."

Kah-tay caught her breath. Wo-ta-kay. A derisive name the Horse People used for a leader too wise for his own good. What did her husband mean? She trusted Squi, but...she'd trusted the Raven Shaping, too.

"If you lead us astray," said Clayfoot, "I will be riding beside you. My lance will be up your ass before you can change shape." He crowded Mah-ki against Bear Paw, forcing the boy's leg in a tight squeeze. "We know a Shaping can be killed. Our encounter with Ironskin at Sacred Pond drew his blood. I hope we don't have to spill yours."

Kah-tay gasped. "Clayfoot!"

Ortig, riding behind her, tightened his grip on her hips.

CHAPTER NINETEEN

Raven plummeted from the tree tops, his wings glinting in the moonlight. A flutter, almost a flourish, put him on Kah-tay's shoulder. She leaned her cheek to the bird for its caress.

Welcome, my friend.

Phaugh! I see you are on the right path.

Clayfoot glared at the bird.

Well, Black-Ass. If you'd been here earlier I wouldn't have had to rely on a boy, who might be a Shaping, for all I know.

I notice you have your lance ready, Clayfoot. Afraid he might turn and bite you? Raven fretted as he paced her shoulder.

Clayfoot sneered. *He couldn't move fast enough.*

Stop it, you two! We have enough problems without your bickering.

Kah-tay urged White Mare forward to Bear Paw's side opposite from Clayfoot and Mah-ki. Her husband withdrew his lance from beneath Squi's bottom. "Are we on the right path to Burning Rocks?"

Of course. The Bird cocked its head at Mah-ki as if sending a secret animal-only signal, then leaped from her shoulder to land on Mah-ki's rump. *There is danger ahead, Muscle-man. A Shaping. It will require your best skill.*

"Ironskin?"

No. Something from an earlier time. It lies in wait.

"Can it be killed?"

Of course. Your new skills will accomplish more than you realize. Just be warned and accept the strangeness of a beast you have never seen before.

167

"Bow or lance?"

Be a hero. Use your knife.

"Buffalo shit! I don't care about being a hero. That's for little boys."

Tato frowned. Anger seemed to boil beneath his usual stoic expression.

"If you are going to carry on a one-sided conversation please do it where I can't hear it." He stopped Bear Paw abruptly, nearly spilling a sleepy Squi. "Tell me both sides of your *co-wat-ca* talk with the bird."

"My talk with Raven is not crazy. He says there is a dangerous Shaping hiding in the brush. It is very close...some beast I have never seen before. And I have seen many."

Tato removed his bow from its deerskin case. "Good. At least I can kill something in this dark hell. It has been too long since I've counted hair."

Kah-tay touched his arm. "You may not have time to enjoy this, my friend. Raven stands poised for battle alongside Clayfoot. Something I have never seen him do."

Her eyes closed after she looked to the tree tops and searched her memory. Her bird-friend had always fought alone when defending her. How strange. In many ways, Raven had changed toward Clayfoot since his disappearance...and his attitude toward her. His fight with Ironskin's shaping was more savage than any she had ever seen. It was as if he were taking a larger role in her life.

Family! Had the Great One told him his duties were to be expanded? A private conversation was in order, but now was not the time. At any moment a vicious beast could leap at them. She knew she would be the target. Kah-tay positioned the white mare between Bear Paw and Mah-ki, signaling she was the intended victim of what lay in wait.

All at once, a mind splitting screech tore the darkness. She cringed. Instead of the terrifying growl she expected, this was far more shocking. Small red eyes gleamed through the brush before the creature leaped. It knocked Clayfoot from Mah-ki's back. Clayfoot appeared dazed when he flung himself at the beast, knife drawn and slashing. She could hear the horrible tearing sounds of rending flesh and bone. Tato shot two arrows, striking the thing in its head.

"Buffalo turds! I missed its eyes." He charged forward, knife drawn, as the bat-like Shaping reached for her.

A quick swipe knocked Tato to the ground, bleeding from his clawed chest. Again the man-sized bat reached for her. Clayfoot hugged its chest, plunging his knife repeatedly. She pointed her finger at the enemy but hesitated. Her power would kill Clayfoot–and break her vow of non-violence. Raven circled the beast's head, pecking and clawing as if trying to draw its attention from Clayfoot and her.

Hugging the white mare's neck, she bent low, and to the side, away from the hideous Shape. "Great One...save us."

Out of the corner of her eye she saw Ortig, now slipped to the ground, holding his upraised palm as if to ward off the creature. Squi rushed past him and pointed his finger at it.

Nothing.

"Milady," he screamed, reaching for her hand. "Help me."

"No! It will kill Clayfoot."

"Not if I'm careful." Squi grabbed her hand and pointed his finger.

Clayfoot became outlined in the jagged blue light streaming from Squi's finger, plunging and slashing at the Shape.

She gagged at the sight of her husband when the creature's attention was drawn to Raven. Clayfoot seemed covered with blood. His or the Shaping's? Dear Clayfoot! He could not be killed, but his recovery or rebirth would be long and painful.

"A curse on you, Evil One." Kah-tay raised her palm at the Shaping. "May you die in the pit you wish for me."

As quickly as it appeared, the Shaping fell to the ground. It shimmered once, then changed into a small man the color of autumn leaves. Its chest looked a mangle of bloody ribbons and deep wounds from Clayfoot's knife.

Clayfoot made a final slash, disemboweling the thing. "Are you safe?"

"Yes, my husband. It was a brave attack you made."

"Nothing will harm you while I live, wife." He wiped his knife on the little red man's leg.

"Tato!" Kah-tay rushed to the side of the bleeding warrior.

His voice croaked. "It is a good way to die...fighting new beasts."

"You are not going to die." She drew her finger along a gash in his chest.

Nothing happened. Terrified, she peered into the dark clearing. "It is this place. My power to heal is diminished."

Speaking in the language of the Home Ortig said, "Create a shield. Remember what little Alua did."

How did he know about Alua-Te-Te and the barrier the infant had placed around herself? No time for questions. Standing, Kah-tay drew her finger from the ground on one side to the ground on the other. She repeated the action much as she had done to protect the village from the Twisting Wind. A crystal bubble formed around her and Tato.

"Heal," she muttered, knowing her companions could not hear her. As fast as she drew her finger along the claw marks the bleeding stopped, and Tato's flesh grew together.

"Do you want scars of this battle?"

"I am a warrior. Of course I want scars. What am I to tell my grandchildren?"

"At your age you want to have grandchildren?"

"Nothing is impossible. As long as I can satisfy–"

She put her hands over her ears. "Don't talk of such things."

"Why? Did you think children grew like fruit on a tree? There is pleasure involved in the making." He surveyed the bubble. "How do we get out of this magic water shell?"

Kah-tay reversed the process of making the shield and they stepped to the forest floor. Immediately, she ran to Clayfoot with outstretched arms.

"You were so brave, my husband." She placed her head on his chest and let a flow of caring love enter his mind.

She felt him savor her expression. "It appears I had help from everyone," he said. His gaze followed Tato when the old warrior leaped to the fallen Shaping. Grunting, he said, "Always the warrior."

The old man removed a sliver of skin and tangled hair from the dwarf-like creature.

Clayfoot shook his head. "Counting hair." Grimacing, he looked around the foreboding forest. "In this place."

"It means a great deal to Tato, my husband. He rushed to your aid and nearly lost his life."

"He will die in battle. If not this one, the next." Clayfoot gathered Mah-ki's reins. "Let's be on our way. My little Te-Te needs me."

"The Evil One is determined to stop us."

Grim faced he said, "He can try," and flung a leg over the horse's back.

Ortig touched her shoulder. "Your husband is filled with power, milady."

"Yes. The problem is–I don't know how much." She drew herself up on the white mare's back and scooted forward to make room for Ortig. "Neither does he."

Ortig's voice had an ominous tone she did not like. "We will all test the limits of our strength in the coming hours."

"You know much more than you tell, friend Ortig. Tell me. Or must I sort your mind?"

Ortig shrugged and sighed. "Sorting is painful, milady. I confess to a certain ability to read thoughts which are blocked, especially when you project mind pictures as vivid as the one of your daughter sleeping behind a self-made barrier."

Frowning and concerned, she said, "You mean you can enter a mind without consent?" Doing such an act was invasion and worthy of expulsion. "Is that the reason you left the Home?"

"Forced to leave the Home, milady." His voice sounded sour. "The Elders didn't know I listened until I made a mistake and advised them not to suppress the faction supporting the monarchy."

"We are fortunate you came to this land."

"It was on command from the Order, Princess. I have been sent to persuade you to return and take the throne."

Kah-tay blocked her mind. Knowing Ortig could enter a normal barrier, she put up a mental shield-wall. If he tried to read her mind against her wishes Ortig would receive a nerve-rending shock. She would hear his cry of pain. If he tried again, she would heal his abnormality and rend his power useless. The throne. Her father wished to end the monarchy. But he didn't foresee corruption of the Elders. What must she do? Alua must come first...then her husband. What they decided as a family.... Her thoughts trailed when she remembered Raven, her friend from the Beginning. After this is over she would consult him. This land would be good if it were not for the Evil One.

She sighed as anxiety gripped her. They must hurry. After pulling the sticky, milk-stained shirt away from her breasts, she urged the white mare forward. Raven's voice filtered through her barrier.

We make a good team, Clayfoot. Did you see how the Shaping stopped fighting you to get at me? You got several hard thrusts with that knife you stole from the—

I didn't steal it, Raven. You know the story. The stranger gave me every thing I asked for—even this horse if I would end his suffering.

Your tricky mind exposed you when you told the mistress that story. You took all his possessions.

Why not? He wanted to die and made it known I could have Mah-ki. He was only a little foal at the time. Should I not take what I wanted? And yes— I did feel I got the best of him. After all—the stranger got death. I'm still alive.

Despite her feelings of desperation, Kah-tay couldn't help but smile. This was the first civil exchange the two had since they discovered mind-speak.

Clayfoot spoke again.

Thanks for your wild pecking at the Shaping's head. It gave me time to cut its heart. Stay close, friend. We are not out of Dark Forest yet.

The Evil One has many plans for us, Clayfoot. The mistress is his goal, and we are doing just what he wants by coming to his kingdom.

I know. But little Te-Te must be fed...and soon. The trap is well set, but we have power to overcome his wily tricks.

It will take all of us to win, observed Raven.

Yes. Can you scout ahead? There will be more of his Shapings to slow our journey. We must stay battle ready.

You talk more like a citizen of the Home every day.

I am a citizen of the Home—by marriage.

Then watch over her while I search ground and sky.

Kah-tay saw a flurry of wings amid the straggly, weird shapes of the forest as Raven took flight. Clayfoot's mind-speak called after the bird.

Don't I always watch over her?

Yes. But sometimes you are such a turd about it.

Raven's mind closed. She knew they would hear its warning or receive a mind-probe vision of what lay in wait.

.   "Lady?" Ortig's voice came low and close to her ear. "Did you break my warning?"

"No. Their conversation was heard by everyone who can mind-speak."

He pulled back and removed his hands from her hips when she wiggled forward. She knew Ortig got the message she did not like this familiarity and sensed his physical attachment change to the mare in order to keep his seat.
.   "What did you wish to say?"

"Only that your husband and the bird are right. More beasts lay in wait. They are but delaying tactics to keep us from reaching Alua in time. We must ride directly to Burning Rocks, fighting a running battle."

"You mean like a retreat...only to Burning Rocks?"

"Exactly."

There was wisdom in Ortig's suggestion. He had a large stake in keeping her alive, too. The Others, the rebels who wanted to restore the monarchy to the Home, were the force behind his motive. The only way he could do that was to help rescue Alua-Te-Te. She thought long moments before deciding.

"I will suggest your plan to Clayfoot. If there is wisdom in it, he will agree." She tapped her heels in the mare's sides. "Clayfoot may have other plans."

She sensed Ortig's grimace and sent a mind-probe. Only his last thought came to her...something about having to consult an outsider about matters better left to the Others.

Her mental barrier went up. *I'll deal with Ortig after Alua is safe in my arms.*

"Clayfoot! Wait. We must talk."

"Yes."

She was startled by his nearness. His voice came from the other side of a large tree. Had he heard them?

"Ortig suggests more Shapings await us. They are but a delaying tactic to steal precious time and wear down our child so she will starve before we get there. He thinks we should—"

"I know. I heard his plan. It is a good one. Call Raven and we will discuss our moves."

After sending a mind-probe to Raven, she received an annoying reply. A vision came of a large cat that lay on the inner edge of Dark Forest. She puzzled over Clayfoot's quick reply...and his near presence. Had he been there all the time? Was he suspicious of Ortig, as he had a right to be, now that she knew his true motive for visiting this land? How much did her husband know? He was already distrustful of the boy. She channeled a thought to him.

What of Ortig? Do you trust him? Do you wish him to ride with Tato instead of me? How did you know of his plan before I told you?

I don't know. Ortig has a special mission. We will consider it after Alua-Te-Te is safe. As for how I knew, I don't know that, either. It just comes to me. If special power has been granted, remember, it can just as easily be removed. He moved Mah-ki closer. *My duty is to protect you and our child. I promised my life for it.*

Raven dropped to Mah-ki's rump just as Tato and Squi appeared out of the shadows. Bear Paw seemed invisible with his strange black on white markings.

"Milady," said Squi after sliding from Bear Paw. "Our conversation is being heard by...." His voice trailed off as his eyes searched the tree line. "I sense a presence among us. It does not belong here."

Ortig slid to the ground. "It has a strange odor. One that I can taste as well as smell."

"Rusting metal?" Clayfoot sniffed the air.

"Yes. Can you smell it, too?"

"No. Ironskin has masked himself from me. Probably Kah-tay, too, or she would have noticed it before."

Kah-tay frowned. A new dilemma had been added to their already perplexing search. Masking. They were fortunate to have Squi and Ortig in their midst. She hoped Clayfoot realized it, but her stamina was growing thin.

Make a bubble, channeled Clayfoot. *Large enough to hold all of us. Raise it off the ground so that it touches nothing in this evil place.*

"What about the horses?" Squi asked. "I hate to think I was riding around on a Shaping that was leading us astray."

Kah-tay scowled. The exuberant youth had much to learn to go with his unusual powers: Which was another gift she determined to explore. The youth was a strange one, as was Ortig. Decisions. So many to crowd her mind, always seeming to slow her uniting with Alua-Te-Te. Her patience grew thin.

Angry, she circled her finger, making an opaque shield around them complete with a rock-like floor. Her arms stretched out, palms up, as she made a lifting gesture.

"Safe," she said tersely.

Her husband looked bewildered but said, "Inspect every corner and wall for night bugs or other creatures," he said. "Shapings can be any thing. Look for Blood Biters on the horses." He ran his hand along the surface of a wall and its corner.

Kah-tay wondered why they didn't charge ahead. They knew where Alua was. Clayfoot could fight the dangers of Dark Forest and its evil inhabitants.

"Ortig," said Clayfoot. "Do you still smell or taste metal? Ironskin has become cunning."

Ortig sniffed and sucked air into his mouth as he paced the room-like bubble. "No. It's gone."

"Good. We must separate and defend against this place until we gain a foothold at Burning Rocks."

Squi waved for attention. "Why don't Tato and I fight Shapings? And Raven and Ortig do the same. Then you and milady can run like the wind to Burning Rocks."

She watched her husband scan the companions for dissent. There was none.

Raven paced the white mare's back. *What of the great cat?*

"The giant cat Raven discovered is nearby. Who will take it as Kah-tay and I race to Burning Rocks?"

For an answer Tato nocked an arrow. "It will be good to add another hair to my lance. Medicine from this place is strong." Turning to Kah-tay he said, "If I fall and cannot receive your healing I bid you farewell. May you find your child and slay the Evil One. Otherwise..." He sucked a deep breath. "I will join you at the place of Fire."

"Medicine or not, we will join you soon, milady." Squi rolled his eyes at Tato. "Between us we have enough strength to kill a stray cat."

Hardly a stray, muttered Raven. He fluttered across the white mare. *Come, Ortig. You and I will seek out the other Shapings.*

Kah-tay shuddered when the cat-monster screamed.

"Hurry. Tato and Squi will fight this one."

She placed her head against Clayfoot's back. Patience was at an end. Anger raged beneath her facade of waiting. They would either reach Burning Rocks, soon, or she would forget her vow of non-violence.

CHAPTER TWENTY

Behind them Kah-tay heard the battle cries of Tato and Squi. She shook her head to clear the strangeness of Tato's voice in her ears and Squi's from her mind. Both sounded victorious as they struck blow after blow at the cat-like Shaping.

She caught a brief image of the animal when Squi first saw the beast. Larger than two men, striped yellow and black, with two large upper fangs, its mouth opened ready to tear the two volunteers to shreds. Willing courage to the warriors, she turned her thoughts to the tangled deceit of Dark Forest. Ahead, just beyond the trees, she got her first view of the meadow. It, too, gave her a sense of foreboding...of black enchantment, hidden beasts, and pitfalls to delay them. She clutched Clayfoot's hips in a tight grip.

They cleared the edge of Dark Forest without incident, Ortig and Raven close behind.

"Look." Clayfoot pointed at a spot on the far horizon, a dim glint in the faded light of the waning moon. "Burning Rocks. They will be filled with fire when the sun shows its welcome face."

"How do you know it's Burning Rocks?"

There was much to discover about this man she had taken as a husband. Each day she became drawn to him...his newly acquired bravery and mysterious intelligence–his handsome features and physical strength.

No longer was he afraid of spirit beasts. Kah-tay smiled, thinking of his frightened attack on Noc-Muks, animals he had never seen, that first day in the meadow at Sacred Pond. They were not Shapings, but interlopers in a land not suited for them. She recalled his victory dance over the still-writhing carcasses. His voice scattered her thoughts.

"The visions come to me, wife. I do not know how. There is something about this place that draws me to it."

"We must cross the meadow with care. I, too, feel drawn to it. Not because of Alua, although that is reason enough. It is something else. Something sinister."

"You told me before we killed the first Shaping in Dark Forest that it was after you. Why?"

"I felt it, husband."

"I think you should use the totem. See what evil spirit waits for us in the tall grass."

Apprehensive, Kah-tay slipped the totem out of its deerskin pouch. Its turquoise center stone seemed to glow in the waning moonlight. The Evil One often interfered during each revelation, showing false visions. His sneering prediction always came that this time he would win. The Great One's favored daughter would finally succumb to the pleasures of this world in order to rule in his dark kingdom.

"This will test all my powers, husband. Please hold the totem against my forehead."

Just as he took the totem, Ortig and Raven galloped through the scrub oak at the edge of the meadow. Clayfoot motioned them to silence.

Do not interfere, he channeled to them. *She will sense it if you do.*

His intense gaze rested on Ortig who acquiesced with a surprised nod. Kah-tay closed her eyes when she felt the cool stone on her brow. Her last thoughts were of Clayfoot. How had he discovered Ortig's ability to override a mental barrier?

Through a swirl of mist, the first vision came with a stench of sulphur. Alua still rested against the wall, motionless. Kah-tay willed her mind for a closer look at her daughter. The child's breath came in small puffs though pursed lips as if she were searching for a nipple.

A dribble of milk oozed from Kah-tay's breasts as a heart-rending pain flashed through her chest. How could anyone be so cruel to a mother and child? For an instant, anger tore her mind. Clayfoot should have killed the child stealer during their first battle. But it is difficult to kill one's brother...even though the brother is the cause of a life filled with misery. Compassion. Another of her husband's virtues, but at a great price.

The vision of Alua faded, replaced by the meadow stretching out before her. It rippled in a slight breeze sending forth a scent of wild flowers. There were no beasts or Shapings. She smiled at the peaceful scene. All at once a frown replaced her smile. Clayfoot lay on his back, arms outstretched, held by a large tree stump on each side. Beneath him swarmed an angry nest of thumb-size red ants, racing to bloody cuts on his chest.

Kah-tay recoiled from the painful vision. After a sharp intake of breath, she realized the Evil One had detected her probe through the totem. He was sending a warning.

He will be mine, too.

No! You shall not have him.

She clenched her fist and Clayfoot sprang free of his bonds. After a roil of mist, Kah-tay saw him hurl his lance in a smoke and flame colored tunnel. Terror-stricken, Ironskin raced down the rocky corridor and....

The turquoise grew warm against her head, signaling the power of the totem was over. She collapsed into Clayfoot's arms.

"Alua is still sleeping," she gasped, "but grows weak from hunger." She shielded her mind. *I will not tell him about the Evil One's plan to capture him.*

"Is that all? From the twists and turns of your face I thought you were fighting Wa-Ha-Na himself."

"I always fight him." She smoothed her tunic, now stiff from dried milk, and pressed her lips together. "We must hurry. The way ahead is clear." Clutching Clayfoot's waist in a tight grip, she hoped he hadn't seen into her mind. With his newly acquired powers, she was never sure.

After a glance at Ortig, whose features were bland, she sought solace in the comfort of Clayfoot's back, snuggling in his man-smell. Neither had seen her vision.

"Go, Mah-ki," shouted Clayfoot. "Stop for nothing."

White Mare, with her lighter load, took the lead. In moments a snake reared above the grass, challenging the mare. Its head and body grew until it was shoulder high to Ortig. Just as it prepared to strike, Raven circled its head, making repeated attacks on the Shaping's eyes. Ortig made twisting motions with both hands as if trying to wrench the beast's head from its body.

Nothing.

Kah-tay lent power through her clenched fist as Ortig circled out of harm's way. The rending sound of torn flesh filled the air. A headless, small red man, with ragged black hair, writhed in the grass.

Thank you, milady. Let us take the lead again. Raven and I make a fine pair.

Mah-ki pranced as his white mare galloped past.

"He is eager to race," yelled Clayfoot over his shoulder.

"Mah-ki knows why we hurry."

"I did not tell him," shouted Clayfoot.

"It must have been Raven."

A black streak ripped toward them. A wild boar, twice normal size. With knife-like tusks, it made ear-splitting grunts as it came. Clayfoot hurled his lance in a difficult cross-body throw, then guided it with his finger. Kah-tay tightened her fist and watched the glistening blade dip. It took on her added power to pin the Shaping to the ground. Its spine was severed.

"Look. It changes to the Evil One's tribe. He must have many warriors to waste fighting battles the little red men cannot win." Clayfoot retrieved his half-buried lance and wiped the bloody blade across the ugly pygmy's chest. As he leaped on Mah-ki's back he said, "Where did he find such worthless warriors?"

"They are born of fire, my husband. Very dangerous Shapings."

"With your power added to mine the lance almost passed into the land of buffalo-running-below-the-earth."

A shout from Dark Forest drew their attention. Tato and Squi charged from the scrub brush. The old warrior waved his lance in a triumphant gesture.

"He has added more hair," muttered Clayfoot.

"You can see it from this distance?"

"Easy." He pointed at the lance. "The small, dark spots along the shaft are *wa-Ni*, his claim to be noticed."

"Filthy thing."

"Not to him. It is a mark to others that he is a true warrior."

They watched Tato slow Bear Paw at the place that had been the snake Shaping. Apparently satisfied, he hurried toward them.

"I thought you would take a memento," she said, "from the little red man who once was a snake."

Tato shook his head. "I cannot take the hair of a man I did not kill. No honor it taking another's leavings."

Kah-tay shuddered. It seemed a barbaric practice to *na-na-co*, count hair as Clayfoot called it. His enforced travels had broadened his knowledge and language. Na-na-co was a term of the Horse People.

"Ride ahead and search out more emblems of valor," she said. "The Evil One is sure to have many waiting to devour us."

Squi cleared his throat. "Milady. Tato carried himself quite well in battle. He deserves the tribute to his bravery." He pushed himself from the spotted horse and walked around the little man who was once a very large boar. "This one has no marks other than the large hole in his chest." His gaze went to Clayfoot. "You have a mighty arm."

"A man's arm grows strong," said Tato, "when he is defending his woman."

How would you know, old warrior. I've seen no evidence of a woman in your tipi.

She channeled the thought to Clayfoot along with the image of racing across the meadow. Burning Rocks was her final thought. A harsh nudge to speed his decision.

"We must hurry, Tato." Clayfoot nodded toward Ortig and Raven, now distant figures in the tall, waving grass. "Remember our mission."

"I have not forgotten. The little girl will be sucking her mother's *ba-ba* before the sun sleeps."

Kah-tay grimaced. She did not appreciate Tato's vulgar reference to her breasts. Of all the Horse tribe, he was worst when it came to language-of-the-earth. However, she savored his confidence Alua would be fed before nightfall.

The old warrior and his boy companion hurried past, apparently eager to tell the story of how he killed the unusual cat. She had to admit it took an equally unusual man to kill a Shaping from another place and another time.

"Do you share Tato's belief we will rescue Alua before the sun sets?"

"All I want is little Te-Te and her mother in my tipi before the sun sets this day."

"You didn't answer my question, husband. You have new powers, unknown even to me. What do you think?"

"Power can be taken just as easily as it was given. I cannot tell the future. I know Ironskin will die this day if I have my wish. The Evil One will fight to protect him–and it will take all our power to defeat them."

"My power may be diminished when we enter his kingdom."

"Then I give you mine. We will find our daughter and fight to the death to bring her home."

Kah-tay placed her head on his back and added her heels to his against Mah-ki's sides.

***

Tato had a dour expression when they stopped at Burning Rocks. He had been there, waiting, for several shadow sticks, he said, and the sun was overhead, setting the rocks ablaze with color.

"No water in this place of little men who cannot fight." Tato leaned against his horse. "Bear Paw is thirsty. So is his owner."

Kah-tay's eyes roved the area. "Where is Ortig?"

"He and the bird are searching for water."

"Use the totem," said Clayfoot.

"It won't work this close to the Evil One's dwelling. If Ortig or Raven cannot find water we will have to do without." She scrutinized their surroundings, suddenly aware of a prickly sensation crawling up her arms.

The Evil One is near, husband. Be on guard.

I feel it, too. Ironskin must have masked himself again. I do not smell or taste his presence.

She inspected the rocky slope to the shelf where the rocks reflected the flame of light from the sun, dreading the climb. It had to done, but first, they would inspect the area for Shapings. To be this close to Alua and not be able to grab her and flee was maddening. Control, she thought. I must retain control.

"As soon as Ortig and Raven return we will climb to the rocks and the cave behind them."

"What cave?" Tato pushed away from Bear Paw and gripped his lance. "I didn't see any cave."

"That is because you searched for more *na-na-co* to fill your lance," said Clayfoot. "We saw the black hole in the side of this mountain while we were still far away."

"You weren't attacked by little red men because of my desire for *na-na-co*, were you?"

"No." Clayfoot turned and searched Kah-tay's eyes. "And I find that strange. Perhaps other forces are at work now that your bravery has been proven."

Tato examined his lance tip with a calloused thumb. "My enemies know when they are defeated."

"Then let us climb the slope and search the cave."

The expression on Tato's face changed. "I do not think my enemies are in a cave."

Kah-tay frowned. *The man is afraid of caves.*

Yes. But we need him.

She sent a mind-probe for Raven and received his vision of a barren plain where yellow-tinged smoke spewed from cracks in the ground. Ortig was waving to Raven, signaling it was time to return. A half shadow-stick later they joined her and Clayfoot at the base of the black mountain.

Kah-tay listened while Clayfoot explained his plan. They were to enter the cave single file and gather together as soon as they reached a wide area. If there was no wide area they were to stay close behind him...and Kah-tay.

She wondered why he paused before adding her, then realized he wanted to pool their power in the event of an attack. Tato and Squi were to follow with Ortig bringing up the rear.

"I'll stay here and hold the horses." Tato grasped Bear Paws reins and reached for Mah-ki's.

"The horses will not flee, Tato. You know that." Clayfoot crossed his arms and sniffed the air. "Is that fear I smell? Who could it be?"

Tato hung his head. "I do not like caves. When I was a small boy I wandered into one and got lost. It was many winters before they found me."

"Many winters?" Kah-tay scowled. "I think it was more like many shadow-sticks, hours we call them, if what I read in your mind is true."

"If you are such a great healer, calm my fear of dark holes in the earth."

"Think of my daughter, Tato. I will enter that place of evil alone, if I must, to save her."

"You will stay beside me?"

"Of course."

"Then let us see how many *na-na-co* I can find in that black hole."

Clayfoot smiled and channeled his thoughts to Kah-tay.

It took great courage for him to admit his fear.

***

Orange light, dim and smoke clouded, cast shadows on the rock walls. The foot path was smooth for which Kah-tay gave thanks. Once, Clayfoot stopped and motioned her to silence. Tato, close behind, bumped into her and cursed.

"Be silent," she whispered. "Don't follow so close."

He gave off a strange odor which she knew was fear. Glancing back, she saw Squi outlined in the tunnel opening, erect, an overconfident grin on his face. Then the boy disappeared, momentarily, in what seemed a puff of smoke only to reappear next to Tato.

Grasp the cord around Tato's waist. Pretend you need a warrior's bravery.

He fears caves. She projected an image of a small boy lost in a cave.

And none of your remarks. At least Tato has enough sense to be frightened. Are you frightened, milady?

As my husband keeps reminding me, only a fool shows no fear.

A mind probe pierced her head! She sent a quick reply. Alua wakening from her sleep! Every thought distorted because of the barrier the child still held in place. She called for her mother.

At least some of my powers are still intact. I must not test them to the limit, else the Evil One will try his deceptions to entrap me.

Her thoughts transferred to mind-speak. This time she did not care if the others knew. In fact, she wanted them to know. Alua was alive and waiting. But her power....

***

The tunnel ended when they entered a wide, smoky room. Its walls were shadowed with moving, dark figures cast by the glow from an open pit. Squi bumped her elbow when he emerged from the tunnel.

"Milady. This is a strange place. Notice the dark place across from us."

Kah-tay turned to follow Clayfoot, but did not see him. Panic-stricken, she groped in the dim cavern, whispering his name.

Silence!

A hand grasped her and she was pulled around a sharp turn.

Clayfoot?

Yes. I can smell metal in this place of yellow stink. Ironskin is near. Tell the others to use caution.

Don't leave me again, husband, unless you tell me. I know what fright is in this place. Tato reeks of it.

She whispered the warning to Tato and channeled to Squi and Ortig. Tension built like flood waters over the men behind her. Clayfoot's mind was closed, but she held his hand and crept forward.

It is not like any darkness I have ever seen."

"Nor I," she said. "But this is my first visit to the Evil One's hiding place in this land. Sometimes he uses a blinding light...or blood."

She felt an unlikely quiver from the boy. Was he frightened? In other circumstances, she would have laughed. The youth was normally unaffected by weird events or animals. Especially Shapings. Power, she thought. How much does the boy have? He, like Clayfoot, had an unfathomable force.

Except Clayfoot's was ever-changing. She turned to watch her husband. How magnificent he stood, arms across his chest. Flame-colored light played over his muscled body! To lose him would be unthinkable. Yet he had promised to lay down his life to defend his family.

A voice rasped from the dark-that-is-not-a-dark.

"Welcome. You will find great pleasure in my kingdom."

Crack!

A brilliant beam highlighted the dense, cloud-like veil. In its midst sat a soot-blackened figure...a confident tyrant, one leg draped across an arm of a glowing throne.

"It is good to see you again, Kah-tay. Have you come to bargain for your daughter?"

She jutted her jaw. "We will not be staying. Alua is not yours to bargain—and you know it."

The Evil One shifted his gaze to Clayfoot.

"So this is your dim-witted husband. How nice of him to accompany you. His strength will serve me, well."

Clayfoot stood motionless, a grim smile on his face. She saw a force emanate from the Evil One, probe him, and retract. An equal force came from Clayfoot, shot to the soot-covered figure, and snipped back to her husband.

The Evil One's mouth gaped. "So. My Equal has granted him power to do battle. How well he masks it."

Clayfoot stirred from his rigid stance. "You were never the Great One's equal," he said. "You pile of buffalo droppings. Now release my daughter."

"*Your* daughter?"

"My daughter. You know very well my promise to guard them with my life."

"Yes. But first you must defeat my servant."

A dull, yellow flame highlighted a familiar figure standing beside the throne. Beyond him came a horde of small, red men grinning like possums about to pounce on a delicate morsel.

The stench of rusty metal became overpowering.

Ironskin!

Clayfoot's mind-speak blended with hers. In a one-on-one battle there was no doubt her husband would slay his evil brother. How much power had been given to them by their masters remained hidden. She prayed the Great One gave Clayfoot all he needed.

185

"Wait!" Kah-tay made a bold decision. "First I want my daughter. Then they fight."

"Certainly." A smirk crossed the Evil One's face. "If you can find which one is Alua-Te-Te. I believe that is the name your dull husband gave her. How quaint." Wa-Ha-Na motioned at the wall beside him.

Immediately, a gathering of ugly, red pygmies flowed from the wall and became exact copies of the sleeping child.

"I knew you would try something like this."

She went to the wall and made a pretense of searching the Shapings for Alua. They were well made copies, but she stopped in front of Alua, now awake from her sleep.

"This is Alua, my daughter."

"Are you sure? Feel how the others long for their mother. Pick again, Kah-tay."

"Fool. She is seed of the Great One, which should be power enough for you to be warned. Know this. She was sealed in blood and water with Clayfoot, her earthly father...and me. She can not be Shaped."

The Evil One motioned to the Alua Shapings. "Take her!"

They flowed from the wall like ants toward Alua.

"They will not touch her!" she screamed.

Kah-tay stretched her upraised palm to halt the horde, and clenched her fist. The little servants of evil halted then surged forward. She felt added power from her companions. In moments the pygmies faded into the wall.

"Come Alua. We will leave this place."

The barrier surrounding the infant dropped. At a signal from the throne, Ironskin rushed forward. Clayfoot stepped in front of his brother, his lance vertical in a sign of battle. The long-dead Spaniard's sharp blade was gripped in his left hand.

"To the death," he said through slitted lips.

Using the distraction, Kah-tay rushed to the rock wall.

I'm hungry, mother. Alua's plea sounded very weak.

I know, little one.

She snatched the infant to her breast, feeling the flow of milk as if it were an underground river about to burst to the surface. She glanced around the smoky room, a lioness defending her kits.

Suddenly, her heart seemed to stop. Alua was too weak to nurse, listless and would not probe for the breast. Frantic, Kah-tay squeezed a drop of milk on the child's lips. Using the last of her power, she willed her daughter to eat.

Calm settled over them as Alua sucked.

The Evil One leered from his throne. "You are not free yet, Kah-tay. You are in *my* kingdom, now. How much power can you summon after that feat? And where are your companions?"

A glance confirmed her worst fears. Clayfoot and the others had disappeared.

CHAPTER TWENTY ONE

Clayfoot motioned with his lance. Ortig would take the left tunnel, Squi and Tato the right. He would take the center.

No noises. Channel all talk to me. Remember, Ironskin has been given the power to mind-speak, but he cannot break a channel barrier. Kill any Shaping by whatever means you can. Raven, you are with me.

Phaugh! This place smells of earth-diggers. I'm to tell you the Mistress is nursing the infant. She sent a mind-vision when she couldn't find you. Her power is....

Whether Ortig heard or not, Clayfoot was unsure. The man knew Kahtay too well as far as he was concerned, but he suppressed his jealousy. Too much lay at risk with Ironskin fleeing the boiling revenge awaiting him.

Besides, until his brother was dead they would remain trapped in the caves. He deduced the Evil One could not touch Alua, but could place twists and turns in the caves to enslave them forever. Ironskin was another matter. The child-stealer could touch little Te-Te. Clayfoot gripped his lance. *This time the liar's blood would cover the ground.*

You believe you can best me in battle, dear brother?

Rage burned Clayfoot's mind. He had broken his order to channel all thoughts of Ironskin. Now, he didn't care. In fact, Ortig and the others would know where he was and that he was in contact with the enemy.

I can always beat you, stealer-of-children. You are co-wat-ka to the Horse tribe. They already know you for what you are. Crazy—and a thief.

To the death, brother. Watch your back. A creature of the caves will eat your flesh.

Clayfoot poked his lance at a thick cloud. Nothing.

Afraid to face me, Ironskin? The Horse People know you are the coward, not me.

Another shapeless cloud drifted toward him. The odor of metal drenched with human sweat assailed his mouth and nose.

What do I care of the Horse People? They mean nothing to me.

Clayfoot closed his thoughts against mind-speak and crept down the corridor. His gaze darted to the walls and murky tunnel ahead of him. Would the traitor show himself? In his heart he knew his cowardly brother would use deceit to win this battle.

A rock struck the wall near him. Clayfoot grinned. He wasn't going to pursue an old warrior's trick to draw attention away from the source of the enemy. His battle with Ironskin would take place on open ground. But it is not going to happen, he thought. The liar will try to surprise me. And knowing that, I will not be surprised. Instinct caused him to swirl in his tracks. A presence sent a chill up his back. He stabbed his lance repeatedly where a man's throat would be.

So. We meet, brother, said Clayfoot. *I don't smell the stink from your iron shirt.*

Suddenly, his lance pressed against skin that looked like it had been roughened by intense heat. It seemed almost like dried meat.

Unmoving, Ironskin stretched his voice over the sharp lance. *You are quick, Clayfoot. I remember our fights when you cut off my hand. It will not happen again.*

No, it will NOT happen again. Out of respect for our father, I spared your life two times. It will not be spared this time.

Before Clayfoot could thrust the lance into Ironskin's throat, the man faded in a cloud of yellow smoke.

Phaugh! I could have told you it was a Shaping. It had no substance.

Why didn't you, Black-Ass? We are in this together.

The bird fluttered to Clayfoot's other shoulder. *Well! He surprised me with his sudden appearance. I will not make that mistake again.*

I hope not. Clayfoot tightened his grip in the lance and continued his way down the hazy corridor.

***

His attempts to contact Kah-tay were puzzling. She seemed to fade from view as soon as he saw her. Her voice grew faint or nonexistent. In fact, he had not felt a probe from Ortig or Squi, either. A feeling of loneliness palled over him at the prospect of spending interminable days wandering the heat-laden tunnels in search of his enemy. Perhaps forever.

Tato is probably talking the ears off the boy, he muttered to Raven. *Ortig is strangely silent. Has Ironskin lured the Wanderer from the right path?*

Stroking the Raven's neck, as he had often seen Kah-tay do, Clayfoot thought of his failed attempts to reach his wife. He stifled thoughts of a lifetime in....

Can you send a probe through this puzzle of buffalo guts?

Raven clutched his shoulder. *I see her, Clayfoot. She is happy–and confident.*

How do you know it is not a vision made up by the Evil One?

Raven fluttered his wings in a shrug. *Perhaps I had better return and see for myself.*

You mean you know your way out of this tangled mass of holes within holes?

Raven cocked his head in a look of disdain. *Of course. Don't you? I'll return before you slay the cause of our anguish.*

Then you better hurry. If my wa-na-tona brother shows as much as a little finger, I will cut it off.

He spared a glance at Raven as the bird disappeared in the labyrinth. Loneliness and fear of failure returned.

"I have resisted the desire to kill my brother all my life," he whispered into the darkness. "Even in my moments of deep despair, when I thought I would perish from misery, I resisted. Now, for the pain Ironskin has caused others...he must die. For stealing a child...he must die. For taking up the standard of Evil...he must die. A faint smile of absolution crossed his face when he remembered Tato's sage advice.

Some men need a good killing.

Clayfoot stepped around a large boulder and recoiled from the scene before him. Ironskin's voice reverberated in his ears. The time had come. He must not fail.

Yes, Clayfoot. Here is our place of battle. You will be successful if you determine which is your target.

Crystal cubicals lined one wall and the far end of the dusky cavern. Ironskin leered from each niche. Every Shaping stood in a different pose, moving and beckoning.

You have one thrust with your lance, brother, said Ironskin. *And one cut with the knife you prize so highly. After that, I will claw your guts out and take your woman. They will serve me and my master for endless winters.*

Clayfoot gritted his teeth and scanned each niche to determine which held the true Ironskin. Rage boiled to the surface like the hot, muddy springs he had seen during his wanderings. *I'll use as many thrusts as I need.*

Phaugh! Do not let the coward goad you into foolish mistakes. Raven settled on his shoulder, his head cocked at the array of Shapings. *The mistress is safe behind a barrier even I could not penetrate. She trusts no one, but sends encouragement to her husband. Now, who could that be?* Raven pranced to his other shoulder. *Also, it's the last of her power.*

Calm settled over Clayfoot like Kah-tay's warm embrace. In her caution, she had sent a message only he would understand. She was safe, at least for the present. He turned his attention to the row of Shapings.

Which was the true Ironskin?

His mood casual, he inspected the imitations of his brother. Raven paced or fluttered when they stopped at each one, scrutinizing, or pretending to inspect the Shaping. Soon, knowing Ironskin's impatience, a taunt would come to speed his decision.

The next Shaping leered, its good hand on a knife, as it worked the talons of a paw where a hand had once been.

Clayfoot grinned and said. *I should have cut it off higher.*

The Shaping uttered a low growl.

Clayfoot feinted a jab with his lance and turned away, knowing Raven would attack if the imitation moved to slay him. His ruse worked. Out of the corner of his eye he saw a lance glint in the flame colored light.

Ortig's words to Tato splintered his mind when the man of the Home explained how he caught the arrow in mid-flight.

Imagine the arrow traveling slow...almost stopped in its flight. Then reach up and grab it.

The lance slowed, seeming to float in its journey to Clayfoot's heart. A side step...a quick reach...and the shaft was in his fist.

Craaaack!

The sound of fire-hardened wood reverberated in the chamber and the lance lay at his feet, shattered.

"I didn't see where it came from," he whispered to Raven. "Did you?"

About...there. His talon pointed to the far end.

Raven's mind-vision showed a clutch of three Shapings. Wide grins split their faces.

"I warned you the last time, Ironskin, if you interfered with my life this lance would follow you to the place where the sun sleeps. There will be no escape."

A roar of laughter came from the row of Shapings.

"I do not fear your lance, Clayfoot. You have not found me. Now I order my Shapings to..."

For an instant, Clayfoot saw movement behind the middle figure. Squi and Tato moved slowly toward the grinning traitor. He lifted his lance.

Suddenly, an unwieldiness pervaded him. Something was terribly wrong. Never had a lance been this heavy. His arm hurt when he forced it higher. Had Ironskin acquired new power?

Look who is here, Muscle-man.

The pressure of Raven's talon guided his sight. Ortig stood in the mouth of the tunnel, both fists clenched in the Home's way of control.

Another traitor has succumbed to the Evil One!

Clayfoot pointed at Ortig. "Fall." A thin, jagged bolt zipped across the flame-lit cavern. Ortig crumpled against the wall, powerless. In the next instant Clayfoot's lance hurtled at the middle figure.

"Follow." He commanded his lance and pointed his finger.

Ironskin's mouth gaped as he bolted to the tunnel. No matter which way he turned the lance twisted its path to come after him. Leaping over a boulder, the iron-clad warrior knelt in the shadow.

Clayfoot crossed his arms over his sweat-covered chest. His teeth bared when the lance snaked around and headed for his brother. A ripple filled the area where Ironskin stood. Immediately, an eagle took flight to the top of the cavern. The lance wavered as if searching.

A screech cracked the smoky interior. *Your precious lance has lost its power.*

The eagle swooped low when the lance swept upward, following the raptor's flight. Over a flaming pit they fought, then dropped back to the floor of the cavern.

"Call it back, I beg you, my brother."

Silence.

Ironskin raced to the end of the room. He whirled, arms spread-eagled against the glowing rocks. Terror split his face as he screamed against the gloom.

" Nooooo!"

The lance buried itself in the center of the armor, ripping through metal and flesh as it pinned the child-stealer to the jagged, searing wall. A stench of burning blood joined the sulphurous mist.

Watch my back, Raven. My lance is a weapon of good charm. I will retrieve it and carry it with me when we fight the Evil One.

Raven left his shoulder as Clayfoot went to Ironskin's writhing body. He glanced, once, and saw the black bird flitting in front of the advancing horde. They stopped at the bird's clawing attack and slowly changed from Ironskin Shapings back to their small, autumn-red forms.

"So, brother. You sought to best me again by turning to evil." Clayfoot grasped the shaft. "You never learn."

Ironskin gasped, "You will never escape."

"No?" He paced his foot against the hot armor and pulled the lance from the rocky wall. "*You* will not stop us."

Clayfoot turned at the sound of a familiar voice.

"This time you will do *na-na-co*?"

"For you, Tato, I will take his hair."

Ironskin's dull gaze followed the knife as he gurgled a death chant around blood dripping from his mouth.

"The song-of-death is not for cowards." Clayfoot slashed his brother's throat, cutting off the sound. A second quick swipe, below a handful of hair, lifted the bloody piece.

"Here." He tossed the dripping scalp to the old warrior. "Something for your grandchildren."

"Hi-yah. It is a worthy totem," Tato cackled as he held it aloft. "I did not take it—but I wished for it. That makes it mine."

A quick grimace crossed Clayfoot's face. When and if they escaped this fiery hell, they would have to endure Tato's endless tales of bravery in the land of evil.

"What is Squi doing?"

"Eh?" Tato seemed absorbed in the gory flesh and hair. "Worried about Ortig, I think."

"So am I."

They found Squi hunched over Ortig, poking the man's flaccid belly. Clayfoot shook his arm.

"What did you do to him?" the boy asked.

"He was trying to interfere with my power when Ironskin threw his lance."

"But why?"

"That is what I'd like to know." Clayfoot's mouth twitched as he knelt beside Ortig. "He is still breathing. I wasn't too careful with my power since it was my life he meddled with. Kah-tay will heal him."

"I hope so. I cannot reach his mind. It–it–seems empty."

"Kah-tay will know." After calling Tato to join them he said, "You and the proud warrior can carry him. We will follow Raven. The bird knows the way to Alua and her mother."

He whistled for Raven who still pecked at the Evil One's retreating pygmies.

Phaugh! You spoiled my fun. I had them in full retreat.

Thank you, my friend. I appreciate your help.

I sense no joy in your victory, Man of Muscle.

It is never pleasant to kill one's brother. My heart is heavy–my stomach retches bile. Clayfoot forced a dry swallow. *Now, show us the way to Kah-tay.*

He plodded after Raven, paying scant attention to his companions. His mind filled with memory of Ironskin. As evil as his brother had become, he was still his only brother–and once, a mighty warrior.

***

Kah-tay returned hate for hate as the Evil One stared at her. Alua had finished nursing and Kah-tay fought the surge of pleasure from the sleeping infant's lips at her breasts. Even the slightest ease of her remaining power would let Him enter the barricade she had taken over from her daughter. Once entered, He could isolate them. Starvation would wear them down.

Sleep, little one. He will not get through the barrier.

Wa-He-Na laughed. "I have patience, proud Princess. Time is on my side. Even you must eat. And it will be many winters before you see your over-confident husband. Even now, my servants plot his death."

"I am not afraid for Clayfoot. He has power...more than you will ever know. Your little red abominations are nothing but leaves in the wind. They cannot–"

"My new servant will assist Ironskin. This kingdom is like a mound of ants, twisting and turning to lead Clayfoot astray."

"What new servant?"

"Surely you didn't think Ortig would help Clayfoot. He is more interested in returning you to the Home as a triumphant queen. I showed him how to accomplish...." His smoldering eyes left hers and seemed to search the dark.

"I'm not interested in the monarchy. Ortig knows that." She cuddled Alua-Te-Te to relieve the infant's belly. "My place is with my husband."

The Evil One grinned. "Your child ate like a ravenous bear cub. It suffers and will grow very ill."

"I am a healer. Remember?"

Alua's loud burp reassured her.

"Your power is diminished, Kah-tay. Soon it will disappear and you will submit to my demands. Perhaps Ortig is right. You would serve me better in the Home, guiding your people in my ways."

Her eyes narrowed. Hatred filled her mind. She refused to mind-speak with him as it would open a chink in the block she placed in her mind. If he gained entry, many false images could lead her astray.

Raven appeared, projected a quick view of Clayfoot, and she returned an image showing her safety. The vision was for her husband's mind, only. The Great Trickster could be sending false images again. But the scene of Clayfoot, his body glistening in the flame-lit tunnel, gave her a sense of security. She pondered his power, wondering why the Great One had been so mysterious in hiding it...even from her.

"I will ignore the evil of this place. My husband will protect...."

A familiar scream of agony echoed in the tunnel. Her gaze flew to the soot-covered figure on the dusky throne.

The Evil One's interest in her seemed to fade. His yellow gaze roved the gloomy, smoke-filled cavern as if searching for an answer. She was tempted to lower the barrier, knowing the sulphurous odor would numb her senses.

No! It could be a trick.

But the scream was one she had heard before. To search the index of her mind would require lowering the mental shield. That was what the Tempter wanted...one slim chance to enter her mind.

"I will not give in to curiosity!"

Shadows from the tunnel broke her self assurance the Evil One could not trick her. Without lowering her protective shield, she watched Raven, followed by Clayfoot, enter the cavern. Squi and Tato carried Ortig. At her husband's signal they deposited Ortig next to the barrier. Were they Shapings? The others, perhaps, but not Clayfoot. He could not be imitated.

The Evil One roared. Flames and smoke belched from the open pit. With a sudden gesture, the area in front of the throne swarmed with red pygmies.

"Slay them!"

The horde surged toward Clayfoot and his companions. Raven hopped on Clayfoot's shoulder, one claw raised to ward off the screaming throng.

"Stop!" Clayfoot pointed his finger and raked power across the oncoming crowd. Some tried to become Shapings before they melted into the flame-colored walls. The Evil One and Clayfoot stared at each other across the open space.

"So, the conquering hero returns."

"I killed my brother if that is what you mean. Ortig has no power to serve you or anyone." He seemed fearless standing beneath the shadow of the black throne. Nonchalant, his finger caressed Raven's neck.

"You will never leave my kingdom until you submit."

"We will find our way out." He continued stroking Raven.

"That bird is useless, now. I can make several Shapings from my little friends to lead you astray." The black figure gestured at the wall across the fire pit. "See the new tunnel? It circles this place forever. Will *your* bird lead you...or one of mine?" Evil laughter rattled the walls of the cavern. Rocks and dirt plummeted around them

Strange, thought Kah-tay. Not one rock fell on her companions. Her husband stood, unshaken, as dust rose and settled. His gaze never left their captor. She cocked her head, wondering about the outcome of this battle of wits. Then Clayfoot's voice, more confident than ever, answered the Evil One.

"You cannot take a life, Wa-Ha-Na. Others must do it for you." Clayfoot glanced around the hazy room. "Where are your servants?"

"I can raise up servants from these stones and—"

"And I will slay them as quickly as they appear." He crossed his arms on his chest. Raven paced across his shoulders, rocking its head from side to side. "It would be wise to let us go free. You haven't seen or tested the power granted us."

"I'm about to find out. You will all starve before you leave. Better you should submit to my rule. Kah-tay will have a kingdom in the Home that will bring you much joy." The dark figure gestured and a scene of beautiful girls danced before him. "They are yours, Clayfoot."

Her husband snorted his disgust and continued to stare.

Suddenly, Alua stirred in her arms.

"Shu–shu, Alua. We must save our strength."

Let me free, mother. Do not hold me. My strength has returned.

Shocked, Kah-tay felt the infant and her cradle board slip from her grasp.

The shield she had so carefully maintained seemed to melt away. Alua floated above her. Dancing in waves of heat, her little cheeks puffed, the child propelled herself to the black figure.

Alua, don't–

He cannot stand against my power, mother.

The Evil One glared. *Get back to your place, child of dreams. You belong to me.*

You do not have the power, Evil One. I will breathe on you and watch as you shrivel and die.

The cradle board rocked as waves of power filled the room. It floated closer to the sooty face. Yellow eyes, that were once commanding, now looked bewildered. Kah-tay stole a glance at Clayfoot. He stood, calm and relaxed, almost smiling, his arms across his chest. He seemed majestic in the dim, flickering light. She probed for supportive power that might be going from him to Alua. Nothing. Had he heard Alua ask...no, *tell* her not to interfere? Her gaze returned to the struggle between her daughter and the evil force.

The infant was so small. How could she have power to lift, and do battle with the one the Horse People called Wa-Ha-Na? Powerless, she watched Alua take in a deep breath. Her tiny cheeks puffed out, then sent a stream of air toward the taunting figure on the throne.

The Evil One flung his arm across his face in a protective gesture. Foul odors filled the room as a piercing shriek rocked the walls.

Nnnnoooo....

Murky yellow fog drifted from the high seat, down jagged rocks, and across the floor of the cavern. It oozed over the edge of the open pit. A hollow voice boomed in the chamber as it disappeared.

My time will come. I will search forever to find your weakness.

Alua floated back to her arms. The infant's eyes were closed.

"Sleep, now," said Kah-tay. "He will not bother us again."

Clayfoot knelt beside her and rubbed his finger over Alua's black hair.

"Little Te-Te," he murmured. "She has been given much power to face Wa-Ha-Na and live."

"Yes." Kah-tay cuddled her daughter, feeling the tenderness...both hers and Clayfoot's.

Tato swept his arm at the rock walls. "If this battle is over, I think we should run like the wind."

Kah-tay shuddered at the grisly scalp still dangling from his fist. But the old warrior was right. The ground beneath them trembled a warning. Clayfoot grasped her hand and tossed Raven in the air.

Find the way out, Black-Ass.

Phaugh! It was such a good fight. The infant is mighty, indeed. I wonder...?

Wonder later. Let's get out of here.

They raced after Raven as the bird twisted its flight upward and out of the sulphurous cave.

***

Kah-tay breathed a sigh of relief. Dungi, Ironskin's horse, nickered to them as they descended the cliff from Burning Rocks. He seemed only too happy to be with familiar people and animals. She smiled when Squi leaped on its back and raced ahead. They hurried from the area. Mind-visions of the Evil One returning spurred them on. Ortig lolled in front of Tato on Bear Paw while Squi stayed in the lead. Her white mare seemed content to carry her and the child to safety, but stayed close to Mah-ki.

"Stop!" Clayfoot reined to a halt beneath a large oak tree. "This meadow is filled with the stench of death. We must proceed with caution."

She stole a glance at Burning Rocks. "They still glow in the sun like a council fire, husband."

"They serve as a reminder of evil." He slipped from Mah-ki's back and shaded his eyes. After a long look at the flaming spot, he scanned the horizon. "We are fortunate to have power on our side. Little Te-Te still sleeps, eh?"

"I can't believe what happened." She slapped his hand away from the infant's balled fist. "Remember how she crushed your finger the last time you tested her grip."

He grinned. "*She* was testing me, I think.

"I think so, too. Hold her while I see to Ortig. He must have received a severe blow to make him senseless." Squi's muffled laugh caught her attention. "What?"

"Ask the man with mighty power. Ortig brought shame on us when we fought the Shapings."

She turned a questioning gaze at Clayfoot, who seemed to ignore her as he played with his sleeping daughter.

"Clayfoot!"

His face looked filled with guilt. "Ortig was trying to stop my power when Ironskin was about to kill me. The power made him fall down.

"Bring Ortig," she said. "I'll sort his mind. Some people," she looked at her husband, "don't know their strength."

After touching Ortig's forehead, she found his mind a thornbush of tangles and sharp-points. Threading her way through the maze, she sorted his thoughts, stopping once to chastise Clayfoot.

See what you did?

Would you rather see me dead?

Of course not!

What would you have me do? I knew you could heal him.

Laboriously, she mended Ortig's mind. When finished, she sank to the soft grass only to find her husband staring at Alua in disbelief.

"Give her to me." She reached for the cradle board.

"A vision of her dream appeared to me. She wants Burning Rocks destroyed...along with the evil kingdom."

"How? Did she say?"

"She saw us joined together...and the earth shaking from buffalo-running-beneath-the-ground."

"I will consult the totem." She slipped it from the soft pouch. Its cool stone gave her the same image. As she returned the totem, Ortig scrambled to his feet and knelt before Clayfoot.

"Do not slay me, servant of the Great One." He reached for Clayfoot's hand. "I only wanted Kah-tay to return to the Home and take her rightful place."

"That is for her to decide." Clayfoot shrugged off Ortig's hand. "Remember, my power is like a wild beast. Untamed. Don't make me use it again. She," he nodded at Kah-tay, "might not be able to heal you the next time."

"Stop it!" She took Alua, rocked her gently as she looked at Ortig. "My place is with my husband. I told you that, before."

Squi handed Dungi's reins to Tato since the old warrior was already holding the other horses. "What about Alua's vision?" he said.

Kah-tay felt Clayfoot's arm around her shoulders as she pondered Squi's question. How were they going to destroy the evil kingdom? Her mind opened. She saw her husband's suggestion. They should sit in a circle and concentrate. Collapse was the word he was trying to form.

Or did the thought come from Alua?

Her husband shaded his brow again to look at Burning Rocks. Moments later, he nodded at Ortig. "Come," he said, "Sit with us and join our powers."

Silent, she motioned Ortig to join the circle. With the child strapped to her back, she sat next to Clayfoot. Squi sat on her other side. She told Ortig to take the open space.

"Our thoughts are to be one," said Kah-tay. "The Evil One's kingdom in this land is at an end. We will think this same thought–the earth must collapse into the pit."

Their minds became one. Power flowed across the meadow, shimmering, a mirage in a thirsty desert. A great wind roared, pushing the flow of energy back toward them.

"The Evil One is fighting us," murmured Kah-tay.

Clayfoot lifted the cradle board from her back." We must add her power to ours," he said. "She will stay between us. Put your finger in her fist on your side and I will do the same on my side. The rest of us join hands."

Kah-tay felt a tingle surge across her chest as the child's energy flowed around the circle. She heard them gasp when Alua's force buffeted their consciousness. Their minds joined with the snapping sound of a broken limb.

Again, power streaked across the plain, rippling the grass like waves on the sea. It seemed to splash against the cliff, flow upwards, then engulf the hillside.

Burning Rocks erupted in a ball of fire, then fell inward as dust and smoke plumed to the clouds. Beneath them, the ground trembled as they continued the destruction of the Evil One's home.

Squi gasped. "He'll not come back to this place."

"He cannot be killed," said Kah-tay. "Let us hope we have driven him to a far land." She placed Alua in the harness and shrugged her in place between her shoulders. The child refused to answer a quick probe to see if she was hungry. It was just as well.

Sleep, little one. You have shown us you are of the Home and its people. But we must live here, now.

"Look!" Squi pointed to the meadow and the distant trees. "It's almost like the Home."

Flowers bloomed where weeds once choked them out. Colorful birds flitted among the trees. A pleasing odor of fresh earth after a spring rain filled he air. Near the tree-line, a herd of antelope raised their heads to stare at the interlopers in their feeding grounds.

A sense of relief came over Kah-tay as they rode to Dark Forest. "The Evil One is gone, my husband. Let's go home."

After Clayfoot mounted Mah-ki, Raven settled on his shoulder. Ordinarily, she would be jealous, but she had something more precious than her lifelong friend. Alua-Te-Te was a loving enigma...an infant with an adult mind.

Raven's mind-speak brought a smile.

We make a good fighting team, Clayfoot. But one thing I wish from you. Please stop calling me Black-Ass.

And what would you wish to be called? Warrior, perhaps? Then stop calling me Muscle man.

Well, that's what you are.

And your ass is black.

Behind, she heard Squi translating their mind-speak to Tato. The old warrior laughed, waving the grisly trophy still clutched in his fist. "They speak the truth. It is good for warriors to laugh after a mighty battle. You must tell us your story when we gather around the council fire tonight."

"No," said Ortig. "We will journey to the North. There is much I must teach the boy. The Horse People may not care for too many visitors from the Home."

"If you travel North," said Clayfoot, "I will draw a place where water leaps from the earth, hot and filled with odor. Mud boils up in wallows, and you can sleep beside it to keep warm—even in winter."

"It sounds like a place of mystery. Just what we need."

"You will need two horses. My brother had another mighty horse—a brother to Dungi. But it is mean spirited. No one can gentle it. It is yours if you can make it accept a child on its back."

Kay-tay nodded, channeling a thought to Ortig.

It is a peace offering. Take it while he is in a giving mood. The horse will be gentle enough to carry any child—even Alua.

I sense you have made a wise choice, Kah-tay, taking him as your husband

.   Yes. And it will last forever.